THE SAXON SHORE

THE DEFENCE OF ROMAN BRITANNIA FROM SAXON AND FRANKISH INCURSIONS

THE SAXON SHORE TRILOGY
BOOK ONE

JOHN BROUGHTON

CHAPTER-BY-CHAPTER GLOSSARY

CHAPTER ONE

Batavians = Germanic people on a large island between rivers in the Rhine-Meuse delta.

CHAPTER TWO

Trireme = a war galley with 3 banks of oars, each oar manned by one man.
Corvus = a boarding ramp taking its name from corvus – the raven, owing to its spike like a beak.

Menapian = a member of the Belgic Menapii tribe dwelling near the North Sea in the Roman period.
Classis Britannia = provincial naval fleet of the Ancient Roman navy, its purpose to control the English Channel and the coastal waters of Britannia.
Bagaudae = groups of peasant insurgents in the later Roman empire who arose during the 3rd Century.
Cornu = Roman horn.

CHAPTER THREE

Capsarii = Roman doctors taking name from doctoral bag – capsae.
Corbilo = important trading port of the Veneti on the Loire about 2 leagues below Nantes.

CHAPTER FOUR

Branodunum Fort = ancient Roman fort to the east of modern Brancaster in Norfolk.

CHAPTER FIVE

Solidus = highly pure gold coin issued in the late Roman and Byzantine Empires.
Denarius = 4.5 g silver coin – 1/72 of a Roman pound weight.

CHAPTER SIX

Antonine Itinerary = a register of the stations and distances along Roman roads compiled for Emperor Antoninus (86-161 AD).
Camulodunum = modern Colchester.
Venta Icenorum = modern Caistor-St-Edmund, Norfolk.
Sitomagus = a town 30m south of Venta Icenorum on the road to Londinium.
Combretovium = present-day Coddenham in Suffolk.

CHAPTER SEVEN

Glevum = present-day Gloucester.
Dalmatia = a region of modern Croatia.
Mauretania = a region embracing more than modern Morocco.

CHAPTER EIGHT

Deva = modern Chester.

CHAPTER NINE

Gesoriacum = modern Boulogne in France.
Ulpia Noviomagus Batavorum = modern Nijmegen in the Netherlands.

CHAPTER TEN

Regulbium = Roman fort near modern Reculver in Kent.
Canti tribe = Britons in Kent.
Portus Lemanis = Roman fort at modern Lympne in Kent.

Vectis = the Isle of Wight.
Metatores = a Roman civil engineer.
Gromatici = Roman surveyors.

CHAPTER ELEVEN

Tamesis = River Thames.
Durovernum = modern Canterbury.

CHAPTER TWELVE

Civitas = citizen community.
Praetorium = high army officer's headquarters.

CHAPTER THIRTEEN

Vindelis = modern Portland Island, famous for Portland stone.
Anderitum = modern west end of Pevensey in Sussex.
Ander Forest = the Weald.

CHAPTER FOURTEEN

Porta decumana = Decuman gate opposite the praetorium, generally the rear gate.
Portus Adurni = fort situated at the north end of Portsmouth harbour.
Ballista ball = ballista, an ancient missile thrower which launched great balls of stone a considerable distance for use against fortifications in a siege.
Clausentum = a small town in the Roman province of Britannia. The site is believed to be located in Bitterne Manor, which is now a suburb of Southampton.

CHAPTER FIFTEEN

Verulamium = modern St Albans in Hertfordshire.
Cornicen = a junior officer in the Roman army, whose job was to signal salutes to officers and sound orders to the legions.

dextrarum iunctio = the joining of right hands in wedlock.

CHAPTER SIXTEEN

Dubris = modern Dover.
Liburnia = a type of small galley used for raiding and patrols. It was originally used by the Liburnians, a pirate tribe from Dalmatia.
Othona = Roman fort near modern Bradwell-on-Sea in Essex.

CHAPTER SEVENTEEN

Chauci = an ancient Germanic tribe living in the low-lying region between the Rivers Ems and Elbe, on both sides of the Weser.

CHAPTER EIGHTEEN

Teutoburg Forest = is commonly seen as one of the most important defeats in Roman history, bringing the triumphant period of expansion under Augustus to an abrupt end.

CHAPTER NINETEEN

Rutupiae = modern Richborough Castle near Sandwich in Kent.

CHAPTER TWENTY

Constantius = Flavius Valerius Constantius "Chlorus" (ca. 250 – 25 July 306), also called Constantius I, was Roman emperor from 305 to 306.

CHAPTER TWENTY-ONE

Liburnae = used as cargo ships in the later Roman empire.

CHAPTER TWENTY-TWO

Principia = headquarters building. This building was in the very centre of the fort. It was where the commanding officer would issue orders to the soldiers, and the clerks would have offices. Also, there was the strong room where the pay was kept.

CHAPTER TWENTY-THREE

Ballista = Roman catapult for hurling massive stones.
Illyria = north-western part of the Balkan Peninsula.
Infera Insula = the legendary once fertile low-lying island of Lomea – the modern Goodwin Sands.
Testudo = a packed formation covered with shields on the front and top.

Gariannonum = Roman shore fort probably at modern Caistor-on-Sea, Norfolk, guarding the Yare estuary.
Rutupine shore = Roman name for the coast around modern Sandwich, famous for its oysters.

CHAPTER TWENTY-FOUR

Noviomagus Reginorum = modern Chichester, West Sussex.
Calleva Atrebatum = modern Silchester, 5 miles north of Basingstoke, Hampshire. Well-preserved Roman walls and amphitheatre.

CHAPTER TWENTY-FIVE

Isca Dumnoniorum = modern Exeter, Devon.

Eboracum = modern York, Yorkshire.

Dumnonia = the Latinised name for a Brythonic kingdom covering modern Devon and Cornwall that existed in Sub-Roman Britain.

Drepana = Helenopolis, a Byzantine town in Bithynia, Asia Minor, on the southern side of the Gulf of Astacus (present-day Turkey).

Samhain = pagan festival, marking the Celtic New Year, the end of summer, and the end of the harvest season.

Mediolanum = present-day Milan in Lombardy.

I

VALDOR BENT TO HAUL HIS EEL TRAP ONTO THE RIVER bank when a hand clamped over his mouth and a familiar voice hissed, "The Romans are hunting for Faldrek; you've got to help us find him. He's only killed a centurion, and the whole legion is hunting for him. Look over there! They've even got dogs to help sniff him out!" The rough hand of the smith's apprentice released its grip. "You're his best friend; you'll know where he'd run to."

Several ideas tumbled through Valdor's mind, but there clearly wasn't time to evaluate which was best.

"I know what I'd do in his place, Heidar," he told the apprentice. "Are you three willing to come with me? We'll take my uncle's boat, find Faldrek, and sail it out of the estuary into the open sea."

"My father's boat? The North Sea?" Johar gasped. "Then what?"

"Then we take our chance and see where the gods, time, and tide lead us."

"Are you mad?" Johar, the youngest of the four by one winter, protested. He was comfortable with the older youths because he could run and throw as well as them, and his muscles were just as well developed from hauling wet, laden nets of fish onto his father's boat.

"I'll come with you, Valdor. There's nothing for us in the village now the Romans have seized our tribe's treasure, and they've forced my master, Thragnor, to work the forge for them. I'll not stay to be a Roman slave! Besides, Faldrek is my friend, too. If the Romans seize him, they'll torture him and maim him for killing a centurion."

"Are you coming with us, Johar?" Valdor shook his cousin's arm urgently. "Look, some of them are splitting from the main force and coming this way."

"Since it's my father's boat you're planning to steal, I'll come so that it isn't seen as theft. Let's go!"

Hidden by the steep river bank from the approaching Romans, the three youths dived into the river and struck out for the islet opposite. Batavian boys all learned to swim like otters in their infancy, and the men were renowned for their incredible ability to swim even in armour, thus taking an enemy by surprise. So, it was not a hard task to arrive at the far bank, scramble up, cross the islet to reach Johar's father's boat, moored in its usual place, and decide there what to do next. The distant yapping of hounds made them hasten their deliberations.

"You two get in," Johar said. "I'll push her off the mud, and you can haul me aboard. We'll row to where we're going for now. We can't risk hoisting the sail; it's white, and the Romans will see it and be after us in a trice."

He gave the boat a mighty shove, but it failed to budge, so he tried again while Valdor used an oar to push into the silt. Johar had to dive into the river again and strike out after the boat that was already being swept along by the current. Strong arms reached for him, and soon he was hauled into the belly of the boat. Valdor had already taken charge of the oars and was pulling strongly with the current, parallel to the bank but in the direction of the village and hence towards the Roman soldiers.

"What do you think you're doing, Valdor?" Heidar grumbled. "You'll have us all taken prisoner."

"Nay, Heidar, you take the tiller and head us out into midstream while I do the hard work."

"Give me an oar; I'll help you," Johar said fiercely. With the two youths hauling on an oar each, the boat shot forward swiftly.

"Now where?" the tillerman asked.

"Torik Isle, over yonder," Valdor pointed. "That's where we'll find Faldrek."

"Never! He'd never have swum that far," Johar argued.

"Listen, Faldrek is a stronger swimmer than any of us, and he was desperate. Besides, I know a place where he would hide."

Gradually, they approached the low-lying holm, a refuge for every conceivable type of seabird, but uninhabited by the Batavians as it was so prone to flooding.

"There's nowhere for him on Torik," said Johar querulously. He was a little jealous of his elder cousin, who had now assumed command in what by right was his boat.

"You'll soon see; I'm not given to flights of fancy, cousin."

The low line of the coast, which was the bank of the Waal, could be seen from Torik, but the movement of anyone ashore was invisible at this distance. Conversely, this was a guarantee that the three of them and their boat could not be seen by the Romans. The value of Johar's advice not to hoist sail was evident now. They ran the boat into a small inlet, where there was slightly firmer ground in the shallows made up of shingle. The boat scrunched into it, and they leapt out to drag it higher, making it impossible for the vessel to be lifted away by the tide.

The turf was springy but not marshy in these summer months, so they set off confidently towards the middle of the islet. The forces of nature had created a hollow at the centre, and as they approached, they saw a thin wisp of grey smoke curling into the air to be instantly dispersed by the sea breeze.

"I told you!" Valdor said triumphantly. "It must be Faldrek!"

The three youths appeared over the brow of the hollow, where their friend leapt to his feet, brandishing a gladius—a short Roman sword. "Hey!" he cried. "What are you doing here? Don't you know, I'm an outlaw?"

"Whose law?" Valdor said truculently, smiling grimly. "We've come to share your fate."

"You can share my dinner, too!" He pointed to a rudimentary turnspit where two seabirds were skewered and dripping fat, hissing in the flames of a small fire made from salvaged driftwood. "Puffins. I caught four. I still have to prepare the other two."

In their village, puffins were regarded as a delicacy, so Valdor's stomach was already rumbling.

"What happened exactly," he enquired of his friend.

"I was grooming our horse when that swine of a centurion crept up behind me. The first thing I felt was a hand on my buttocks, and then he spun me around and started kissing me on my mouth. Yuk!" He dragged me into our house and pushed me onto the bed. Luckily, mother was out; she'd gone to Aunt Ysilis' to help make bread and prepare some crabs. Then he started to strip off his armour until he was naked." Faldrek's voice broke, and his lip trembled. "It was clear he wanted to rape me. In fact, he said that if I was a good lover, he would see that I was well-treated in the legion. They plan to round up all our people aged over sixteen winters because, he said, we make the best warriors in the Empire—"

"So, that means us as well," Valdor looked meaningfully around his companions' serious faces.

"Ay, anyway, that was when I surprised him by leaping up to grab this," he brandished the gladius, "and plunged it into his heart."

"Good riddance," said the apprentice smith, "I'd have done the same!"

"Hang on," Johar looked astounded, "Are you saying that you swam all this way carrying the sword?"

"Ay, what's the problem?" Faldrek replied proudly. "You just have to keep a tight grip on it."

He used the murder weapon to slice the puffins, but it made no impression on the hungry youths, who devoured the fowl with relish as their host prepared the other two birds. Soon the fat was spitting in the fire again as Heidar, expert with flames, added just the right amount of wood for good roasting without burning the flesh.

Chewing on his meat, Faldrek swallowed and asked, "I suppose the Romans are hunting for me?"

"Ay, they are, but I reckon they won't think of scouring the various isles and islets because they won't think anyone could swim this far. I think they'll search the nearby villages and while they're at it, they'll round up lads of our age and older as auxiliaries in their army.

"So, what are we going to do? We can't stay here too long."

"We have our boat," Johar said proudly, and Valdor's plan is to sail out of the estuary into the North Sea."

"Aye? But what then?"

"We'll leave it to the gods to decide our fate, my friend."

After much discussion, they decided to spend the night on the holm, also because not even the Romans would attach importance to a white sail in the early morning, which would be seen as a fisherman sailing out to cast his nets. The mild season permitted them to sleep under the stars, and the hollow hid the glow of the fire from the mainland so that they could sleep around its warmth. Heidar organised the collection of driftwood and maintained that he needed little sleep, so he would keep the fire burning through the night. The other three were weary from their efforts and soon fell into a deep sleep.

The following morning, Valdor gathered his friends together to make a solemn oath. His grey-blue eyes, typical of his tribe, stared intensely into others of the same hue, except Heidar's, which were an unusual deep blue.

"We must swear before the gods that whatever we have to face,

5

we'll endure it together, united: each individual should act for the benefit of the group, and the group should act for the benefit of each individual."

Four arms stretched out in unison and hands clasped over the other, "I swear!" they chorused and grinned into each other's faces: each face that of a young man who had grown through infancy and childhood together. Trust for each of them was of supreme importance and in the comforting glow of comradeship, at least momentarily, they were able to dismiss the frightening thought of what a future far from the reassurance of their village, family, and the routine of their chosen trade might bring. A moment's thought told them that was no longer any reassurance. For Faldrek, a return certainly meant a cruel death and for the others, a harsh life in the Roman legion under Emperor Maximian.

Valdor, who had tacitly assumed command of the little group, said, "Come on, men, the sun is lighting up the river, it's time to row out into midstream and raise sail. We'll be out in the North Sea by noon. Look, there's an ebb tide to help us and the current is in our favour!" He hadn't mentioned the breeze, but when they hauled in the oars and, as before, Heidar took the tiller, when Johar ran up the sail, it flapped and filled with the wind. Since the breeze was contrary, coming from the North Sea, Johar called to his tillerman, "We'll need to tack downstream. Keep the bows in that direction for the moment. I'll tell you when to turn."

Nobody questioned his decision because among them, he had the most experience of sailing. If they were to survive this voyage, they would have to heed his advice. The fisherman's son settled down in the bows to keep an eye on the direction and perhaps any debris that might damage the small vessel.

By midday, they had reached the choppy water at the mouth of the estuary, sliced through it and into the calm water in the lee of the islands positioned like sentinels guarding the entrance to the great river complex. From the bows, Johar pointed excitedly, calling to Heidar to change course. They headed towards an area where the sky was full of mewing gulls and diving gannets. The diving birds were plunging into an area of water that seemed to be bubbling and boiling. "Mackerel!" Johar shouted and pointed excitedly as the boat ploughed into the area, the fisherman's son twirled a net over his head and cast it among the easily netted fish.

Moments later, he had hauled the bulging net aboard, tipping the teeming fish into a writhing, glittering heap on deck. His exultation was brief, as a large gull swooped down and snatched one in its bill, soaring away with its prize. Soon, all four youths were using oars as weapons to fight off the famished persistent predators. Johar was the first to use his wits instead of his muscles, grasping a mackerel and flinging it into the sea, diverting at least a dozen of the gulls to swoop and compete for the prey. His friends joined him, throwing squirming mackerel into the sea. The breeze came to their aid, driving them towards the shore of an island. Johar seized the respite to cover the fish with old cloths so that the gulls, unable to see fish, mewed and sped off in search of prey elsewhere.

Valdor took charge now, "Heidar, take us into that inlet, we have more fresh fish than we can eat for lunch."

Johar had a gutting knife on board, so he prepared selected fish whilst Heidar took charge of lighting a fire on the sandy beach. Never had they eaten so much fish in one meal, and they had plenty to store in a barrel of salt that Johar's father kept on the boat for occasions when he had fish that advanced beyond the requirements of the village. "In this way, we'll have rations for when we can't catch fresh food," Johar explained.

"Let's sail over to the outermost island," Valdor said, "we can spend the night there and above all, we can find a freshwater spring or we'll die of thirst. Have you got an empty barrel on board for water?"

The following morning, they found a spring oozing from a cleft in the rock and slowly filled a medium-sized cask with fresh water, blessing Johar's father for the useful equipment found on board the vessel. They carried the cask aboard and then shoved off into the relatively placid waters of the bay. Strong strokes on the oars took them around the northern tip of the island and into the face of a strong south-westerly wind. The sail filled with a snap and the boat shot forward.

Johar approached Valdor, grasping his arm, to turn him so that he faced back towards the land they had left.

"Now what? Cousin? It's all very well leaving our fate to the gods, but should we not have a *plan*."

"I was thinking that we should cross the North Sea and try our luck in Britannia. They say the people there are similar to our tribes."

"But Britannia is under Roman ru—"

Valdor followed his cousin's gaze and understood why he had broken off mid-sentence and was standing, mouth open, peering into the distance. A rectangular sail clearly stood out against the horizon and it belonged to a much bigger ship than theirs.

2

THE NORTH SEA, AD 286

AS SOON AS THE LARGE VESSEL CAME INTO SIGHT, THE four companions realised to their dismay that it was a Roman war galley. That observation was not exact because the galley was a Carthaginian trireme captured in battle during the Carthaginian war, little more than a score of years before. Still, it contained a complement of 190 men and was a formidable fighting vessel armed with a ram, catapult, fire pots, and archers. It possessed a tower from which to direct attacks and reinforced wooden sides. An innovation was the *corvus*, a thirty-foot-long boarding plank, four feet wide with a spike at one end. As the trireme neared the fishing boat, the corvus came crashing down to impale the wooden deck, just missing Johar standing in the bows. Roman legionaries swarmed down the boarding plank, at least a dozen of them, wielding swords and wearing armour. The four youths had one sword between them. Resistance was out of the question and, laughing, the legionaries herded them up the ramp into the galley. The remaining warriors searched the vessel, but the only thing they removed was the barrel of salted mackerel, which they carried up the steep ramp, taking it aboard the trireme.

Valdor gazed with amazement at the ranks of seated rowers and the drummer in the stern, there to beat time for the coordination of the many oars. He imagined that the galley could fly through the water without the aid of the large rectangular sail that now flapped uselessly in the breeze because the crew had slackened the stays for the boarding. The crew were now busily engaged in recouping the *corvus*—no easy task because the spike had embedded deeply into the wooden deck of the fishing boat. It required a team of twenty men to release it by hauling on ropes. With a squeal of steel on wood, the spike came free and, at last, the fishing vessel, of no interest to the Roman commander, was allowed to drift free. The fate of Johar's father's boat was in the lap of the gods, whereas the fate of his son and companions was firmly in the hands of the galley commander.

Forceful hands pushed them towards the tower in the stern and half-shoved, half-hauled them up the ladder. The legionaries thrust them before the commander of the galley. Here was their next surprise because the curly-haired and curly-bearded stocky man in full Roman regalia was not a Roman, neither was he a patrician. His coarse-featured visage spoke of humble origins and his accent was known to the youths. Before them stood a Menapian, a member of a tribe the Batavians figuratively 'rubbed shoulders' with in Belgic Gaul.

The rough-mannered commander grinned, "Well, well, what a prize! Who would have thought it? We close in on a fishing boat; nothing more than a tub containing a few salted mackerel and find a real treasure—four Batavian warriors!"

Faldrek was about to protest that they weren't warriors when Valdor nudged him in the ribs, and he swallowed his objection.

The commander, who had noticed the gesture, fixed his eyes on Valdor and astonished him by addressing him in his own language. "You have something to hide from me, young man, but Marcus Aurelius Mausaeus Carausius has a way of finding out everything. Do not dispel my goodwill. Tell me what you are doing so far from home?"

"Commander Carausius, sir," Valdor gained confidence because he could use his own language freely, "we are fugitives from the Romans, who seized our village, but one of my dear friends here slew a centurion who tried to rape him."

To his surprise, Carausius laughed heartily, "Ay, some Romans, especially those of noble families, have this peculiar vice." He slapped his thigh as if sharing a joke, "I prefer women to satisfy my carnal needs as I expect you four healthy Batavi do, as well. Am I right?"

"Ay, sir, you are. Will you not punish us for the death of a centurion?" Valdor asked meekly.

"Listen, young man, it would be a waste! I know the worth of Batavians in battle. I venture you are all horsemen who can swim, too?"

"Indeed, we grew up with those skills, lord."

"I knew it! I will give orders for you to be equipped, and you will form part of my bodyguard. That is a special privilege. As for the centurion, I am not interested; the swine had it coming to him!" Carausius spun to face Faldrek. "It was you who slew the Roman, was it not?"

"H-how did you know?" Faldrek stuttered.

The commander guffawed. "Easy, you are the pretty boy of the four! If you like, I can scar your face to spoil your looks, you just have to ask," he roared with laughter again. "I'm only joking, don't worry!"

"Thank you, lord," Faldrek found the wits to add. "We'll serve you faithfully."

The commander shouted orders in what they recognised as the Latin tongue, and the galley stopped wallowing in the waves to shoot forward under the power of 120 oars, to the pounding rhythm of the insistent drum. More orders and the crew stretched the rectangular sail by hauling and fastening the stays.

Suddenly, the commander looked at the four companions and switched to their language again. "You rascals took me out of my way, but I believe you were worth it!" He addressed Johar. "That boat was yours, was it not?" Johar's jaw dropped in amazement. "Ay, sir, but how could you know that?"

Carausius bellowed with laughter again, a trait they would come to know and appreciate. "Easy, one should always pay attention, especially in the presence of strangers. I saw how your eyes followed the tub as we set her adrift."

"It was my father's livelihood, lord, but I expect he will not need it now that the Romans have seized our people."

"Think no more of them," Carausius said, casting a weather eye to the south-west. "A new and better life awaits you. Your father will find his place in the legion if he is anything like his son. You four and I will become friends." He shouted orders in Latin again. They did not understand, and the sharp-witted commander recognised this. "I have ordered them to kit you out with armour and weapons. As of now, you are part of my bodyguard. Soon, I will summon your superior officer. He is a good man but does not suffer fools gladly. You'll find him brusque but fair."

"Suits me!" Valdor murmured, not intending Carausius to hear, but the officer's hearing was as sharp as his wits.

"I'm glad we deviated to pick you up," he said. "I'm more at ease with my own kind. We are on our way to meet the *Classis Britannica*. I am to command that fleet in the English Channel to eliminate the Frankish and Saxon pirates who have been raiding the coasts of Armorica and Belgica." He stared hard at Valdor, meeting his puzzled eyes. "Why me in command? You might well ask, young fellow. I'll tell you. We Menapians are fierce fighters like you Batavians, and although I have no great fondness for the Romans, I distinguished myself," he beat his chest proudly, "during Maximian's campaign against the Bagaudae rebels in Northern Gaul, earlier this year." He smiled grimly. "Add to that my previous career as a pilot in these waters, and you see, there's nobody better to command the fleet."

Modesty might not have been his strong suit, but the commander had impressed the four youths, each of whom was eager to seize the opportunity Fate offered him. To strengthen this feeling, four legionaries deposited arms and armour at their feet.

These same soldiers helped the lads strip out of their dirty clothes and pull a deep crimson *tunica* over their heads, next they strapped a *balteus*, a kind of apron belt, around their waists, from which dangled the *baltea*, studded leather straps. "These are the insignia of my bodyguard," Carausius said. "The mere sight of them should instil terror in the foe," he grinned wolfishly. Expert hands positioned a leather cuirass over their torsos so that, with the steel *lorica segmentata*, all four took on the appearance of fully fledged Roman soldiers. Two details were missing: the *caligae*, the army sandals, and the *galea*, the helmet. The eight men on the tower had a good laugh because the *caligae* fitted them perfectly, except for Heidar, whose feet were too big; not only that, the *galea* was too small for his head. The legionary hurried away to fetch replacements as Carausius guffawed. "Friend, what is your name?"

"Heidar, lord."

"Well, Heidar, you are a big lad for your age; it must be hauling all those nets that have built you up."

"Pardon, commander, but I am no fisherman, but a smith by trade."

"A smith! By all the gods! Today is my lucky day! I know we will give you many opportunities to practise your trade in the months to come. Ha! Here are your sandals and protection for your head."

As soon as Heidar was fully kitted, Carausius spoke again. "As part of my bodyguard, you are exempt from pulling on the oars. If you hear two blasts of the *cornu*, you drop everything and rush up onto this tower, swords drawn. You'll notice that for the moment you have no *scutum*, no *gladius*, and no *pilum*." He saw the confusion on their faces. "You'll soon learn the terms for your equipment. In our tongue, I refer to shield, short sword, and javelin in that order. When you meet your centurion, Galenus Cato, after his sleep," he smirked, "he will issue you with arms and no doubt, sleeping quarters since he's an expert on the subject." The smirk reappeared. "Meanwhile, off you go down on deck and familiarise yourself with the ship. If you see a soldier with the same *baltea*, make his acquaintance at once, for he will be your comrade at arms. Besides, you might need to find your way back with all speed."

The four companions gingerly, but noisily, stepped down the ladder to the deck, getting used to the clattering hobnails under the soles of the *caligae*, which made it easy to slip on wooden surfaces.

Once on deck, Valdor held up his arms, looked down his body ostentatiously, and then peered at his friends. "Will you look at us! Proper Roman soldiers, who'd have thought it this morning when we were filling our water cask?"

"Who indeed?" Faldrek said. "It looks like my career of killing centurions has come to a sudden end."

"Hush! Only our commander must know about that," Johar said anxiously.

"My cousin is right, the least said about that, the better."

"Isn't that the coast of Britannia?" Heidar asked.

Valdor resisted the temptation to gaze at what might otherwise have been their destination and said, "The commander seems a fine fellow."

"Aye, we're lucky. He's a Menapian—almost one of us," Johar said.

"Take nothing for granted," Valdor cautioned. "We'll have to show our worth. He's as likely to send us to our deaths as protect us. He's a quick-witted type, that's for sure. He notices the slightest detail, so let's strive to show him our true worth."

They wandered right to the bows, where a sentinel stared at them. "Here, aren't you those fishermen we rounded up earlier?"

Valdor wasn't going to let the opportunity pass. "Fishermen, nay, we are part of the commander's bodyguard, so show some respect or my comrade will throw you overboard."

"The commander might not take too kindly to losing the sharpest eyes on the ship," came the sour retort.

"Sharpest eyes?" Valdor tormented him. "Then, why haven't

you spotted those sails in the distance?"

The man spun around, a look of anguish on his face, his hands reached for a *cornu* dangling from a leather cord, which he unhooked and blew two shrill blasts. "Thank you," he smiled at Valdor, who in turn, spun around and startled his comrades by setting off at a dash, jumping over anything in his path. His companions, suddenly realising their duty, chased after him to reach the tower in the stern. Valdor took the ladder two rungs at a time and almost stumbled at the commander's feet, but the willing hands of other bodyguards hauled him to his feet.

"What the devil? Why has the lookout sounded the alarm?" Carausius snarled.

"Because I spotted sails in the distance, over yonder, Lord. Aye, see over there beyond yon headland!"

Carausius's eyes narrowed as he peered. After a moment's concentration, he said, "By the gods, lad, you have sharp eyes. And you say that *you* spotted them, not my lookout?"

"To be fair, Commander, we distracted him with our presence in the bows. If not, I'm sure he would have seen them first."

"What's your name, lad? I like your honesty."

"Valdor, Lord."

"Valdor, eh? Men, this is Valdor and he is Heidar, a smith. They, with their friends, are your new comrades."

Valdor stepped in quickly, pointing, "Johar and Faldrek. We are Batavians," he said proudly.

"Ay, and Batavians are not to be messed with," the commander said sternly. "You will treat them as brothers."

The red-plumed helm of a centurion appeared up the ladder.

"Ah, Centurion Galenus Cato," the commander said. "We have four new recruits, Batavi, worth their weight in gold in battle. This one, Valdor, out-spied my lookout, hence the warning."

"We'll see their battle worthiness if those are enemy ships," the centurion said grumpily, his sleep disturbed, glaring at Valdor, who met his gaze without flinching.

3

OFF THE COAST OF EAST ANGLIA, AD 286

THE TRIREME DREW CLOSER TO THE FLOTILLA OF SHIPS waiting a mile off the coast of East Anglia. Valdor counted nine vessels, all war galleys. His commander ordered a small boat to be lowered to carry a messenger, instructed to summon the nine captains and their escorts aboard the Carthaginian flagship. Soon, several small boats arrowed towards them.

In moments, a swarthy Roman officer stood before Carausius, and next to him a crimson-plumed centurion. The captain's lip curled, and in a sardonic voice, he said, "What's this? Are we to take orders from a barbarian thug?"

No sooner had the words left his mouth than Valdor's sword was in his hand. The centurion reacted just as quickly, drawing his gladius. "How dare you draw your sword at a Roman officer, barbarian?" He leapt forward, delivering a scything blow, which but for Valdor's agility would have been fatal. As it was, it left a gash in his leather cuirass without penetrating his flesh. Valdor's same nimbleness allowed him to jump, twisting off the deck and deliver a downward chop by surprise, which severed a tendon in the centurion's wrist, causing him to scream and drop his gladius with a clatter on the wooden boards. In a flash, as the centurion held his useless, bleeding arm to his chest, Valdor's sword was at his throat. The Batavian glanced at his commander, who reacted quickly, "Spare him! That kind of wound is two a sestertius in the army, and we have the *capsarii* to stitch him up and have him fit for combat in no time. It would be a shame to lose a centurion on my first day in charge, Valdor."

Valdor glared at the centurion, removed the blade, and bowed to his commander.

By now, other captains had reached the command tower, and word had rapidly spread about what had happened. The swarthy captain now changed his tone, "Commander, I believe you were about to give us instructions; pray continue."

Carausius also glared at the offending captain, but in a loud clear voice declared, "Caesar Maximian has named me commander of the *Classis Britannica*, tasked with cleansing the channel of Frankish and Saxon pirates. So, we'll sail in search of them off the coast of Armorica. My ship will lead the flotilla, and I expect you to remain within hailing distance of each other. When we sight the enemy, I will issue further orders. We sail upon three blasts of the *cornu*."

There was nothing to question, so the captains, murmuring sullenly among themselves, beat an orderly retreat to their small boats, which were hoisted aboard the galleys. As soon as the last of them was on board, Carausius raised three fingers to signal to the lookout to give three blasts of his horn. That done, he shouted crisp orders to get the galley underway, leading the small fleet south-eastward towards Armorica.

On the voyage, the commander took Valdor aside and confided, "I will not forget your action, my lad; it made an immediate difference to my acceptance as commander. Those captains realise that if a commander inspires such loyalty in his men, he is to be reckoned with. You have a great future ahead; you have my word."

"Thank you, Lord. May I seek out my friends?"

"Ay, but remember, two blasts of the horn and you are to be back beside me on the instant."

"So be it!" Valdor bowed and descended the ladder, turning over Carausius' words in his head with mounting excitement. A matter of days ago, he was a nobody even in his own village; now, it seemed, he was a favourite of a high-ranking Roman officer.

In the open sea, they passed the occasional Roman trading vessel, but there was no sign of pirates. They scoured the north-western coast of Armorica, paying particular attention to the great estuaries.

Valdor spotted a comrade with the insignia of the bodyguard and strolled over to speak with him. He was in luck because many of the crew could not speak his language, but this man, a seasoned mariner, had picked up enough over the years to hold a rudimentary conversation. After rounding a large headland and changing course, the older man said to him, "We're heading to a great river we call the Liger that the locals call the Loire. There are several ports at the mouth, but the most important is Corbilo, the busy trading station of the Veneti tribe. I say, is it true that you chopped the hand off a centurion?"

"People exaggerate," Valdor said. "I had to disarm him, so I cut into his wrist, but the last I saw, he still had his hand. He attacked me first."

"I heard you defended the honour of our commander. That will stand you in good stead with all your comrades. So, it's true that the Batavi are great warriors."

"Well, we need to be put to the test in battle for you to decide that," Valdor said modestly. "But you remind me, I must seek out my friends."

"The other Batavi? I saw them playing dice at the front of the ship not long ago. Stay strong, my friend."

"You, too."

Valdor gazed at the bustling port of Corbilo, which held his attention for a while. Lumpers carried crates of fish from boats up steep steps to the quay, while others rolled barrels into warehouses. He had never seen such a busy place and on so large a scale. He thanked the gods that his life had changed so dramatically. His reverie came to an abrupt halt at the twin blast of the horn, so he skipped over coiled ropes and hastened to the ladder. Again, he was the first of his original companions to mount the ladder, but once on the tower deck, he was met by the broad grin of his new friend who, in a lowered voice, said, "Look over there, the other side of the estuary!" He pointed to a fleet of ships tied together. "Those are Frankish vessels or I know nowt about ships! If I'm right, they'll be raiding in Namnetes territory. That's a valley area full of rich country houses. But let's hear what the commander has to say. The other captains should be here for orders, soon."

His words proved correct, but Carausius' orders did not please them.

"Hark! We'll not chase inland after the pirates. We'll let them plunder and bring back their spoils, which we'll relieve them of in a trice. We'll slay them in battle hereabouts. Meanwhile, we'll sail across the estuary to cut loose their ships, which will be lightly guarded and we'll use our rams to sink the lot of them. Any questions?"

One bold white-haired captain stepped forward to express the perplexity doing the rounds among his colleagues. He stared down his aquiline nose, saying, "Commander, I fear the emperor's wrath when he learns that you did nothing to protect the Namnetes' villas."

"Captain, do not dare question my orders. *I* am the voice of the emperor here and as such, I tell you that when he learns we have destroyed a whole Frankish fleet and its crews, he will be more than satisfied."

Muttering among the captains caused Carausius to lose patience. He bellowed, "Return to your ships and carry out my orders! Within the hour, I do not want to see a single Frankish ship still afloat."

Valdor marvelled that his commander did not take part in the operation but contented himself with a watching brief. Ramming was not so straightforward as he had imagined. Each galley was equipped at the bows, below the waterline, with a long spike, essentially a sharpened tree trunk. But to use it effectively, the attacking vessel needed considerable speed, generated with the sole intention of caving in the side of an enemy ship so that the seawater flooded in and sank her. The first ship had the easiest task because she targeted the outermost of the moored vessels and, sail filled by the strong breeze, drove into the smaller craft with a mighty crashing of rending timber. Valdor listened to the orders being called and watched as scores of oars backed the galley away from its victim. Panicked shouts came from other Frankish ships, whose skeleton crews attempted to cut their boat free. The first to drift out into the estuary was immediately rammed by an incoming galley surging forward at high speed.

The smaller, lighter and therefore, more manoeuvrable Frankish vessels were able to avoid ramming, but not the grappling irons that flew towards them. Roman soldiers poured aboard and overwhelmed the undermanned vessels. Working at great pace, the boarders soon scuppered the ships by springing the planks below the waterline. In these operations two or three Romans drowned because they were unable to flee the onrushing waters in time and went down with the ship, but the number was negligible compared to the Frankish losses. Soon, not a single Frankish craft of the twenty-two moored vessels remained afloat. Even the irascible Carausius expressed his satisfaction and hailed the nearest captain, telling him to moor where the Franks had tied up previously. Shortly, all ten galleys were moored alongside each other so that it was easy to step from one craft to the next, which Carausius did to congratulate his captains in turn. To each, he ordered a scout sent inland to look out for the returning pirates and with instructions to report back without being seen as soon as they spied the foe.

Carausius sent out Johar with another of the older bodyguards. When they returned together, all smiles, the older man reported to the commander. "Before sunset lord, look the sun is low, by the time it touches the sea, they will be here. I estimate that there were eight hundred of them and they were carrying a large box on two poles."

"Ha, the booty!" The commander turned to Johar, "do you agree that the enemy has eight hundred men?"

"Aye, I'd say that's about right, lord."

"Then, we outnumber them for sure," he smiled grimly.

The accounts of the other scouts tallied, so Carausius ordered three blasts of the *cornu* and led his crew onto the shore. He employed the tactical system based on small and supple infantry units called maniples. Each maniple numbered 120 men in 12 files and 10 ranks. The maniples drew up for battle in three lines, each line made up of 10 maniples and the whole arranged in a chequer-board pattern. Nobody organised this better than Carausius, hence his burgeoning reputation as a military strategist.

The Franks possessed high-quality weapons, especially their long swords, but unlike the Frankish professional soldiers, did not wear chain mail. This was an advantage for the Romans along with their superior numbers. Had their commander brought horses, he would have used the cavalry to protect his flanks. Instead, he urged his captains to position their hardiest men on the right flank and took his bodyguard to hold the left.

Johar whispered to his cousin, "I'm scared, is there anything I should know?"

"Aye, that we are stronger than they, and will win the day. Keep your shield high and meet force with force. Remember, I'm next to you and will guard your flank. Look, Heidar is on your other side. You no longer need to be scared."

The Franks came at a rush, hurling insults, oval, colourfully-painted shields raised. Their first mistake was to hurl throwing spears and axes at the solid wall of Roman *scuta*. These formidable curved shields proved impenetrable, causing the weapons to fall harmlessly to the ground. The Romans did not waste their spears, preferring to use the *hastae* to stab the onrushing enemy between shields. So, the Franks crashed onto a wall of spikes. The survivors were forced backwards by the *scuta* and the *gladii*, the famous short swords used so effectively in close engagements.

The chequerboard line-up of the Roman formation proved devastating as the Frankish pirates had never encountered anything similar. They were already outnumbered and, adding disorientation to this, the battle was soon swinging towards a Roman victory. To combat the Roman formation, the Franks split their force to attack the flanks. It was the worst thing they could have done as the central maniples swung out behind them to drive them from behind onto the well-formed flanks. The four Batavian companions acquitted themselves bravely, a fact noted by their equally ferocious commander. Three of them killed for the first time, the strong Heidar, several times.

At last, an eerie silence, broken only by the shrieks of scavenging birds, fell over the battlefield as the twilight brought by the setting sun enveloped the survivors, casting long phantom-like shadows before them.

"Quickly, you four," Carausius indicated the Batavians, "come with me." He set off through the bodies at a run until there remained no more corpses. The comrades had no idea what he was about until in the distance, about four hundred yards ahead, they spied four Franks each holding up a pole, transporting a large chest.

Carausius pointed, "Their spoils, ours now!" They redoubled their pace and within shouting distance, the commander warned them fluently in their own language, "Set down that chest if you want to live and disappear from my sight. We'll slaughter you like swine if you make a fight of it."

Evidently, the Franks' greed outweighed their wisdom, for they drew their swords and stood shoulder to shoulder. The sight of their gore-spattered adversaries should have terrorised them, but they were determined to keep their ill-gotten gains.

The sheer ferocity of Carausius and Heidar was probably enough for victory without the support of Valdor, Johar, and Faldrek, but it was the latter who first struck down and killed a foe. The engagement was short and sharp and the outcome inevitable. With all four Franks dead on the ground, Carausius ordered the Batavians to hoist up the poles and carry the chest to his ship. They laid their *scuta* neatly on top of the chest and weary, fit to drop, plodded back to the battlefield, where many Romans were picking weapons, especially the prized swords, and items from the corpses of fallen Franks. To the relief of the four companions, their commander called four of his bodyguards who took over carrying duties. Even so, they had to help them load the chest onto the galley as it needed lifting high to clear the gunwales. That accomplished, they were entitled to rations of wine and bread.

But Valdor could not enjoy his refreshment in peace since he spotted the captain of the neighbouring ship storming aboard, his expression wrathful. Sensing trouble, Valdor set down his beaker and tossed his remaining crust overboard for a swooping gull to devour before hurrying to the tower ladder.

He was in time to catch the same puce-faced, patrician captain shouting at Carausius, "First, you let the pirates rampage at will through the province, then, not satisfied, you seize their bounty and bring it aboard *your* ship. We *all* fought in the battle." He thrust his contorted face into the commander's so that their noses were almost touching as he shouted, "Do you think we'll passively accept this? Well, you're mistaken!"

The commander stepped back and wiped his spittle-flecked face, leering at his enraged subaltern, and said, "What are you going to do about it?"

"The emperor will hear about this!" He raised a huge fist and took a step forward to deliver the blow, but Valdor's hand clamped around his wrist and hauled him, off-balance away from Carausius. Valdor meant to take advantage of the man's loss of equilibrium to toss him to the deck but, as misfortune would have it, the captain's sandal caught in a small gap between planks and he staggered at the moment Valdor heaved. The result was disastrous because the captain precipitated down the ladder, striking his head on the way to lie still at the foot of the steps, his head at an unnatural angle. Valdor shot down and placed two fingers on the officer's neck searching in vain for a pulse.

Carausius joined him and the Batavian shook his head, "I-it was an accident, I didn't mean to slay him."

The commander placed a fatherly hand on his shoulder, "I saw that it was an accident! But where were the rest of my body-guard? Only you, Valdor came to ensure my safety and I shall not forget that. Now, I'm twice in your debt. Hurry, find and fetch four of your comrades with a blanket. They'll carry the body back to his ship. I'll accompany him to appoint a new captain and explain how this one lost his temper and stormed away in a blind rage, losing his balance and falling down the ladder in a terrible accident that was his own fault."

"Thank you, lord."

"Nay, thank *you,* my brother!"

4

LUCKILY, CARAUSIUS COULD NOT HEAR THE MURMURS of discontent on the other vessels of his flotilla. His own crew thought the world of him because they admired his strategic military superiority compared to previous generals.

As they approached the coast of East Anglia, the commander summoned Valdor to the tower. They were alone up there, and Carausius spoke with confidentiality to The Batavian.

"Valdor, I can only imagine the grumbling on the other ships. You see, I made my name as a land-based soldier and led my men to victory against the Bagaudae rebels, using the same tactics as against the Franks at Corbilo. These naval types have never taken me to heart, and they resent me holding the Frankish spoils." He placed a hand on Valdor's arm and stared into the earnest grey-blue eyes. "Why am I telling you this? For two reasons: to urge you to watchfulness because those sailors would as soon slit my throat as shake my hand; secondly, because I don't want you to judge me ill. I do not lust for treasure any more than the next man; indeed, I intend to share the Frankish loot with my crew and with—oh, never mind, you'll find out soon enough."

"Lord, I promise to be watchful and will also speak about the need for alertness to my three friends."

"Look, yonder is the fort of Branodunum; can you see its walls? Severus Alexander built it and two others along the coast some three-score years ago to help protect traders from pirates. At the moment, the garrison is made up of *Equites Dalmatae*, Dalmatian cavalry. I remember you saying that you and your friends grew up riding horses."

"Ay, lord, it's true, although—"

"Tell me."

Valdor hesitated as if reluctant to criticise anyone. "My cousin Johar is not as proficient as we others because he had to spend much time at sea with his father."

"I'll bear that in mind. I have a surprise for you and Heidar once we set foot in that fort. See, to the west and north of it is the *vicus* where the civilians live and work outside its walls. The inhabitants belong to the Iceni tribe. I have a lot of time for them; they are fierce warriors if you get on the wrong side of them, as their queen, Boudicca, proved by defeating a Roman legion and burning Londinium to the ground, but that was in a past century. The southern wall, facing the sea, is on the shoreline and it serves as a harbour. I have brought the fleet here as I will not tolerate mutiny in the ranks, and I have a special fondness for cavalry."

I wonder why he is telling me all this?

Once moored at the harbour, Carausius issued orders that only his crew should disembark, while the others were to remain aboard their respective ships. The commander inspected the loot obtained from the Franks and called several of his officers to whom he handed coins and gems to distribute among the crew. Valdor and Heidar each received a large Byzantine gold solidus, whereas Johar and Faldrek were happy with a smaller Roman gold *solidus* bearing the portrait of Augustus Diocletian.

At a certain point, the commander closed the trunk and ordered it to be carried ashore. The lookout, on his command, strode with his horn to the southern gate and blew a peremptory blast, at which the doors swung back and Carausius marched his men, carrying the remainder of the spoils into the rectangular fortress. At the eastern end, there was commotion with many men cheering and laughing.

A couple of officers strode to greet Carausius. Judging by their elaborate crimson plumes, they were of high rank, Valdor thought. His conjecture proved correct when they introduced themselves respectively as the camp prefect and a tribune. To them, Carausius delivered the spoils to be shared among the cavalrymen.

"What's going on over there?" The commander pointed to the raucously cheering assembly.

"Ah, yesterday we received a new consignment of horses," said the tribune, "and among them is a spirited black stallion. Nobody has managed to break him in yet. Assuming anyone succeeds in mounting him, the beast bucks so hard that it is impossible to stay on its back. Remember, I have some of the finest horsemen in the Empire and yet..."

Without asking permission, Valdor strode over to the compound, leaving Carausius to deal with the camp officials. He pushed his way through the crowd to the front, just in time to see an unfortunate cavalryman thrown backwards off a stomping black stallion, its muzzle flecked with white foam. Valdor climbed into the compound over a three-barred fence without consulting anyone. Meanwhile, a soldier had snared the stallion with a lasso, so Valdor walked up to him and took the free end of the rope. "I'll ride him," he said confidently. The soldier, like the rest, had never seen this cocky fellow before, so, not knowing him, tamely handed over the rope.

Valdor strolled carefully over to the stallion, making sure to keep well within the horse's sight. The stallion was stamping and snorting angrily, but Valdor's first action was to remove the noose from over its head and then, he gently caressed the restless animal's muzzle. He put his head close to the horse and, smiling, looked him straight in the eye before slowly, slowly, moving to whisper in its ear. The onlooking crowd had become rapt in silence, which helped him soothe the beast. He continued to pacify the horse with gentle words before again, slowly, slowly, moving to stand, arms outspread in front of him, gently clicking his tongue. An awed murmur came from the gathering when the stallion steadily stepped towards the stranger and nuzzled his chest. Again, Valdor whispered in the horse's ear and suddenly, sprang onto its back, threading his fingers into its mane, leaning forward and whispering his magic words into its ear. With a proud neigh, the stallion responded to the gentle heel kicking of its rider and to the astonishment of the assembly, set off around the compound at a trot. Valdor sat upright and, holding tightly with his knees, waved to the crowd, which raised a cheer. Valdor's delicate pat on its head kept the stallion calm, and he let it trot where it wanted as there was no bit nor reins to guide it. Soon, the splendid mount stopped of its own accord, and Valdor leapt down to caress the sleek coat and speak more calming words. Another nuzzle and their friendship was sealed. "Thank you, my friend; I shall call you Sparax," he said to the stallion, earning himself another whinny and a happy toss of the head.

Ignoring the pressing questions in a language he could not understand, Valdor broke free and came face-to-face with the broadly-grinning Carausius.

"Well done, Centurion," the commander said.

"Lord, I don't understand."

"Centurion Valdor, you have been promoted, and the tribune has gifted you yon stallion since only you, it seems, can domesticate it."

Valdor, for once, was speechless. "W-what?"

The tribune, an officer of considerable learning, came to his rescue. "Come, Centurion, I will accompany you to withdraw your new equipment," he placed a playful finger in the slash in Valdor's cuirass and tugged. "By all accounts, you owe the legion a new centurion! The camp prefect is designating the seventy-nine men under your command. You know that a century is made up of eighty men; well, your Decurion is also withdrawing his uniform, there, with him, that makes eighty."

"Heidar, my decurion?" Valdor had regained his tongue.

"Aye, but expect him to be excused service whenever the prefect requires him to man the forge. I believe there's some call for an able smith."

"Oh, Heidar is able, alright, for he learnt from Thragnor, the best smith in Batavia."

"You Batavians are full of surprises, but take my advice, young man. Your feat with the stallion has earned you much goodwill, but don't underestimate the Dalmatians; they too are a fierce race of combatants. They will expect you to be better than them in courage and compassion, not merely in horse-riding. You are evidently young and will be viewed with diffidence."

"Rightly so, I have never commanded men."

"*Hard, but fair; kind but hard.* Make that your motto, and I'll have to look over my shoulder lest you rise further!"

Valdor laughed, but his head was spinning, yet, he sagely managed. "Lord, you need never fear for my loyalty."

"So, I gather from your commander. I do not suffer fools and would not have consented to your early promotion if I did not agree with Carausius. He is a fine general. I'm sorry that he might leave us so soon."

"I know nothing of that, lord."

"I know, but here we are. Greet your decurion, and I'll requisition the armour with a centurion's insignia."

The tribune marched into the building Heidar had just vacated.

The former smith greeted him. "Valdor, you'll never guess!"

"I will. You're a decurion, and you can't believe your luck!"

"H-how did you know?"

"I know because I am your centurion. From now on, you obey my orders, Decurion!"

Heidar mock-scowled. "Nothing new, then! Oh, by the way, the prefect is giving me a horse!"

"I like your feathers, very impressive!" He pointed to his friend's plumed helmet, tucked under his arm.

"Ay, but I can't wear it yet; apparently, it's not the done thing in the camp when we're off duty."

"I must go; the tribune's calling me!" He dream-walked into the building and, several minutes later, emerged with a *galea*, distinctive with its traverse crimson crest, and carrying a vitis, the vine-stock that a Roman legionary centurion wielded as a cane with which to punish his soldiers. *Hard, but fair; kind but hard,* he told himself, *I'll probably never use this on my men, except on Heidar!* But that was a private joke because a centurion would never, surely, punish a decurion with a whip!

The two friends strolled aimlessly around the fort, taking in details like the rounded corners with internal turrets backed by earthen ramparts that strengthened the walls, not less than four feet in thickness, built of stone, brick, and tiles used together.

The troops were housed in timber-built huts. The quarters of the tribune and the camp prefect were spacious buildings of brick, and although the friends had not yet seen inside, the latter might almost have been a mansion in Rome itself thanks to its handsome chambers with tessellated floors, its baths, and underfloor heating.

There was a central street, in which provisions, clothing, and trinkets could be bought. The Romans did not permit the dealers to remain within the fort after sunset, but the shops were tenanted by day and did well for business, not only with the soldiers but also with the neighbouring Britons. Many of the women in the soldiers' huts were Britons. "I'll bet their children will be soldiers, too, when they grow up," Heidar said.

From the nearest corner turret, Carausius emerged.

"Centurion, Decurion!" he bellowed at them, "Over here, smartish!"

Taking time only to exchange glances, the friends ran at once to their commander.

"Quickly, up the tower! I want you to see something."

Together with Carausius, they gazed down at the harbour. "What do you see?"

"Our ships, lord," Heidar said.

"Ay, but what don't you see?"

Heidar frowned, looked puzzled, and glanced at Valdor, who said, "Eight-*nine*! One is missing!"

"Exactly! What does that mean?"

"One of the captains has disobeyed orders and sailed—"

"Correct, Centurion, and I know why."

"You do?"

"Ay, we must prepare for war. He'll have sailed off to meet Emperor Maximian's forces in Gaul to denounce me for not protecting the Namnetes from the pirates and for keeping the spoils to myself." He bellowed a laugh. "He would be angrier if he knew I had given the bounty to the Dalmatians. But I need the loyalty of these cavalrymen."

"Those other four ships did not come with us," Valdor pointed at four identical two-masted vessels, smaller than the galleys but with deep rounded hulls.

"They will join our fleet because they are specially built to transport horses. In our next battle, Centurion Valdor, you will command a cavalry unit. Those ships have stalls below deck along the whole length of the boat, and above deck, there are slings designed to restrain a nervous horse even in the heaviest seas."

"I think Sparax will be better off above deck in the open air."

"Sparax?"

"Ay, my stallion. I would like to travel with him at sea to keep him calm."

"Nay, you travel with me to keep me calm! Or do you have a short memory, Centurion?"

"You are right, lord, my primary task is to guard your safety."

"Those ships look smaller and slower, but in reality, they have two triangular sails that drive them forward at a faster rate than our galleys. Having cavalry available in battle will make my strategy so much easier. Do you remember how our best soldiers covered the flanks? Well, that task will go to the Dalmatian cavalry."

"Do you truly think that Emperor Maximian will declare war on you?"

"I can't be sure, but the captain who has fled is the highest-ranking in the *Classis Britannica*, apart from myself, that is. He's resentful of me and renowned for his political manoeuvring, so I expect he will persuade the emperor that I am a traitor."

"But that's ridiculous!"

"Ay, Valdor, we know that, but my friend, the corridors of power in Rome are awash with the blood of innocent men.

5

BRANODUNUM FORT, NORFOLK, 296 AD

SEVERAL WEEKS PASSED IN WHICH VALDOR AND HEIDAR refined their respective roles with helpful advice from fellow officers. Valdor took delight in training his cavalrymen to form up as required by Carausius. He found ways of putting the formation to the test by mock battles and stressed the importance of keeping a tight formation. A revolutionary aspect was his insistence on occasionally training without horses. Other cavalrymen might have resented this, but Valdor had a way of gaining support through his personality. *Hard, but fair; kind but hard.* The Dalmatian horsemen fulfilled his demands, and he was convinced that he had an elite group ready to face the most testing circumstances in battle.

Relaxed, he conceded himself more free time, so that one bright morning, he decided to survey the view from the top of the south-western tower. He saw a sail and watched a galley anchor close to the South Foreland point. He recognised the vessel as the *Leopard*, the galley that had fled the harbour months ago. His eyes narrowed as a small boat with a single occupant and two oarsmen started to row towards the approaches of the harbour.

He hurried to find Carausius, who took the news badly. "We must intercept that boat before its captain can turn the fleet against me. He must be confident of Maximian's support to sail boldly back here. Centurion, I have noticed you training your Dalmatians to fight without horses, bring them aboard my galley. We'll seize his messenger and then face Captain Leander Russus before he can overturn me."

The oarsmen carrying the messenger did not know that they were in a race against time, an advantage that Carausius possessed. Swiftly, Valdor urged his Dalmatians aboard, their morale high at the thought of impending action even without horses. Carausius soon had the full complement of oarsmen in position and the galley cast off, shooting out of the harbour. Valdor stood in the bows with a coiled rope in hand. In a deep voice that belied his stature, he called down to the rowing boat, "Here's a rope, climb aboard at once, or we will ram you and send you to the bottom to feed the crabs!" He was close enough to see the expressions of fear and horror on the three faces. Moments later, one of the oarsmen grabbed the rope and jumped into the sea. Three strong Dalmatian cavalrymen hauled him to the galley and up its side until he jumped onto the deck. Valdor coiled the rope again, and although he misjudged his cast this time, it fell close enough to the boat for the second oarsman to dive into the sea and grasp it. Valdor's third throw was perfect as the rope landed on the boat. The messenger was soon hauled onto the galley and confronted by Carausius.

"You will tell me what message you bring and for whom it is intended."

The messenger's face was a picture of misery. "Lord, my message was not intended for you, but for Captain Cyrillus Drusus."

"As I feared. But you can confirm that the vessel you sailed on and now standing offshore is the *Leopard*, commanded by Captain Leander Russus?"

The messenger did not meet Carausius' eyes but lowered his head and muttered, "Ay, I can vouch for that."

"I command the *Classis Britannica*, so any message for

Cyrillus Drusus is also of concern to me. So, you will tell me your message at once."

"Nay, lord, I cannot. My captain said it was for Drusus' ears only. I dare not disobey orders."

Carausius glared and snarled, "If you care for the lives of your companions and your own, you will give me that accursed message." He signalled to the two Dalmatians who each had an oarsman by an arm. They dragged the unfortunate fellow to stand trembling before the enraged commander, who drew his gladius and pressed its blade to his throat.

"Wait!" The messenger cried desperately. "I'll give you the message, lord, but I beg you to recognise, I am but the bearer of tidings."

Carausius withdrew the blade from the oarsman's throat, and he, who had steeled himself for a mortal blow, visibly sagged with relief, held up by the two cavalrymen.

"Out with it, then!" the commander roared.

The messenger wiped his brow with a shaking hand. "Caesar Maximian declares that Marcus Aurelius Mausaeus Carausius is..." his voice caught, and he paled... "a traitor to the Empire and decrees," as if to shed a great burden, the messenger shrieked, "his immediate execution!"

"This means war!" Carausius bellowed, and raised his voice to a roar everyone on board was meant to hear, "I, Marcus Aurelius Mausaeus Carausius, declare myself Emperor in Britain and Northern Gaul, which area will be known as the *Imperium Britannicum*. There are now three Augusti: salute Imperator Caesar Marcus Aurelius!"

The Dalmatians drew their swords and raised them above their heads. "Hail Caesar!"

The oarsmen on each deck beat their fists on their benches and repeated the cry over and over.

"We have our Emperor of the North," Valdor said to Heidar. "And now, it's off to war."

The new emperor heard him and grinned. "Too true, my

friend, and with stalwarts like you, I shall prevail." He turned to the Dalmatians. "Put these three in irons, for the moment, they know too much! Prepare for battle, Centurion, we'll attack Russus' galley."

Valdor ensured there were four javelins for each of his Dalmatians and inspected them as they lined up behind their shields.

"Shall we prepare the catapult and pitch, Lord?" Heidar asked.

"We shall not, Decurion. I do not wish to destroy or sink the galley. It will be useful in the forthcoming war. Neither do I wish to annihilate the crew. Those who can be spared in victory will follow me! I want Leander Russus' head. A *solidus* goes to he who severs it from his body." Only the men close to Heidar heard this, but the words engendered a great ferment among them. A gold solidus was the equivalent of six months' pay for a legionary, few of whom had even touched such a coin, as their pay came in silver denarii.

Normally, a war galley approaching an anchored vessel would steer amidships to ram the stationary ship, but their new emperor had been explicit; he wanted to preserve the *Leopard* at all costs.

Instead, they came swiftly alongside, observing the pandemonium aboard the enemy vessel, whose rowers rushed to gather arms. Carausius ordered the *corvus* to be dropped. The long spike knifed into the deck, and the emperor watched as the first across was the man with the transverse plume: Valdor. He was closely followed by the decurions. He smiled grimly; the role of a centurion in the Roman army was not all prestige. On the whole, they were short-lived for this very reason; they put duty and glory before personal safety.

Valdor, and the rest of the vanguard knew they would find Leander Russus on the tower at the stern, overlooking events to send tactical orders to the men on deck. Having disposed of the first onrushing defenders, Valdor pushed Heidar forward, took several steps backwards, and issued orders. The response to his command was a hail of javelins falling into the oncoming defenders followed by his Dalmatians forming into a wedge as practised on the training ground. He placed himself at the head of the wedge and set the pace with a slow forward march.

The sight of the relentless and deliberate oncoming wedge formation unmanned the relatively inexperienced crew, who responded by dropping their weapons and squatting on the deck, despite the hysterical shouting from the tower and the flailing vine whips of the centurions, determined to make a noble fight of it. Valdor chose the nearest centurion, still busily flogging a recalcitrant man, and slew him, distracted with his arm raised. Heidar led the wedge around the squatting and, in some cases, bleeding men. "Go to the bows!" he shouted. "You will be spared."

The demoralised crewmen needed no further encouragement but fled from the vine whips past the grinning foe to stand huddled in the front of the ship. A Dalmatian decurion broke formation, first to slay a resisting enemy centurion, then to bound up the steps where several bodyguards defended their captain. Fortunately for the decurion, inspired by lust for a solidus, several other decurions followed his example to make an even fight of it. Valdor hastened to join them, but with the difference that he bellowed, "Halt, lower your weapons, the Emperor Marcus Aurelius has decreed that those among you who wish to join his legion will be spared today. Look below on deck, there is no further resistance. The day is lost, and the emperor's victory is secure. Join your brothers and fight for the glorious Emperor of the North!"

He read uncertainty on the faces of the bodyguard surrounding their captain, so added, "I, too, was a captain's bodyguard, a nobody, but raised to centurion by my generous emperor. So, I know how hard it is for you to abandon Leander Russus, but remember, the traitor was he, not our new emperor. He deserted the fleet to run off with falsities to Maximian. The bounty we won was shared among the men."

"Pay no heed to this liar!" Russus shrieked. "Fight like men!"

"The cause is lost, lord," one of the guards said to the corpse of Drusus, who had fallen to the blade of a Dalmatian decurion while everyone was distracted by the debate. The same decurion was now busy hacking the head from the body. Valdor took charge *Hard, but fair; kind but hard*, "Come, my comrades, we must return to port." He led the way down the ladder and addressed the cowering crew, "The battle is over, you now serve the Emperor of the North, Caesar Marcus Aurelius," he had a moment of inspiration, "who promises you a donative within the space of a month."

These words were greeted by raucous cheering, handshaking among themselves, and wide grins.

"But now," bellowed Valdor, pointing to the victorious galley, "Greet your Caesar and then back to stations. We will raise the *corvus*."

As the 'Hail Caesar' rang out, to be met with the recognition of a hand wave from the swarthy, stocky, curly-haired and curly-bearded figure on the stern tower, Valdor took Heidar aside. "I'll leave you with your thirty men to guard this ship, although I don't expect trouble. Have them sail to the harbour and then row to their berth." He turned to others of his men. "Prepare ropes around the *corvus*. We'll cross it, back to our ship and free it to stand upright."

The struggle to free the *corvus* was as difficult as expected, but after adding extra muscle, they succeeded.

Valdor hurried to his emperor, "Caesar, it is clear we won the day, but at a cost."

"What? I saw none of our men fall."

"Thank the gods, that is true, but I promised the crew a donative within the space of a month, to obtain their loyalty."

Carausius slapped him on the back and grinned. "My friend, you are a diplomat and should wear the imperial purple, but don't let my words go to your head! What you promised to these rebels, I'll extend to the other crews immediately. Oh, what's this?"

"The head of yon galley's captain, Caesar," said the decurion, "I slew him myself and removed the head."

"I shall keep my promise, Decurion, but I will need you to

bring your grisly trophy to a captains' meeting that I will call in port."

"So be it, Sire," the decurion bowed and moved away to show the head to the few curious Dalmatians.

The two galleys arrived together in the harbour, gliding perfectly into position. Carausius spoke quietly to Valdor, issuing commands for their arrival on the quay.

The first of these was to convene the captains on the quay. The second was to intimidate them by encircling them with Dalmatian troops, and this was followed by the decurion, bearing the deceased captain's head by the hair, breaking through the ring of steel, accompanied by Valdor. The centurion raised his voice, "In the name of your emperor, Caesar Marcus Aurelius, I inform you that any of you who do not swear allegiance to him will meet the same fate as the traitor Leander Russus." On cue, the decurion raised the head of the rebel captain and showed it at close quarters to the aghast assembly.

"But," continued Valdor, "those of you swearing allegiance will receive, along with all your crew, a donative within the space of a month." He watched as the captains put their heads together, and before a conspiracy could brew, he added, "the same news has been delivered to your ships."

As Providence would have it, at that very moment the raised voices of eight galleys chorused repeatedly, "Hail Caesar Marcus Aurelius!" The crews' loyalty had been obtained by blatantly appealing to their desire for silver. One of the captains stepped forward and in a loud voice called out the same refrain. He was soon followed by the others, except one, a white-haired fellow with a swarthy complexion, Cyrillus Drusus, who drew very close to Valdor and thrust out his chin, "I'll not follow a barbarian with the features of an ape." No sooner had the words left his mouth than Valdor's blade had pierced his heart. Although he had slain him, Valdor could only admire the man's courage and loyalty, if not his folly. He wiped the bloody blade on the captain's cloak, then sheathed his sword and, with a nod, dismissed his men, remaining alone with the captains. "I need not remind you that today you have sworn loyalty to the glorious Emperor of the North. I will make it my personal mission to destroy any of you who reneges on their word. I swear this by all the gods!" *Hard, but fair; kind but hard.* He drew his gladius and kissed the blade to solemnise the oath.

6

BRANODUNUM FORT, NORFOLK, 296 AD

THE FOLLOWING MORNING, THE GARRISON AWOKE TO the sound of hammering. Shaking off his sleepiness, Valdor peered out of his window to see the carpenters erecting a dais in the courtyard. He correctly imagined that the emperor meant to address his men. So, it came as no surprise when the southern gate opened to admit an orderly procession of sailors from all the galleys. Soon, they were joined by the soldiers of the garrison, including the Dalmatian cavalrymen.

Everyone waited in anticipation for the new emperor to make his appearance, and he came, with the cloak of imperial purple thrown over his shoulders and with a peaked diadem of office upon his head. Suddenly, the throng of soldiers and mariners fell silent as the emperor raised a hand.

"Comrades, I renew my pledge of a donative within a month. But let us not be deluded; we know that there are now three emperors: myself, Maximian, and Diocletian. I can count on the goodwill of Diocletian because last year, here, in Britannia, I won a famous battle after he assumed the title of *Britannicus Maximus*, and he is grateful and respects me. But, influenced by lies, Caesar Maximian has decreed my execution, which means he is preparing for war. Well, let him know that I can count on three legions here in Britannia, all of which are superior in discipline and strength to anything he can muster. Comrades, we shall prevail. But first, before we move, I shall honour my pledge. I ask only that you bear with me for a few weeks because, as you know, it takes time to gather a decent amount of silver. It is my priority!"

These words were greeted by a thunderous roar of approval, which stopped as if by enchantment when the emperor raised a finger and thumb above his head, holding a gold solidus that caught the sunlight and flashed brilliantly.

"Comrades, see how Caesar Marcus Aurelius honours his word. Step forward, Decurion!" bellowed Carausius, turning to grasp the arm of the Dalmatian decurion. "This man slew my enemy, the treacherous Captain Leander Russus, who spread poisonous lies against my person and turned Maximian against me. I pledged a solidus to the man who brought me his head. Here is the coin, Comrade, take it with your emperor's gratitude." He embraced the embarrassed soldier to deafening cheers. Carausius enjoyed and milked the moment, waving to the approving throng. Suddenly, he raised a hand and silence fell again. "I seek an artist, one capable of capturing my portrait. It is an opportunity for one of you to gain some coins. If there is a competent artist among you, step forward!"

Three men stepped out of the crowd and approached the dais, stopping to bow before their emperor.

Valdor felt sympathy for the three men. He considered Carausius his friend, but by no stretch of the imagination did he have godlike features; rather, his were coarse and pug-like. It was difficult to gaze upon Carausius and not consider him a barbarian thug, as expressed by the late, unlamented Captain Drusus, of Roman patrician birth.

Rather they than me! But why does he want a portrait, now?

He was soon to find out. An hour after the parade ground dismissal, Carausius summoned him to his chamber. He found the three artists there, charcoal in hand and portraits ready for exhibition.

"Ah, Centurion! Come in, I require your opinion. Which of these three portraits, place them on the table, Comrades, do you prefer?"

Valdor looked at the honest renditions with some trepidation but, after a brief hesitation, pointed to the one on the left. "I find this one captures you well, Sire."

"Ah, then we are in agreement, good Valdor," Carausius said, to his relief, a sentiment he kept closely hidden. "Even so, I am grateful to you other two. Here is a smaller recompense for your efforts, which anyway, will grace my wall." He handed them each two denarii. "As for you," he said to the chosen artist, "I require your further services. Take another vellum and draw a large circle. Imagine it to be the reverse of a coin but it must show three profiles: mine," he laid two silver denarii on the table and tapped each with his forefinger, "those of Maximian and Diocletian— a new version of a Triumvirate and underneath, the legend CARAVSIVS ET FRATRES SVI— Carausius and his brothers."

When the artist had finished, the emperor said, "Now, back to my portrait, write the legend PAX AVGGG, the peace of *three* Augusti."

Mmm, cunning devil! That implies that he is recognised by the other two current Augusti, thought Valdor, *smart move!*

He didn't have time for further reflections because the newly self-appointed emperor turned to him, "As you see, Centurion, I will have my own coinage, and it is your duty to take all of your cavalrymen to the mints in Londinium and Colonia Claudia Victricensis, and I want none of their excuses. If need be, slaughter the lot of them, but come away with all of their reserves of silver and gold transformed into my coinage. Your Dalmatians will ensure safe transport back to Branodunum. Do not fail me, Centurion Valdor. You are becoming my right hand!"

"I am humbled, Caesar, and your wish is my command."

The artist rolled up the two sheets of vellum and bound them together with a red ribbon before scooping up the six denarii given to him by his generous emperor. Valdor felt the gold solidus in his pocket and decided to visit the stalls in the camp to change the coin into more practical silver denarii before departing the fort. He bowed out of his emperor's presence, bearing the precious sketches. At a stall, he bought an expensive whetstone, costly because it had two degrees of roughness so that sharpening a blade could be done more precisely. This enabled him to change his coin easily. At another stall, for just one denarius, he bought a pendant image of Epona, the sole Celtic divinity worshipped in Rome itself as the patroness of cavalry. He took off his helm, bowed his head, and allowed the British woman stallkeeper the satisfaction of looping the leather thong over his head. *Epona, may you protect me in battle!*

Next, he summoned Heidar. "Assemble the century. All my men are to ride to Colonia Claudia Victricensis on an important mission. Encourage them by telling them we are going to collect the emperor's donative. Soon, they will receive it, but only if we return with it safe and sound."

He wandered over to the stables, realising that he hadn't seen Sparax for several days, a rarity because he loved his stallion as he might a brother if only he had one. There was a married sister back in Batavia. He wondered if he would ever see Alodia again. Would he have nephews or nieces that he would never see? His destiny was now in the hands of a terrestrial god, namely, Caesar Marcus Aurelius, or as he knew him first, Carausius. His emperor pressed a map into his hands.

"Use this, it is a copy of Iter IX of the Antonine Itinerary and the only reliable guide to our roads in Britannia. If you ride south to *Venta Icenorum*, you will have the precise route to *Camulo-dunum*, the site of the first mint and thence to *Londinium*, where the second mint is located."

Valdor took the map gratefully and saluted his emperor with a clenched fist to his chest.

At the stables, he caressed Sparax's sleek coat and pressed a silver coin into the young Briton's hand, the one which groomed his stallion so assiduously that the horse's forelock felt like silk thread. He whispered to the stallion, whose gentle whinnies showed him how much his horse had missed him. "We're going a long way, my beauty, but fear not, I'll look after you."

His century set off out of the southern gate and took up a gravel-surface road some fifteen yards wide with a ditch either side and headed southwards to *Venta Icenorum*, the trading capital of the Iceni tribe. Their early morning departure meant that they arrived in sight of the flint defensive walls by mid-afternoon, by which time, every one of them and his steed was weary from the ride. The town, with its forum, two impressive temples, and baths was a thriving combination of Romano-British activities. Rather than thinking of relaxing in the baths, Valdor thought of the well-being of Sparax and the other horses, so it was a relief to find a welcome in the Roman fort, where willing servants rubbed down, fed, and gave drink to the animals. The camp prefect told Valdor that the walls had just been completed in response to constant Saxon raids. Valdor reassured him that the *Classis Britannica* was on hand to deal with the pirates and that his mission was to fetch the pay for the fleet.

Having seen to the well-being of their horses, Valdor and his decurions and some of the legionaries availed themselves of the hot and cold baths to reinvigorate their aching bones. Afterwards, Valdor and Heidar joined with Johar and Faldrek to find a tavern with acceptable red wine. Their first attempt had them spitting vinegar in disgust and threatening the innkeeper, who blamed the Saxon pirates for the depredation of his best wine. However unwillingly, he told them where to find a tavern that had enjoyed better fortune than his. The streets took them past a temple with massive stone pillars. Valdor wanted to look inside, but his companions were not enamoured of the idea, so he gave Heidar three denarii and told him to start without him. He secretly hoped to find a shrine to Epona, but wasn't to know that her altar was in the town's other temple, so he contented himself by making his devotions to the helmeted statue of Minerva, the Roman goddess of war and wisdom. He prayed to her to watch over him and his close friends in battle and to give him the wisdom to fulfil his centurion duties with sagacity.

The latter part of his prayers took an immediate blow as he allowed himself to drink more of the excellent red wine than could be legitimately described as wise. As an incentive for their continued consumption, the innkeeper provided them with salted meat, cheese, and bread.

The next morning, Valdor ensured that his dearest friends rode close to him because apart from the previous evening, he and Heidar had rather lost touch with the other two. Their long-standing friendship meant that there was no envy or resentment about the promotions the other two had enjoyed. Before them, but on good roads, stretched a ride of 54 Roman miles to reach *Camulodunum*. After 30 miles, they came to *Sitomagus*, an important market town as the name *long market* suggested, the stalls stretched along the road for almost two miles, in which Valdor allowed those of his men who wished to peruse and purchase to do so without reprimand. They could always gallop to catch up with their comrades.

Apart from this brief diversion, the journey proved to be uneventful. Fortune favoured them at *Combretovium*, a Roman fort, which was garrisoned only by cavalry. This fort was at the crossing of the River Gipping and, as the camp prefect lamented, it was undermanned also because nothing ever happened since the Britons in the area were pacific and largely civilised. The official was happy to accommodate his visitors for the night and allow his grooms to pamper the steeds.

Over another excellent wine imported from Ostia, and forti-fied by fermented British elderberries, the prefect and Valdor hatched a plan. On their return from Londinium, whenever that might be, the entire garrison would forsake *Combretovium*, unite with Valdor, and ride to swear allegiance to the Emperor of the North. Their conversation was not as private as Valdor imagined because as he was retiring to his quarters in a rectangular timber building, he encountered three centurions who eagerly pressed him: "Is it true that we'll transfer from this godforsaken place to Branodunum? And will there truly be the prospect of an engagement? We're fed up with rotting in this place, Centurion."

"Valdor is the name, I'm Batavian by birth. But goodness, how quickly news travels in *Combretovium*!"

"So, it *is* true!" said another eagerly. "When do we leave?"

"Within the month when I stop here on our return."

"I'll bet our good prefect did not tell you the whole truth, Centurion."

"Hush!" said another, arousing Valdor's curiosity.

"Hold your tongue, Marcellus!" said the other, making it imperative for Valdor to discover what was afoot.

The one called Marcellus stuck out his chin defiantly, "We have nothing to be ashamed of, Centurion Valdor, but it's like this: the men here are a part of the disgraced 3rd legion, punished by being disbanded in 238 and sent to useless places like this because of its role in putting down an African-based revolt against Emperor Maximinus Thrax in favour of the provincial governor Gordianus. Capelianus was a legate in the legion and the officer who was falsely accused of misusing his legion to attack Gordian. It was a necessary action and I blame Maximinus for the current crisis in the Empire. He was the first emperor who hailed neither from the senatorial nor from the equestrian class. Now we have your Carausius..." Valdor's hand strayed to the hilt of his gladius, a reflex noticed by the others. Marcellus added quickly, "...of whom I have heard only good things.

"Centuriones, our emperor will be delighted to welcome you into our ranks and I, who have fought under him, can assure you that he is a great general. I, too, will welcome you as comrades." He extended a hand and had his wrist clasped three times in time-honoured fashion.

"It is time I retired because we have an early morning start, so I'll bid you goodnight." He set off for his quarters but soon heard a footfall behind him, so he spun around just in time to see the flash of a blade and throw himself to the ground. Rolling over before springing to his feet, gladius in hand, he crossed swords with a helmeted figure—the single plume indicated a decurion. The idle life at Combretovium could not match the disciplined training at Branodunum, so Valdor rapidly gained the upper hand and sent his opponent's gladius clinking on the paving stone. Pressing his blade to the decurion's throat, he uttered one word, "Why?"

"Because you wish to dishonour the 3rd legion, by inducing us to desert our duty."

"Truly, the 3rd is dishonoured already, festering here, doing nothing. My intention is to restore honour to your legion by placing you in the forefront of battle. But you'll need training to be ready, judging by what I've just seen. Since we are in the throes of a misunderstanding, Decurion, I am prepared to accept an apology and let the matter drop." Valdor slowly lowered the blade but kept a tight grip on the weapon.

"Forgive me friend, I misjudged your intentions. The 3rd legion has a glorious reputation and my only desire is to uphold it."

Valdor sheathed his gladius and smiled, offered his hand and they clasped wrists. "We need more honourable men because war is in the offing with Maximian, not to mention the Saxon and Frankish pirates that infest the Channel." He slapped the decurion's upper arm before bidding him goodnight, said, "Reassure others who might share your earlier doubts that they are uniting with a formidable fighting force. Good night, Decurion."

Pleased with the outcome of his visit to Combretovium, and departing on refreshed horses, the journey was easy on a gravel road whose ditches were 60 feet apart. Before noon, they arrived at the river Colne, where five temples graced the crossing point. Delighted by how things were faring for him and his men, Valdor was convinced that he had been guided by Minerva to the agreement at Combretovium and was determined to visit her shrine to give thanks in prayer. Rightly, he chose the largest temple and immediately found himself face-to-face with the larger-than-life statue of the helmed goddess. "O Minerva, I beg you to continue to guide your humble servant so that he accomplishes his mission to the glory of Rome," he whispered.

"Lead us to glory in battle and preserve us," came a deep voice behind him, and Valdor turned in time to see Heidar's bowed head.

"Come, let's cross the river and find what is in store in Camulodunum."

His fearless stallion waded across the ford confidently, setting the tone for the other horses so that, soon, they were before the north gate of the stone-walled town. Valdor called his *cornicen*, the horn blower, who produced a prolonged, deep vibrating sound from his curved horn. It proved immediately effective as the gates swung back and the cavalry rode into town. Valdor, who had not imagined such a bustling city existed in Britannia, led his cavalry along the *Cardo Maximus*, the well-paved main north-south street with drainage channels and fronted by houses and shops. It included footways, and the rest of the Colonia was gridded into about forty blocks known as *insula*, all with paved streets and colonnaded paths between. Valdor was impressed while at the same time concentrating on his stallion's hoofs skidding on the paving stones. They certainly slowed his progress as he did not want any of the horses to slip and become lame.

The vast, busy population reminded him that this city enjoyed the status of *Colonia* rather than *Municipia*, meaning that legally, it was an extension of Rome and its inhabitants were Roman citizens. Many of them were, in reality, retired legionaries. Next to one of these greybeards, Valdor halted his horse and called down, "Good fellow, where is the building where coins are made?"

The man saluted the centurion and replied, "Continue to the main crossing of the *Decumanus Maximus*, the main east-west street, turn right, and it is the second building on your left."

This information proved correct, meaning Valdor and Heidar entered the main portal, leaving his cavalry at ease but on call in the street. Clasping his rolled vellum, Valdor mounted the stairs to the first floor, where he found an official. He handed over the drawings and gave instructions.

The man looked uncertain and even rebellious, "But you don't have written authorisation, and we cannot utilise all of our reserves to produce what you want."

"What need is there for written authorisation when our emperor's profile speaks for itself? Dare you disobey him?" Unsheathing his sword, he said, "Decurion, go back downstairs and bring the whole century up here to persuade this disobedient servant of the empire that we mean what we say!"

"Centurion, that will not be necessary," blurted the official, "I'll set the die cutters to work at once and fire up the forge."

"That's better! And make sure that each denarius weighs precisely four and a half grams. I shall check carefully. When will the coins be ready?"

"The die will be prepared directly on the anvil, and the forge will rapidly melt the silver. Hark, Centurion, if you want a vast quantity of coins, we'll have to debase the silver somewhat with copper. It's normal practice. We can treat the coins with acid to bring the shiny silver to the surface; even an expert will not know the difference. The die cutter can hammer the mould, producing one hundred coins an hour."

"I want at least 40,000 denarii, so decide how many die cutters to use. The emperor requires me to go to Londinium to have more coins minted. I shall return in six days and expect to find that many coins, so calculate well; otherwise, it will go badly for you, as our emperor has authorised me to slaughter anyone who does not cooperate in this important matter. Let me remind you that I have a century of bloodthirsty Dalmatian cavalry outside just waiting for an excuse to use their weapons."

"Go to Londinium in peace, Centurion. Upon your return, your coins will be bagged up and waiting for you."

"They had better be!" Valdor snarled and marched out of the room.

7

CAMULODUNUM TO LONDINIUM AND
BACK TO BRANODUNUM FORT, AD 286

VALDOR LED HIS CAVALRY THROUGH THE MONUMENTAL archway of the west gate and remembered the camp prefect's words. This was the *Porta Clausa*, built to commemorate the crushing victory of Emperor Claudius in 61 AD when he terrorised the local tribesmen by using war elephants. The name of the city in Latin was *Colonia Claudia Victricensis*, so named after Claudius' victory, whereas Camulodunum was a Romanised version of the Brythonic name, just as the *Balkerne Gate* was the Porta Clausa to the locals. The past glory of the Empire in Britannia could still be read in such Camulodunum structures as its vast circus, but Valdor had plans of his own to re-establish Roman supremacy in Britannia under Carausius. If that meant riding to *Londinium*, which by all accounts was as large and important as Camulodunum, so be it!

The Antonine Itinerary indicated a road running westwards called Stane Street, which led to a three-way interchange, one of which led directly to Londinium and was known as the Great Road. An engraved milestone indicated 70 Roman miles—70,000 paces of a Roman soldier. He sighed at the thought of the 139-mile return journey awaiting them, stretching back from Londinium to Branodunum Fort. But that was in the future, for his mission was less than half completed at this stage. But would he achieve success in time for his emperor?

The journey was swift and uneventful, owing to the remarkable work of the Roman engineers who had made a road surface ideal for rapid military transfers. The journey remained uneventful until the Great Road brought them to the Thames crossing, where an entire Roman cohort emerged onto the north bank. Valdor blinked; there was something different about this force. In an instant, he understood—the skin colours! These legionaries were, for the most part, black, others brown. The centurion who rode towards him and hailed him was not black but distinctly swarthy.

"Hail friend, we are the *Auxilia Palatina*, fresh from victory on the Danube. I am Centurion Ibrahim Ibn Attab—that's my true name in my own language. Emperor Diocletian, in his infinite wisdom, has rewarded us by sending us without pay to the confines of Britannia." His voice dripped with sarcasm, and his dark eyes were hard. "This valiant cohort is to garrison the Aballava Fort at the western end of the wall, built when Emperor Hadrian reigned." His sincere disapproval became obvious when he said bitterly, "What sense is there in all this? It's freezing cold here, so why send men from Mauretania to the frozen north of this accursed land to act as *limitanei*? But enough of my moaning. What of you?"

"I am Centurion Valdor, a Batavian, but my men are the *Equites Dalmatae*, Dalmatian cavalry. We are on an important mission for Imperator Caesar Marcus Aurelius, Emperor of Britannia and Northern Gaul."

"Hold!" the Mauritanian interrupted, his expression revealing his perplexity but also hope, "Are you saying there is a new emperor? Where is he based, in Londinium?"

"Nay, we are with the *Classis Britannia*, the fleet based on the coast 140 miles hence."

The Moor's eyes glinted with slyness. Half-turning in his saddle, ensuring that his men had joined him, he said, "Well, this changes everything. But tell me, maybe our new emperor will spare my men from chill exposure in the northern fastnesses. Why are you heading for Londinium?"

Valdor looked at the centurion from head to toe. *I cannot trust him. I will not tell him!*

"Centurion Ibrahim," Valdor smiled, "as I said, we are on an important mission for our emperor that will detain us several days in the city."

"It must be *important* to send so many men to accomplish it. What is the nature of your assignment?"

I'm damned if I'll tell you.

"I am not at liberty to reveal it."

The unmistakable irritation was plain in the swarthy countenance. Although his eyes did not, Ibn Attab's mouth smiled, "I'll tell you what we will do. We shall make an encampment hereabouts and await your return after these *several days,* then, we'll accompany you north to the emperor, for I wish for an audience with him."

Valdor hid his feelings and gave the Moor a friendly smile, all the while eyeing the newcomer's cavalry and massed infantry. "Very well, Centurion, I cannot be certain how many days it will take, but we'll meet here when my mission is fulfilled," he lied.

I must devise a plan. I cannot risk the coins with a whole cohort of Africans in the offing.

The officers clasped wrists, and Valdor then led his cavalry to the great river Thames, across it and south to the Aldgate, one of seven gates in the Roman-built walls girdling the city.

His encounter in the mint was even more hostile than that received in Camulodunum. This time there was bloodshed, not only inside the building but outside, too, the Dalmatians had to fend off a part of the garrison summoned urgently by the mint officials. Their resistance disappeared like slush in the rain when Valdor, without hesitation, struck down the obstructing prefect in charge of the mint. Suddenly the obstruction ran away like melting snow and changed with the sun into cooperation. Valdor displayed the sketches of the emperor's profile and demanded haughtily of an official, "How soon before you provide me with the 40,000 denarii?"

"If we work also at night with all our available men, I can have them done within forty-eight hours, Centurion."

"Mmm. See that you do; otherwise..." he jerked a thumb at the blood-soaked corpse and left the rest unspoken.

"Have no doubts, Centurion. I'll oversee the production myself."

"Good man! Two days is enough for us to obtain a solid cart and two strong carthorses. Hark, I need to know, apart from the Great Road, is there another that leads to Camulodunum?"

"Ay, there is. You can take the Ermine Street, which leaves through the Bishop's Gate."

"Perfect!"

Centurion Ibrahim Ibn Attab, you'll not get your thieving hands on our silver coin!

Two days later, Valdor selected thirty Dalmatians, took them to a tavern, and bought them each a couple of beakers of the best red wine to ensure their goodwill, returned to the mint, and oversaw them load the new cart with bulging bags of silver coins. Prior to the loading, he had them accompany him upstairs to the production centre, where he ordered the weighing of a randomly chosen denarius. It was exactly 4.5 grams, which satisfied him. The brutish features of Carausius on the coin seemed to smile up at him in approval.

Unfortunately, on exiting the main door, Valdor and his decurions did not spot the black-faced figure lurking in a shady portal of a nearby building, so they set off for Bishopsgate without undue preoccupation. The Ermine Street crossed the river just below Cricklade and would have taken them to Glevum, but they found the intersection with its milestone indicating Colonia Claudia Vitricensis.

They had been on this road at the steady pace dictated by the sturdy carthorses for a while when in the distance, the drumming of galloping horses assailed their ears, and, swivelling in his saddle, Valdor saw a cloud of dust raised by the selfsame hoofs. He rapidly issued orders: "Halt! Defensive formation around the cart, weapons drawn!"

Centurion Ibn Attab's eyes were anything but friendly, "Centurion Valdor, you broke our agreement! Did you think you could elude my spies? I now know your mission was to obtain coinage for our emperor. But hark, instruct your men to sheath their weapons because we come in peace and wish to *buy* from you and not steal your coins. We wish to buy the emperor's goodwill by pacifically accompanying you to your base wherever that is."

Can I trust this man?

"Where are your infantry, Centurion Ibn Attab?" Valdor asked, scanning the road behind him.

The Moor laughed, "They are fast, but cannot keep pace with my cavalry. I will leave a horseman to order them to march to... where, Centurion?"

"To Camulodunum, but beware, Ibn Attab, do not incur the wrath of Caesar Marcus Aurelius. His coins must arrive undiminished at our base."

I'll not inform you where that is until I'm good and ready!

"And so, it shall be! I do not blame you for your mistrust, brother. I would have done the same." The deep brown eyes were sincere and met Valdor's grey-blue eyes without faltering.

As one, the Dalmatians sheathed their swords at Valdor's gesture—in itself, an impressive display of leadership—and the Moors, obeying Valdor's command, delivered in Latin, much to his satisfaction, formed up behind his Dalmatians, and the steady advance continued. For a while, he chatted with the Mauritanian centurion, without revealing their ultimate destination because he had a plan that depended upon his calculations: *Ibn Attab commands these eighty cavalrymen, but he has a cohort, so there will be 400 infantrymen. They must not know that our destination is Branodunum until I gather reinforcements at Combretovium.*

First, however, they had to add to their load by calling at

Camulodunum. A surprise awaited them there. The western gate, the one with the monumental archway, by which they had left the town and now approached, had been bricked up during their week's absence. Valdor could see no structural purpose in this as the monumental archway revealed no lesions or other reasons. Since the walls contained three other gates, Valdor led his men around them as far as the southern entrance. He halted them there, distant from the mint, and took his most loyal Dalmatians, the ones from the tavern, with him in case of trouble, and the carthorses and cart. The bricking of the archway, he discovered, was simply a precaution to strengthen the walls, for it was regarded as a weak point. After checking and withdrawing the coins, he had them loaded with those from Londinium and returned to the bulk of his force, where a shock awaited him.

He had left just over a hundred men but now found five hundred! The Mauritanian infantry had arrived, and he was in time to hear Centurion Ibn Attab address them in Arabic—loyally, although he could not know it—: "Men, we are no longer going to Hadrian's Wall..." he had to raise a hand for silence such was the positive murmuring caused by his words. "...and we are no longer serving Emperor Diocletian, but the new Emperor Marcus Aurelius, who will recompense you for your toils." This remark was greeted by unrestrained cheering until Ibn Attab raised his hand again, now, for the benefit of Valdor, he spoke in Latin, "as from this moment, you will obey the orders of Centurion Valdor, your new commander." He pointed him out, lest anyone was in doubt. Again, these words were greeted by murmurs, this time a neutral sound. "I have promised them a reward from the Emperor of the North," Ibn Attab explained to the new commander.

"I shall see that they will have it if they obey me," Valdor replied.

It was just after noon, so Valdor went to the camp prefect and asked about the possibility of spontaneously feeding nearly 600 men. He expected a rebuff but was surprised to receive a positive reply and, to ensure the Moors' loyalty, Valdor was able to accommodate them in the refectory in turns of 50 men. Fresh bread and seasoned cheese accompanied by red wine was simple fare, but manna to the famished infantrymen. They gobbled the food, so the turnaround was fast. Within an hour, Valdor was ready to lead the 25-mile march to Combretovium. The infantrymen could march at almost three miles an hour; the well-disciplined *Auxilia Palatina* neither flagged nor complained, so thankful for the long hours of daylight, Valdor brought his men across the river Gipping and across the triple ditches of the Roman fort of Combretovium as twilight cloaked the land.

When the approaching force sounded a triple blast of the *cornum*, the gates swung open and the camp prefect rode out on a fine white charger.

"I am pleased you honoured our agreement, Centurion Valdor, although I expected no less from you. But I see you are now leading African legionaries."

The interrogative tone of this statement made Valdor answer in Latin for the benefit of the Moors within earshot, "Aye, we met at the Thames, where Centurion Ibn Attab and his valiant men decided to follow your example by swearing allegiance to the Emperor of the North. But, heed me, Prefect, the men are weary after tramping this morning from Londinium."

"By the gods! That's some feat! They can sleep in the fort as we have many unoccupied beds in the barracks. Pray give orders," he wheeled his horse, waved a signal to the gatekeeper, and the second door swung back.

To obtain the loyalty of men, sometimes it is more important to be lucky rather than a capable commander. Valdor was endowed with both virtues. His arrival with extra men coincided with the Roman desertion of Combretovium, so there was no problem about eating and drinking what provisions remained, for the Provisioner was not concerned about the morrow. After the previous lean days of near-famine, the Mauritanians felt that the gods had supplied them with the best officer in the world. Even if

Valdor could not speak their language, the flashing white teeth of ready smiles soon convinced him of his popularity among his new troops.

The following day, at the halt station of Venta Icenorum, he endeared himself further. In possession of 80,000 denarii, he felt it incumbent upon himself to issue one silver piece to all of his new additions, which cost him less than 1,000 denarii. He allowed his troops an hour's break to do as they wished with their pay. Most drank it away, others paid for sex, but he saw some at market stalls purchasing trinkets. Wherever he went, he was greeted with joyous smiles and friendly nods.

They arrived at Branodunum Fort in ordered ranks, the cavalry flanking the infantry at both sides. Never had Valdor dreamt that he would lead men and never had a sound rung so sweetly in his ears as the triple blast of the *cornum* outside the northern gate. Proudly he led his troops into the fortress to be greeted by his beaming emperor, who asked: "What do you do on a mission, Centurion, breed soldiers?"

"They need pay, Sire."

"We all do, Centurion, and so it shall be!"

Valdor was glad to be home but he was not alone as Sparax whinnied a happy neigh as the three Batavians hurried to embrace their returning friend. They managed this without taking their eyes off the bulging money bags. In this, they were not alone, as soldiers and sailors alike waited for the emperor to fulfil his promise.

8

THE EMPEROR ORDERED A ROOM TO BE EQUIPPED WITH shelves, groaning under the weight of bags of silver coins, with a desk where an official doled out denarii after entering the recipient's name in a ledger. Upon receiving his shiny coins, each man signed his name or placed his mark against the sum. It was a long process, for all the legionaries, whether established or newcomers, were in line to receive their pay together with the sailors. The centurions collected first, followed by the decurions before the lower ranks entered. As one of the first to get his pay, Valdor decided to pass the time by climbing the south-eastern lookout tower to breathe in the sea breeze, and from where he could survey the harbour and its approaches.

He was surprised to see the increase in moored vessels since his absence. Undoubtedly the fleet had swollen due to the capture of pirate ships. He recognised the shallow-draughted Saxon vessels and the shape of the Frankish two-masted river craft, which somehow the marauders managed to keep afloat in the rougher North Sea. To add to this mixed score of shipping were Roman trading vessels. Had they been captured or levied by the emperor? He didn't know for sure.

His surprise increased when his eyes shifted to a shipyard.

59

Faintly, he could hear hammering. One galley was near completion and four others under construction, one of them little more than a keel. *The emperor must be concerned about Maximian's threat. I need an excuse to speak with him, especially now that he has given me command of both the Dalmatian and Mauritanian cavalry. I'd like to know how close we are to war.*

His excuse came in the most unexpected form. As his eyes turned inland, he saw a legion marching on Branodunum. A well-disciplined march it was, too. He could see the SPQR eagle standard from his tower and, unless he was mistaken, another with II proudly displayed. So, this was the legion II Augusta, stationed in *Glevum*, the Cambrian frontier town the Britons called *Caerloyw*. The question was, did they come as enemies, loyal to Maximian, or as deserters prepared to throw in their lot with the new emperor, Carausius?

Valdor dashed down the winding stairs and to the emperor's quarters, which was no more than a spartan chamber equipped with a bed in one corner and a desk under a window. A fire burnt in the centre of the room, for the sea air had freshened now that summer had given way to autumn. It was difficult to imagine what luxurious quarters Emperor Diocletian must enjoy when he gazed at this rudimentary room, little better than the legionary's barracks.

"What is it, Valdor? Have you not been paid your fair share?"

"As to that, lord, I am more than happy. Nay, I come to warn you of the arrival of an entire Roman legion. I believe it to be II Augusta but cannot be sure until it is right under our walls."

"How come it is always you who informs me, Valdor? Are you the only one awake in this fortress! How long before they reach us?"

"I'd hazard a quarter of an hour."

"So soon? We'd better prepare the men."

"They won't like that! They are being paid."

Carausius roared with laughter. "That's true, so we'll bar the gates and anyone, like you, who has received his pay will take his arms and draw up behind the gate."

Valdor decided that now was the time to raise his query.

"Caesar, I also saw that you are building new galleys and have added to the fleet. Are we about to sail to face Maximian?"

Again, came the bellow of a laugh.

"How can Maximian assemble a fleet? He gave me his! Nay, *we* do not sail, *you* sail with your cavalry, Valdor."

The conversation terminated abruptly as three sharp blasts of a *cornum* rang out from outside the gates.

"More of that later, Centurion. Quickly, I must wear the purple! We'll mount the gate tower and see with what we have to contend." He snatched up the imperial diadem and rammed it on his head. It lent the coarse features an undoubted dignity and authority. Valdor ran to keep up with the emperor's stride. Stocky, he might be, but he could move rapidly, as under the toga were thighs of iron.

Standing at the battlements before Valdor arrived breathless, Carausius said, "Look at the emblems, every shield bears the Capricornus and the other emblems are Pegasus and Mars. You were right, this is *Legio II Augusta*."

"I like the horned goat on the shield," Valdor said irrelevantly, "I must acquire one."

"When we've defeated them, my friend."

But there was no need. A hand pointed up to the battlements and a strong voice cried, "Hail Caesar, Imperator Marcus Aurelius: Legio II Augusta at your service!"

"Valdor, put on your helmet, go out the gate, and see if we can trust them enough to welcome them into our ranks."

"I'm on my way, Caesar." Valdor beat his chest with his fist in the standard salute and hurried down to get his plumed helmet. Confidence increased by wearing the insignia of his rank, he ordered the gates to be opened and rode out on Sparax to meet the commander, who introduced himself as Legate Vitulasius.

"You have a fine steed, Centurion, my congratulations. I thought I saw our emperor over the gateway?"

"Indeed, lord, he came to see whether II Augusta had come in peace and friendship."

The legate smiled, "Your emperor will be pleasantly surprised because, to my knowledge, XX Valeria Victrix, based in Deva and, therefore, not far from the territory of the Silures, whence we came, will follow our example and swear allegiance to the Emperor of the North."

"You know that it may mean war with Emperor Maximian, Legate, are you prepared for that eventuality?"

"I have spoken with my counterpart in Deva, and he fully understands the implications of our decision."

"You are most welcome in the *Fortress of the Crows*, as many call Branodunum. I shall not presume to command your horn blower, but the gates must be opened to your legion."

The legate bowed in acknowledgement of the courtesy and cried, "Three blasts, *Cornicen!*"

Even as the third resonant note faded, the great gates swung back.

"Your men will be weary, I'll see to refreshment for them, but first, I must accompany you to the emperor, ride with me."

Once they arrived inside the compound, stable boys met them and led the beasts away while Valdor took Legate Vitulasius to Carausius' quarters.

The newcomer knelt before his new emperor and, having formally given his name and rank, said, "I have come to deliver the Legio II Augusta to you, Caesar. As their commander, I swear allegiance."

"Let it be known, Legate, that any disloyalty in the ranks will be punished by death," Carausius said bluntly.

The high-ranking officer looked around the spartan quarters and said approvingly, "Reports do not lie, you are a true soldier—hard but fair."

I have heard that before, thought Valdor and smiled.

"You are most welcome to Branodunum, Legate. I have only one other condition to stipulate. My centurion here desires a *scutum* of the II Augusta. He has a liking for goats!"

The famous bellowed laugh surprised the legate, but soon he would grow accustomed to it; meanwhile, he assented immediately, "I shall find you a *shield* without battle scars, Centurion."

Valdor felt that circumstances were favouring his emperor day after day, and with his good fortune, his own went apace. Now was not the time to ask what the emperor had meant earlier by *you sail with your cavalry*. That could wait until the morrow. Now he had to see to the welfare of the II Augusta. No one knew better than he what toll a cross-country march took.

Once he had dealt with that, he was free again.

Although the three friends from his village were still dear to him, it was inevitable that he had become closer to Heidar, his trusted decurion. There had to be a certain detachment from Faldrek and Johar to avoid rancour among the other legionaries. Valdor was well aware that he should display no favouritism, but an opportunity arose to draw nearer to them when Carausius summoned him the following day.

"Have the II Augusta been adequately accommodated, Centurion?"

"Ay, they have, Caesar. It's just that—"

"What?"

"It's not in my place, but since Legate Vitulasius informed me of the likelihood of *Legio XX Valeria Victrix* coming to swear allegiance—"

"He did not tell me this!"

"Forgive me, Sire, he must have believed I had referred the matter..."

Carausius smiled, "Well, it *is* good news."

"Ay, lord, except—"

"Except?"

Valdor was hesitant as he didn't wish to risk the wrath of his fiery emperor. He did not want to overstep the mark. But he knew that keeping Caesar waiting for his reply was a sure way to arouse his temper, so he blurted, "We are overcrowded in Branodunum as it is, Sire. With XX Valeria Victrix, we'll need to construct new barracks."

The roar of laughter, always a possible reaction from Carausius, surprised Valdor.

"When you said it was not in your place, you seemed as timid as a serving wench, Centurion. I do not doubt your courage or spirit, so I take it that your emperor intimidates you," he smiled smugly.

"Nay, Sire, not *intimidate*, it's a question of respect."

"Well, let me tell you something, young man, your emperor respects your views, so be bold and air them whenever you see fit. As proof, now I shall order work to begin on constructing ten *contubernia* with larger officers' quarters attached." Again, came the formidable roar of laughter, followed by, "Also, *you* and your cavalry will ease the problem."

"Sire?"

"Think about who you wish to take to *Gallia*. Precisely to *Gesoriacum*—the place your people and mine call Boulogne—my spies tell me that Maximian is building war galleys there in preparation for an invasion of Britannia. Your task, Centurion, is to reduce the new vessels to ashes. Once you have done that, my orders are to proceed to your old village and to destroy any of Maximian's Romans in the area. I will not have an enemy on my doorstep. As yet, I have not worked out the details of my invasion of Gaul. I've decided to wait for news that the enemy ships are burnt. Then, likely I'll join you in Gallia with all the men at my disposal. Let's hope the news about XX Victrix is correct! I also have Frankish allies I can call upon."

He has truly taken me into his confidence.

As if he had noticed Valdor's concentration stray, Carausius said, "I want you to take all four horse transports because it'll be strictly a cavalry campaign until further orders, but you may also take two galleys both for defence and attack," he said enigmatically. "Why don't you take the Moorish infantry, they covered themselves in glory on the Danube. I've discussed that campaign with their commander, Centurion Ibrahim Ibn Attab. He has the makings of a fine general; Diocletian did me a favour sending him to Britannia. Oh, and take your Batavian friends with you. They know the area between the Rhine and the Waal; they could prove useful to you in capturing the area. Go and make preparations, you sail at dawn tomorrow. Judging by the red sky, it'll be a fine day tomorrow. Fare thee well, my friend, and," his pugnacious face thrust into Valdor's, "do not fail me and keep me informed."

"Your will is mine, Sire."

Valdor took his leave, bowing out of his emperor's presence, smiling wryly at the bustling courtyard where only the Mauritanians were undergoing drill. *They'll be glad to get some action.* With this thought, he hastened to find Heidar. After discovering that he had finished in the forge for the day, he reflected and had a good idea where he would find him. His intuition proved correct but with a bonus. His friend was, like himself, as a child brought up by the sea. Military discipline meant that he could not leave the fortress to wander along the shore at will, so the next best thing was to watch the sea from a tower. He found him on the south-eastern turret, beloved of Valdor, in the company of Faldrek and Johar. All three were staring out to sea when Valdor made them jump by saying, *"Ave Socii,"* translating, "Hail comrades," for the benefit of Faldrek, who had difficulty grasping the Latin tongue.

"Valdor!" they exclaimed in unison.

"Will the sea be calm tomorrow, cousin?"

Johar smiled happily. He had overcome his initial jealousy at Valdor's rapid promotion and now felt that his cousin bowed to his superior knowledge on matters regarding the sea.

The former fisherman looked at the sky, sniffed the air, and said, "I'd stake my life on it!"

"Good, because I bring orders from the emperor. Tomorrow,

we sail at dawn and that's not all, the latter part of our mission will take us to our village."

"I doubt we'll be welcomed with open arms," Faldrek said grumpily.

"The gods only know where the menfolk are, but I'd love to see my mother and my aunt,"

Johar looked pointedly at his centurion cousin.

"We'll be on a mission, and while we mustn't be under any illusion about the womenfolk's well-being, we'll make time to find out. That's a promise, Johar. Now, orders! Heidar, have the Dalmatians accommodate their horses in the transport ships. Johar, Faldrek, take your horses on the ship and decide whether to place them above or below deck. Sparax will travel above, I've decided, especially because the weather will be fair. I must away to organise the Mauritanians, Centurion Ibn Attab will add his cavalry to ours."

"The Moors have fine steeds and know how to handle them," Heidar said.

Johar's eyes were still fixed on the sea, but he said, "I wonder if they are used to sailing, though."

He needn't have worried because Ibn Attab was quick to point out that Mauritania boasted two seas: the Mediterranean and the Atlantic. "We also have desert and mountains," he said wistfully. "But shall we see action, Centurion?" He asked this with the same yearning in his voice.

"We're not going to so much trouble not to wield our arms, my friend."

"My men will be overjoyed."

Valdor gave instructions for the cavalry and explained, "I will command the cavalry, but the emperor has chosen you to command the infantry. It seems you won his admiration when you told him about the Danube campaign."

"And he mine because his questions were astute, which only a competent general would have asked."

"Excellent, we sail at dawn, Centurion. Please explain the

arrangements to your cavalrymen. Then, it's each to his respective tasks."

Among Valdor's first tasks, to the perplexity of his men, was the sequestration of every small rowing boat they could lay hands on. These were carried aboard each ship along with many bales of straw, covered with oiled cloths to prevent them from becoming damp.

The following morning, with dawn's orange-streaked sky and millpond sea, encouraged not only the mixed crews and horses to settle but also the purple-clad figure standing on the battlements, watching his ships leave the Fortress of the Crows. Of all these souls, perhaps he was the only one who wished that he was aboard one of the ships. However, wisely, he didn't embark because he wanted to assure the allegiance of XX Victoria Victrix, which, according to his scouts, was only an hour's march away. The imperial diadem sparkled orange in the low sunlight, and Valdor, on the stern tower, pointed it out to his bodyguard, Faldrek. The centurion waved and, although uncertain, thought that Carausius returned the salute.

9

GESORIACUM AND ULPIA NOVIOMAGUS BATAVORUM, GALLIA, AUTUMN, 286 AD

On a high cliff near the beach stood a two-centuries-old lighthouse, built on two storeys in the reign of Emperor Caligula. Once spotted from the sea, Valdor had confirmation that they had reached their destination, but Carausius' words came to mind, "My scouts tell me that the new ships are being built on a beach of white sand, some twelve miles north of the port." To find the beach, Valdor veered his flotilla of six vessels northwards and scanned the coast for the tell-tale white sand.

The improvised shipyard was easy to find, and while his keen eyes sought signs of defence, his lookouts confirmed what he had seen for himself: there were no or few defenders. Carpenters went about their business, hammering nails and carrying a shaped wooden bulkhead to construct the hull of a galley. Others were adding what appeared to be the finishing touches to four complete war galleys, as yet without masts. Valdor calculated that the position of the low sun suggested there was an hour of daylight available before it set. It made little difference to him whether he destroyed the galleys before or after sunset, given the poor state of defence.

Logically, if he attacked immediately, he could make use of the port of Gesoriacum on the Liane estuary overnight. It would be more comfortable moored in the placid harbour than riding at anchor offshore, and the harbour was, after all, the official base of the *Classis Britannica* and, therefore, theirs, not Maximian's, by rights.

Decision taken, Valdor ordered pitch to be melted and poured over the straw filling the rowing boats, thus arousing the crews' curiosity. As soon as his men completed these preparations, the six ships towed two rowing boats each close to the completed galleys, half in the sea and half-stranded on the beach. Within twenty yards of the prey, confusion reigned in the shipyard as carpenters abandoned their tools and ran for the safety of the shore, screaming warnings. Valdor's archers picked off most of them while he ordered the straw to be lit. Black smoke puthered into the air, to be swept away instantly by the sea breeze, but before long, the fire caught, and the legionaries propelled the fire-boats among the war galleys. The effect was devastating: twelve blazing rowing boats crashed into the new hulls so that the raw wood caught instantly.

Carausius wanted the galleys reduced to ashes, and that was what he would obtain, judging by the leaping flames, snapping and crackling along the hulls. Valdor regretted that he had not reserved a fire-boat for the last of the galleys—the one the majority of carpenters had fled, so he improvised, sending a standard rowing boat with six men and three fire tubs filled with molten pitch. He watched as his men carried the tubs onto the beach and smeared the structure of the emergent galley with pitch before setting it alight. The late daylight turned artificially to night by the black smoke shrouding the beach, but the flames from the completed hulls provided a flickering red light for the coughing legionaries to carry out their task. Valdor's scrupulousness was repaid as the pitch caught and the last of the galleys became the pyre to Maximian's carpenters' efforts. The task completed, Valdor had only to wait to survey the extent of the damage.

To do this, he ordered the ships to stand off—blessedly far enough from the choking smoke to the relief of his crews and the few restive horses on deck. The last of the flames coincided with the sunset. The hulls remained little more than useless charred and smouldering skeletons, quite beyond salvage, so Valdor ordered his oarsmen to veer the ships to head for the estuary while keeping a wary eye on the headland, now illuminated by the lighthouse.

Arriving safely in port, the six vessels tied up together at the wooden quay. A surprise awaited them there, as an arrow thrummed into the tower deck at Valdor's feet. "Scuti!" he cried as one nearby crewman fell dying, clutching an arrow embedded in his chest before everyone sheltered behind raised shields. Valdor rapidly ordered his men onto the quay in serried formation to seek and exterminate the archers. He went to Sparax and led him onto the wooden jetty, mounting the stallion and taking command of his Dalmatian cavalry, who were quick to join him. Their mobility allowed him to find the fleeing enemy rapidly, who consisted of less than a score of Roman archers. The horsemen quickly surrounded them; the archers wisely did not attempt to shoot their arrows at such a superior force. The odds were overwhelmingly in Valdor's favour, so he ordered the enemy to lay down their bows. A decurion disobeyed and raised his weapon, determined to kill this arrogant centurion who had destroyed the new fleet. Before he could shoot the arrow, Johar's javelin had pierced his chest, and he fell to the ground.

Thank you, cousin!

"Hark! In the name of Emperor Marcus Aurelius, *Restitutor Britanniae*, unite with us and be saved, or fall on your swords!" Valdor bellowed and thought, *A score of archers will be useful.* But this wishful thought was not to be because three archers had the nerve to kill themselves by holding a gladius to their chests and falling upon the blade. He ordered the remaining comrades to fling the corpses into the harbour and regretfully watched the three bodies splash into the depths—food for crustaceans.

Suddenly, a Dalmatian scout galloped up, swivelled in his

saddle, and pointed back over his shoulder, "Centurion, an entire legion is marching this way from the garrison!"

Valdor quickly ordered Ibn Attab to form his infantrymen into ranks and flanked them with his cavalry. He was ready to confront the enemy legion.

Soon, hundreds of flickering torches held aloft, made of reed fasces dipped in sulphur and lime, appeared over the dunes. The fiery light reflected off the shiny steel armour, but what intrigued Valdor was the absence of spears or drawn swords. His men had spears and swords at the ready behind their shields.

A tribune rode forward alone, hand raised in a gesture of parley. He selected Ibn Attab as the centurion to speak with, but the Moor gestured towards Valdor, who urged his stallion across.

"Centurion," said the tribune, "We are *Legio III Gallica* and come in peace. We know you are sworn to the Britannic emperor and that you burnt the new ships constructed for Emperor Maximian. In theory, we are sworn to serve him, but we are without pay, except for debased, worthless bronze coins with a silver wash. The men are restless and have no stomach for a fight with their brothers. Yet, I cannot surrender Gesoriacum to you as you probably wish. Is there no manner of avoiding bloodshed?"

Valdor smiled grimly, his thoughts racing: with the burning, he had accomplished the first part of his mission. This legion outnumbered him, so avoiding a fight appealed. He replied, "Tribune, as you say, neither do we wish to fight our brothers. If you agree, we shall stay in the harbour overnight and sail away to northern Gallia at dawn. Does that suit you?"

"We can always claim that we never saw who burnt the new ships and leave it at that. But hark, if you wish your men to be more comfortable for the night, we have entire *contubernia* vacant, as the old fortress was razed and a new one built in 274. Since then, we have never been at full capacity."

"It's a kind offer, Tribune, but for an early departure, it's better my men are onboard rather than in your barracks." *Besides, I don't trust you!* The two men clasped wrists in a sign of agreement, and the naval garrison of Gesoriacum wheeled and tramped back to their fortress.

At dawn, Valdor led his flotilla northwards, and his thin smile greeted the sight of the blackened remains, stark against the white sand. His heart sang, not only because they'd accomplished their mission so thoroughly, but also because they were now directed to his home village on the Waal. Hopefully, he would see familiar faces, but he was prepared for the worse.

By early afternoon, driven by a favourable south-westerly breeze, bearing an irritating drizzle, his ships turned into the Rhine estuary and then, into the Waal, its confluence also at the mouth of the Rhine. Valdor explained to his excited Batavian comrades that his idea was to moor near their village and swim the horses ashore. Each would then ride to his own house, with hope in his heart.

Johar expressed what they all felt, "Likely, there'll be nobody to welcome us, we must be prepared for disappointment."

The ships moored, and Valdor urged a reluctant and restive Sparax into the water. The stallion's huge lungs kept him afloat, and instinct had his legs trotting underwater so that soon, the relieved animal was climbing the low bank of the Waal. Familiar terrain and sights moved Valdor almost to tears. Although not even a full year had passed, much had happened since they fled to Torik Isle. His stallion thundered into the village's only street, and at the sight of a Roman centurion, young children bravely stood their ground and stared while the few womenfolk screamed and fled indoors. Relieved to see life in his village, Valdor rode directly to his parents' home. The door was firmly closed, so he tied his reins to a fence and knocked.

His mother, arms white with flour up beyond her elbows, squealed in fear at the sight of a centurion, but suddenly, her jaw dropped, and she cried, "Valdor, my son!" He gently backed her into the house and closed the door behind him with his free hand. His nostrils breathed in the mouth-watering aroma of baking bread.

"Why are you dressed like that? Did you slay a Roman centurion and take his uniform? The gods forbid!"

"I have done that, too, mother, but I wear this uniform as of rights. I left you as a simple country lad, now, I return as an important Roman officer: I'm the emperor's favourite," he said proudly. "It's a long story, but in the name of Jupiter, what are all these sacks, and what are you doing?"

"Every day, the Romans bring sacks of flour from the fortress, and I bake bread for the legion based there. They give me a pittance for my trouble, but I do it for your father and the men of the village, who form part of the garrison. My bread is appreciated, and, in this way, I'm allowed to enter the fort once a month to see your father."

"So, he is alive and well! The gods be praised!"

"Ay, and most of the others, too. He tells me that he has a hard life, always drilling and occasionally marching to fight insurgent tribes inland. Do you remember the smith, Thragnor?"

"Ay, of course."

"Oy! Now look, this bread needs to come out of the oven, or it'll be ruined," she took a long-handled wooden peel and saved the well-baked loaves, sliding them onto a table containing at least another dozen. "...anyway, as I was saying, sadly, Thragnor died from a spear thrust between his ribs when they fought a Germanic tribe last month. Our men—if we can call a Roman legion such—won a crushing victory but lost the poor smith—is Heidar...?"

"Ay, he is well. What of his family?"

"His mother and younger brother still live down the street," she jerked her thumb before sliding the peel under a raw loaf and transferring it into the oven. At the same moment, Johar walked into the house, his expression glum.

"Greetings, Aunt Namuta! My heart sings to see you well. But my house stands empty, Valdor."

"Your mother died of the ague last spring, Johar, I'm sorry. It was just after you boys left. The Romans had captured our shaman, so there was nobody to cure her. But your father is well. I saw him a few days ago."

"Well? Where is he?"

"In the fortress of Noviomagus, a league or so up the river. He's a legionary, like my Caurus."

"Are they well?"

"Ay, until they fall in battle."

"Mother bakes bread for the legion, Johar," Valdor waved a hand at the mountain of loaves, "but hark, I have a plan. I'll tell you when Heidar and Faldrek get here." He turned to his mother, "Ma, do you know which legion is stationed at Noviomagus?"

"I seem to remember *Legio XXII...* something or other."

"Thank the gods! *Legio XXII Primigenia—*"

She turned, her brow glistening with sweat as she removed the loaf from the searing oven and added the bread to the pile. She turned to gather two short logs and placed them on the fire under the stone hotplate, speaking as she did so, "Ay, that's them...XXII Primigenia."

"When do the Romans come to collect the bread?"

"Any time, soon. They exchange the bread with fresh sacks of flour."

"Well, today is your last consignment," he said enigmatically.

A knock at the door ended the conversation. "That'll be the carter to take the bread." But she was wrong, as in walked Heidar, followed by Faldrek. "A sight for sore eyes!" she cried as Heidar embraced her.

"What are you doing? There's enough bread here to feed a legion!"

"Exactly!" she chuckled, and Valdor explained. When he had finished, he put an arm around Heidar's shoulder, "Good and bad news, my friend, Thragnor died in battle, but our fathers are safe in the garrison at Noviomagus, a league hence. You will see them soon." He explained his plan.

"Do you think it will work?" Johar asked anxiously as he watched the tears of joy roll down his aunt's cheeks.

"Legio XXII Primigenia is an old-established legion with a proud story, and that alone gives me hope. Ma, when your carter arrives, carry on as normal and say nothing about our visit. You three, outside with me! We'll ride down the road towards the fortress to greet the carter."

"What about our mothers?" Faldrek asked hopefully.

"Later, once we've completed our mission in Noviomagus. Ha, look! Unless I'm mistaken, here comes the carter."

A chestnut draught horse clopped towards them, hauling a cart laden with sacks. "Whoa!" cried the carter, bringing his horse and vehicle to a halt.

"Hail, carter!" Valdor greeted him, "we'll give you a hand to unload at Namuta's house."

"How do you know—"

Valdor laughed, "It's a long story, but come, we'll ride beside you and you can answer my questions as we go."

In this way, Valdor discovered that the commander of Legio XXII Primigenia was a prefect named Gnaeus Cordius Nolus, and Valdor was delighted to hear that he was a veteran of the Danube campaign. Also, the legion was not at full strength, boasting six, instead of ten cohorts, so slightly fewer than 3,000 men. This information suited Valdor's plan perfectly.

At his mother's house, the four soldiers each shouldered a sack of flour and delivered it into the delicious aroma-filled kitchen. The carter went outdoors, only to return with empty sacks, which he began to fill with fresh bread. When his sacks were full, Valdor hugged his mother and whispered instructions, "We'll be back tomorrow morning, early. Have them here and ready," he ended.

Outside the house, he said to the carter, "We'll accompany you to Noviomagus, friend. Decurion, ride to the ships and tell Centurion Attab to join us." Heidar thumped his chest and rode off to fetch the Mauritanian.

When he drew near the ships, he saw that the men had created an encampment by the river. He made his way to the centurion's tent and passed on his instructions. The Moorish officer called for his charger and leapt on its back. Together they galloped after the bread transport. Fine as Heidar's steed was, it had a struggle to keep apace of the sleek Arab mare. Head-to-head, they came within sight of their comrades and the cart. Ibn Attab slowed to a gentle trot to Heidar's relief since he did not want to injure his stallion or himself.

Valdor turned to wave over the centurion, noting, not for the first time, the pleasant but stark contrast between the Mauritanian's swarthy skin and the fine white transverse plume of his helmet. The white was the insignia of officers of the *Auxilia Palatina* and made a welcome change from the standard crimson that Valdor and Heidar and the officers of most other legions vaunted.

"Centurion, we are making for the fortress of Noviomagus, the stronghold currently held by the Legio XXII Primigenia and commanded by an old acquaintance of yours, unless I err."

The Moor looked perplexed, "As far as I know, I have no friends in the XXII Primigenia."

Valdor laughed, "Be that as it may, but when we arrive and you greet the prefect, you might have a surprise! I hope that I am correct, however, because our task is to persuade Legio XXII Primigenia to accompany us to Britannia."

"Excuse me, Centurion Valdor, but do we have sufficient berths for an entire legion?"

"Doubtful, but they have six cohorts. It will be a squeeze, but the crossing is short to Branodunum. We'll manage, somehow." But both centurions calculated without being in possession of all the information they needed.

Apart from lying close to the border with Germanic tribes, the fortress of Noviomagus had a splendid strategic position on high ground, surrounded by other hills; it commanded views over the river Waal and Rhine valley.

As a daily habit, the carter trundled straight to the main gate, and the small unit of legionaries rode beside him. The carter was worried that he might be reprimanded for bringing strangers into the fortress, but the camp prefect's curiosity was aroused by the white plume and dark skin of Ibn Attab. When he strode up to the Arab steed, he gazed at the newcomer and cried, "So it is you, Centurion Ibn Attab! Do you not recognise an old comrade from those glorious days on the Danube?"

The Moor's flashing white teeth answered before he spoke, "Centurion Gnaeus Cordius Nolus! But I see they have elevated you to a prefect—congratulations!"

"There is little to congratulate, old friend. I am here in command of a mixed bag of Italians and auxiliaries. We have at least two cohorts of barbarians! And don't get me started on the weather," he cast a baleful eye at the dark rain clouds that merely threatened a downpour but instead offered a dispiriting damp mist-like drizzle.

"You will be grateful then, Prefect," Valdor seized his opportunity, "to obey Caesar Marcus Aurelius' order to bring your men to Britannia with my small fleet." He held his breath, but when the reply came, it was unexpected.

"Welcome to Noviomagus, Centurion. From your accent, I hear that you are Batavian, so I should welcome you more correctly to Ulpia Noviomagus Batavorum: the name given this fortress by the great emperor Trajan some two hundred winters past. The Batavi make fine soldiers and have all my respect," he smiled ingratiatingly at Valdor.

"Indeed, your legion contains my father, uncle, and friends, Prefect. I am anxious to reacquaint with them when our business is done."

"Do you have written orders for the transfer, Centurion?"

"I do not. Take my word as your guarantee. I can also warrant for better weather in Branodunum." He looked at Heidar for confirmation, but the decurion looked uneasy and, keeping his head down, muttered, "Not much better!" At which, the prefect guffawed, "Any improvement will be welcome."

"I doubt you will have time to enjoy the British sunshine,

Prefect, for Carausius—er, I mean, Emperor Caesar Marcus Aurelius—is on the verge of war with Maximian."

"Splendid! At last, real warfare! We're tired of walking into cowardly traps and ambushes in the German marshes and forests. I hear Carausius is a remarkable general."

"You have heard correctly, Prefect."

"He has the good sense to appoint Batavian officers, so it is settled!"

"It is. We shall accompany you to Britannia. I fear it will not be a comfortable crossing for your men as we have but two galleys and four horse transports."

"You say that because you have not strolled around the harbour. We have two triremes in the port."

The look of sheer relief on Valdor's face made the prefect guffaw again.

He's sure to get on well with Carausius! Our poor ears!

"Heidar, ride back to the ships. They are to be ready to sail an hour after dawn."

"Nay," the prefect caught Heidar's arm. "There is time before nightfall for you to reunite with your father and to eat with my officers. We have the delicious fresh bread you brought from your village and good red wine from Italy."

Only Ibn Attab did not have relatives in the legion, but he spent a pleasant couple of hours with Gnaeus Cordius Nolus reminiscing about the Danube campaign.

The others did not have to seek out their relatives, who had sidled up to the small party and lurked a discreet distance away from them until the prefect dismissed them.

"Valdor!" his father cried and almost tripped in his haste to embrace his son. There were tears in the older man's eyes, "Your mother and I were unsure we'd ever see you again. Yet, here you are—and a centurion, too! I hope you treat your men better than some of these!"

"Hard, but fair, father, kind but hard. But we have a lot to catch up on. I have spoken to mother today, so I know most of your news. You will hear mine. But the best is that I am taking you to Britannia with mother and will find you employment far from the battlefield."

The next two hours passed in an instant, it seemed. The same was true for Valdor's three friends until they were all called to the refectory for simple but wholesome fare and the welcome red wine. Prefect Cordius Nolus joined Valdor, his expression anxious.

"I understand the emperor's need for my men, but surely, it is not his intention to leave Noviomagus ungarrisoned?"

Valdor thought quickly. He had pondered the problem on the way from the village, but his local knowledge was too limited to be precise. He said, "I believe we have Frankish allies who wouldn't hesitate to take command of this fortress, although I confess, I don't know how to approach them."

"Your emperor is wise. It is a splendid idea. I will send an emissary at once to the Franks' chieftain. Tomorrow, he will find the gates open. I'll give orders to embark at dawn."

"I have only one request, Prefect, and it is in your power to grant it if you are so minded."

Prefect Cordius Nolus looked askance at Valdor, for he was not used to granting favours, but pulled an earlobe and looked down his nose, "Ask, then."

"Prefect, will you grant the transfer of our relatives to my legion? It is a question of but ten men or thereabouts."

"Is that all you ask, Centurion? You have my immediate assent!"

"Thank you. I hope we shall become friends as well as comrades. I'll gather the men concerned and ride back to our ships. Will your ships join us soon after dawn?"

"They will. Take the bread cart to transport your relatives; our cavalry has no spare horses."

The two men clasped wrists, and as he organised the men into the cart to transfer to the ships, Valdor thought, *Things are falling nicely into place for we four simple Batavian country lads!*

IO

VALDOR EXPECTED TO BE CHARGED WITH ANOTHER mission when he returned to Branodunum, but the emperor embraced him warmly for what he had achieved and quipped that on every mission, his centurion returned with more men to strengthen his position in Britannia. He did not, however, keep the XXII Primigenia Legion and their two war galleys but sent them to the south to strengthen the garrison of a shore fort called *Regulbium* in the area of the Canti tribe, known as Kent. This, he explained to Valdor, was for practical purposes because Branodunum was now overcrowded and Regulbium understaffed as a garrison.

Now that the autumn had advanced, there was little danger of pirate incursions, Carausius explained, citing an old rhyme passed down from seafarer to son:

> *"Never let your keel be wet*
> *When the Pleiades have set;*
> *Never let your keel be dry*
> *When the Crown is in the sky."*

Certainly, most maritime traffic ceased by the end of October, for the North Sea could change rapidly into a raging beast as sudden gales whipped its surface into huge waves capable of capsizing even the most stable round-bellied trading vessel.

"When the spring comes, Valdor, I mean to sweep the Channel free of Saxons and Franks."

"I'll enjoy that, Sire."

"*You?* You will do no such thing! I have another task for you, but I shall not inform you until I make my announcement at the end of Yuletide."

Valdor knew better than to object because it was unwise to stir up Carausius's wrath. Yet, he yearned to tell the Emperor of the North that he had acquired sea legs and a certain prowess as commander of a war galley; still, wisely, he held his tongue.

Carausius lit the Christmas brand—or Yule Log—on Christmas Eve to mark the end of the 40-day Advent fast and the start of the midwinter feast. The log burnt for the next 12 days, which were a holiday for everyone—bar slaves and bonded labourers.

The fire in the hearth crackled as a living symbol of the household's prosperity, and a special midwinter fire was a tradition also on the Continent, including pagan areas. When it was over, the emperor ordered the ashes to be scattered outside the walls of the fortress as protection against storms and weather damage, as he looked to prolong the magic of the midwinter fire.

This ceremony enacted, to Valdor's surprise, the emperor summoned Caurus and took him aside, far from intrusive ears. Valdor watched, peered across the hall, as the Emperor of the North embraced his father, clasped his wrist, and handed him a bulging bag of coins. The centurion waited until the emperor dismissed his father before hurrying after him to the small house he had managed to have allocated to his parents in the *vicus* outside the walls.

He watched his father slip into the building and hesitated outside the door, listening to his mother's delighted squeal, and his bafflement increased. He knocked and walked in without waiting to receive permission to enter. His mother's triumphant expression on seeing him startled him somewhat. "Father, what's going on? I saw the emperor embrace you and hand you a bag of coins."

Caurus first looked uncomfortable, then ran his fingers across an eyebrow, bowing his head in thought, but Namuta spoke eagerly, "Your father is in difficulty because the emperor has ordered him not to speak about what he has decided. You will have to hear it directly from his mouth, my son. Oh, I'm so proud of you! Be patient and all will become clear."

"But, mother, all that money?" Valdor pointed to the bulging linen sack with drawstrings his father had set down on the table. "What is the meaning of this?"

"My dear son, it is a fee the emperor has paid me to honour a long-standing Roman tradition. He needed to compensate me in return for my agreement. I'm sorry I am not at liberty to explain. As your mother said, be patient and have faith, for it is a marvellous thing! Emperor Marcus Aurelius is truly a great man!"

"Ha!" Valdor was extremely irritated—*after all I've done for them, they shun me and will not share a secret!*—he glared, turned on his heel, and strode out the door, slamming it behind him.

The centurion brooded all afternoon and asked himself a hundred questions. What would his father do with the money? Why was his mother proud of him? What did Carausius have in mind? Given his parents' reaction to the emperor's scheme—which he could only describe as ecstatic—it had to be something extremely positive involving him. Yet, the emperor himself had excluded his participation in the forthcoming Spring campaign. He would not gladly accept the role of camp prefect here at Branodunum. What use was a promotion if it meant a static life organising the daily routine of a shore fortress?

Suddenly, a thought struck him; tonight, the emperor had organised a feast to mark the end of the advent fast. At last! After forty days without a glass of red wine, he could indulge, but it was not the thought of wining and dining that gripped his imagination, but the memory of Carausius's words. He would make an announcement concerning his future in the Spring. He need only be patient for an hour or two.

It was less than an hour before he learnt something directly from the emperor. The Emperor of the North repeated an earlier gesture by taking Valdor aside as he had done Caurus before him. Instead of the usual booming voice, Carausius pushed forward his somewhat brutish face close to Valdor's and spoke low: "Centurion, from the day I met you, you have been loyal and true. You have shown concern for my wellbeing and, not only that, you regularly demonstrate how much you care that my reign is a success, by reinforcing my position at every opportunity." He paused, and his eyes pierced Valdor's, who muttered, "I only do my duty, Caesar."

At last, the bellow of laughter had everyone in the hall turning to stare, so the emperor gently pushed Valdor out of the glow of the torch in its sconce on the wall and into the shade, where he lowered his voice so much Valdor strained to hear him.

"Hark! Everyone does his duty, even I do! But it's *how* one goes about it that counts. You have been exceptional, Valdor, my boy! So, I have decided to adopt you as my son. I have paid your father as *pater familias* the requisite compensation according to Roman law. All that remains is for you to agree and for us to sign and seal a document with the lawyers. What do you say?"

"Caesar, I am lost for words! It is an honour for me to be your heir. I am shocked."

"Do not be! Did not the great Emperor Hadrian adopt not one, but two sons, at different times? But heed me well, your new position will bring enemies that you do not yet have. Do not speak of this to anyone until my announcement during the feast."

"But—"

"Enough! Come, take your seat at my right hand. The camp prefect can sit to my left!"

The meal passed in a blur for Valdor as his stomach readjusted to the ample rich food and strong drink. The emperor had ordered a priest to recount the Nativity, which further aroused Valdor's perplexity. He had not been baptised, although the idea had crossed his mind on occasion; like his father, he was still a pagan, and his bafflement came from the concept of a god that allowed his son to incarnate only to die cruelly—Valdor had seen the victims of crucifixion first-hand—and all this, without seeking vengeance on his oppressors. Thor would have smitten them with his hammer, sending lightning to burn his tormentors on the spot like a smith's steel sends sparks flying. Valdor had seen mighty oaks split and charred by lightning. Many in the hall were Christians and, overawed by the tale of angels, a comet, and shepherds, crossed themselves in awe. The priest ended the tale for the ages and sat beaming around the crowded gathering as, with one hand, Carausius called attention to himself by banging his wooden beaker hard on the table several times, and with the other, hauled Valdor to his feet.

"Friends," he boomed, "today is one of the happiest of my life for I have decided to adopt Centurion Valdor as my son and legitimate heir. Behold Caesar Valdor Aurelius!" This announcement was met at first by a stunned silence, which Valdor took to mean envy and hatred. His emperor's words still rang in his ears. *Your new position will bring enemies that you do not yet have.* But he need not have worried: not yet, at least, for suddenly people rose to their feet and bellowed "Hail Caesar! Hail Caesar Valdor Aurelius!" applause thundered around the hall. Men copied the emperor and banged beakers on tables until the noise was deafening and only stopped when the emperor raised his hand.

Valdor looked around the high table and only grins met his gaze. He was a popular centurion, but it pleased him most that there was no sign of envy on his close friends' faces, just simple happiness for his lot.

The emperor cried, "Friends, I have not yet finished with my announcements. There is more! As you know, our coasts are infested by pirates from Saxony and Francia. It is my task to liberate Britannia from these marauders and to facilitate this task,

I have constructed more war galleys and thanks to my son, we have more legions to man them and sweep the brigands from the seas. Besides, I now announce the new office of my son. I appoint him Count of the Saxon Shore—*Comes littoris Saxonici per Britanniam*," he announced solemnly in Latin so that everyone would understand.

Valdor's jaw dropped, but quickly he controlled his gaping. After all, such an expression was unworthy, but the position was dignified of the next Caesar. But what did it entail exactly?

That was what the emperor explained as they finished the roast swan and conversations became private again.

"I almost envy you, my son; my campaign cannot begin until the North Sea calms in the spring. You can begin work as soon as you wish, tomorrow if you want! I'll prepare a document stating your role explicitly with my seal attached, so that you meet no internal obstacles."

"But father, what exactly does my role entail?"

"It's complex; we have three shore forts: here, at Regulbium and at Portus Lemanis in the land of the Canti. These fortresses all guard estuaries against Saxon incursions, but I need them also to protect us against an attempt at the reconquest of Britannia by the Empire. I task you to study these three forts and to build at least another six at strategic estuaries as far as the Insula Vecta or *Vectis*—the large island on the Solent. Then, we'll need signal stations with roads to them and strategically placed depots. You will be entitled to withdraw and use the necessary funds, my son."

"As always, I shall carry out the task to the best of my ability, father, and hope that I'll see some action as a result."

"Always the man of action, like myself! I feel sure you will be called upon to fight Maximian unless I can first deal with him. There's news of him gathering troops in *Gallia*. I'm convinced that his first move will be to retake your old homeland, Valdor. In that way, he'll be a constant threat to Britannia, not to mention the other side of the coin, he'll want to defend the Rhine and Waal estuaries from a possible invasion on my part. I have to decide whether to surprise him by moving first. It's painful to me to have to wait for the fair-weather season."

"On the other hand, there's no sense in losing men to a watery grave. Anyway, father, I think I'll walk around this fortress to understand its construction, seen through different eyes. Tomorrow, I'll take Sparax down to Regulbium. I'm told that it is exactly a day's ride from here. I can renew some old acquaintances and confront the layout there with this fortress."

"Nay, stay a few more days so that we can get to know each other better."

"Thank you for everything you've done for a poor country lad."

"The merit is all your own, Count Valdor. In any case, you have to wait for documents to be drawn up—not least, the one that will enable you to withdraw the huge sums needed for building. They'll also prepare another one, entitling you to levy taxes in my name. Only to be used in absolute necessity, mind. It's easy to lose popularity when money raising enters the equation." The famous roar of laughter echoed rather hollow with concern.

Valdor decided to pace out the length and breadth of the fortress and concluded that the walls enclosed an area of roughly two and a half hectares. He had already considered the height and strengthening of the walls but noted that each side of the rectangle was interrupted by a gate, each flanked by two towers. The necessary buildings and the road layout next concerned him. The main road was paved and ran from north to south; at its centre was the *praetorium*, the headquarters building because it housed the *praetor* or base commander and his staff. Just strolling around the camp, Valdor realised the scale of the task he was about to undertake and at once realised he could not do it on his own. He had to create, not one, but at least, six fortresses like this —so, he would need to call on experts. Upon enquiring for an engineer, a soldier led him to a grey-haired man, who had laid out this very stronghold some score years before. He was one of the experienced officers called *metatores*, who explained to him that a camp could have one of two basic shapes: a square, or a rectangle like this one. The rectangular layouts were larger and designed to contain two legions, not one, each legion being placed back-to-back with headquarters next to each other. Laying it out was a geometric exercise conducted by the metatores, who used graduated measuring rods called *decempedae*—10-footers— and *gromatici* who used a *groma,* a sighting device consisting of a vertical staff with horizontal cross pieces and vertical plumb lines. The lined face grew even more wrinkled as Valdor explained the need to construct several camps. He said, "Count," surprising Valdor by using his new title, "you will need to gather a group of expert engineers and begin ideally in the centre of the planned camp at the site of the headquarters tent or building known as the *principia*. Streets and other features are marked with coloured pennants or rods. We can oversee the work done by legionaries drafted for the manual labour," he smiled, confident in his ability to undertake this phase of camp construction.

"You will ride with me tomorrow, my friend. I'll place you in charge of creating my first *castrum*. The prune-like, wrinkled countenance activated smile lines around the eyes and mouth. "Lord, you do me a great honour, for it has been too long since my services have been required."

Valdor had made a mental note of the layout of Branodunum Fort, the roads, buildings: the tribunal for courts martial and arbitration, the guardhouse, the storehouses for grain (*horrea*), for meat (*carnarea*), the barracks, stables, workshops, and the *questorium* for the safekeeping of plunder and cells for captives or hostages. A sudden thought struck him, and he turned to his companion, "Won't we first have to find running water, maybe a stream to divert for the latrines?"

The visage again cracked into a smile, "Ah, I see you are of a practical bent, Count. Fear not, one thing about Britannia we cannot deny is that this soaked country of rheum and agues does not lack water! Another of the first things to be done will be to dig a well for drinking water—again, not an arduous task."

"I take it you can ride, Engineer?"

"Ay, Sire,"

"Then, meet me at the stables at dawn. We'll take an escort of a dozen men to Regulbium. *I'll take all my friends.* When we arrive there, we'll confront the two fortresses and together decide whether there are improvements we can make on our first fortress. I'm sure you'll find gromatici and metatores among the men there, and I'll make it clear to them that they'll work under you. We'll discuss your pay and rank once we start work on the first project." *I make it sound easy, but first I'll have to identify the site.*

Before anything else, he went to find his Batavian comrades to tell them to prepare to leave at dawn. He worried about the reception his new status would reserve for him, but he need not have. His cousin was the first to remind him, "Remember the oath we took on Torik Isle: *whatever we have to face, we'll endure it together, united: each individual should act for the benefit of the group, and the group should act for the benefit of each individual.*"

"I have not forgotten, Johar, and now that I am a Count, I have the position to raise you all in rank. Each of you will be a centurion. I will accompany you to withdraw your uniforms, new galea, and the necessary *vitis*, but friends, make my motto yours, I implore you: *Hard, but fair; kind but hard.* Remember this, and you will be successful officers like me. Now, decide for yourselves, each of you will choose three trusted comrades to ride with us at dawn to Regulbium. Once there, you'll each take command of a century."

"Am I dreaming all this, cousin?"

"Nay, Johar, ask former decurion Heidar whether this is a dream. Together, we'll do great things. As the new Count, I know that I can rely on tried and tested comrades, or better, on old friends."

The four repeated the gesture of long ago on Torik and placed hands one on the other and grinned as of yore.

II

THE WINTER MADE THE BRITONS' TRACKWAYS impassable quagmires, but the Roman engineers, the best in the world, had created arteries that had a metalled curved surface off which the rain ran into lateral ditches. The band of legionaries already knew the route to Camolodunum from Valdor's previous journey. Nevertheless, the long ride south was dismal in the incessant downpour. It dampened enthusiasm for conversation, enabling the cloaked Valdor, under his hood, to reflect on his life.

He dwelt on his new responsibility and, above all, on his youth. He had been catapulted to prominence thanks to the affinity he had evoked in the emperor. That, too, was curious because Carausius would not have become emperor had he not rebelled against Maximian. How strange was Fate! Now, he was effectively the second highest-ranking person in Britannia and was still only on the threshold of his twentieth winter. Therefore, it was reasonable for him to harbour doubts about his capabilities. He would have liked to take the route south along the coast to consider which estuaries might need a new fortress, but the bad weather had botched that idea. This setback did not help his self-confidence. He needed the gods to send him something to ignite the flame of self-assurance.

Whether it was the work of the gods or of Fate (were they one and the same thing?) the event came in the most unexpected way. They had travelled the old British track, the splendid Watling Street, made wide and practicable by the Roman engineers—the rain had eased off for some time—and they were drawing close to Regulbium when smoke darkened the already dull sky: a village was in flames! This could only mean one thing in these troubled times—a pirate incursion! Valdor led the gallop, intent on fighting the raiders, but when they came to a rise overlooking the great river *Tamesis,* Valdor saw that the Legio II Augusta, his old comrades from the garrison of Regulbium, had the situation in hand.

He stared in disbelief, the barbarians were surrounded and fighting desperately for their lives, but among them, surely there was a woman! A female warrior! Was that possible? He galloped over to the fray and in ringing tones ordered the centurion to halt the combat. The tigerish woman had affected him so deeply that he could not understand his own actions.

"If they lay down their arms, take them as slaves, Centurion. Whoever they are... I want that woman."

Valdor's imperial purple confirmed the rumour that had reached the centurion's ears. Here in person was the emperor's adopted son. There could be no gainsaying *him*.

"They are Jutes, lord, barbarians who use women in battle—whoever heard of such a thing?"

The surviving Jutes, standing among their fallen comrades, realised that they had to choose between feasting at Odin's table or remaining alive, laid down their arms. "Bind the woman! I want her for my slave," Valdor ordered. He grasped the trailing rope from her bound wrists to force her to walk beside Sparax or be dragged along the ground. She walked. He could not see the hatred in her eyes because she had smeared a pigment from ear to ear that created a black band across and around them.

The centurion rode beside Valdor to offer gratuitous advice. "Do not underestimate the ferocity of the woman, Sire. The Jutes call such demons *skjaldmaer*, or as we would say, *shield maidens*. She will attempt to strike you with any blade that comes within her reach. Taming her will be harder than trying to skin a wildcat alive!"

I shall tame her if it's the last thing I do! His next words did not reflect this thought: "I'll bear your words in mind, Centurion. Thank you for obeying my orders in the heat of battle. I'll not forget it; indeed, I'll have Legate Vitulasius promote you."

"It was my duty to obey, lord. The legate will appreciate some hardy slaves, in any case. There's maintenance work to be done in the fortress and it will fall to them as soon as the weather permits. The gods only know what folly drove them to risk drowning by crossing the North Sea in this intemperate season."

Valdor completely forgot about his mission to study and compare the layout of the Regulbium fortress. He was too obsessed with his female prisoner. After greeting Legate Vitulasius and explaining his mission, he ordered four female slaves to bathe the captive and dress her in clean clothes.

When they brought her back to him, he was struck by her beauty without the black mask and her proud bearing. Neither did it escape him that the biggest of the slave women now had a red gouge running down one cheek. He would certainly beware his untamed tigress' claws.

The fact that he was Batavian helped him, for she was impressed that so youthful a barbarian warrior had risen to power; also, she found him most attractive. He had little difficulty understanding her Jutish tongue although a few words escaped him. As he admired her long barley-coloured hair flowing in waves over her shoulders and cornflower blue eyes, he realised that this was the first woman he had ever been attracted to. He discovered that her name was Svafa, the daughter of a jarl. Her slim, but muscular arm shot out and, grasping him behind his neck, hauled him towards her. Before he could react, her tongue was inside his mouth. He had no experience of kissing a woman and this lascivious action rocked him to the core, but he loved it! Without realising it, he was responding with his tongue, engaging in a loving battle. At that moment, although he knew it not, Valdor had found the love of his life.

Despite the soft breasts pressing against his chest, he broke free. He needed to find out more about this siren from the north before surrendering to her undoubted charms. He led her to his chamber and was impressed by her strength when he resisted her attempt to push him onto the bed. Her eyes burnt with resentment and anger, but he soothed her, "Svafa, if you are to be my woman, I need to know more about you, and you about me."

"What do you need to know, Valdor? I am a woman and you are a man! I am Jarl Hibald's daughter and will not give myself to just anyone."

"I am the second most important man in Britannia. I command everyone except my emperor, Caesar Marcus Aurelius. Will you concede yourself to a future emperor?"

"You are younger than I. How old *are* you, emperor's son?"

Strangely ashamed of his youthfulness, he conceded defensively, "Almost twenty winters, and you?"

"I'll wager you have never been with a woman! Are you afraid of women, Valdor? I'm five and twenty."

"Nay, I'm afraid of no one. But if a woman were to frighten me in battle, it might be you! I saw you fighting near the village your people raided and was impressed and..." he said slowly, "... attracted, I suppose."

"Batavians are fierce warriors. I dare say you are a mighty one. Why don't we wrestle?"

He laughed, "We'll do that when I'm ready. First, I want to know why you left your homeland."

Her lip curled, "*Me?* Because my father ordered me. He is in Valhalla now, thanks to your Roman friends. But he sailed to escape the doom of our village. The sea has engulfed it and there is no tillable land to support our folks. That is why we sailed over the raging sea. I grew up with tales of how fertile this Britons' land is and how we would one day take it for ourselves. The dream didn't quite match the reality, did it, Valdor?"

"Let's wrestle!" He kicked her leg from under her and threw her off-balance onto the bed before diving upon her. She snarled and wrapped arms and legs around him, writhing so forcefully that she overturned him and pinned him down. They struggled, trading move and counter-move. Valdor could not believe the strength and vigour of this apparently slight jarl's daughter. At last, exhausted, they lay still, and she paid him a compliment, "Only my brother could beat me in a wrestling match in our village. You have not beaten me, but I could not overcome you, either."

"How come you, a woman, are so strong?"

"Training. As a girl, I lifted rocks, increasing their weight with every passing year, and wrestling the youths and even the men. Do not underestimate me, Valdor," she echoed the centurion's warning, "I have killed men in battle, at least two today! Have you fought in battle?"

"Ay, and killed my share of foes."

"I knew it, emperor's son. Come, love me!"

Again, her tongue sought his, and her thighs locked around him. What did he know? He was still a virgin but would never admit it. Nature took its course. With this wildcat, how was he to know that lovemaking could be gentle and slow? Svafa was uninhibited, passionate, and demanding, but Valdor adored what her body was doing to his. If he thought maybe he loved her, now he was completely in her thrall. The gods had answered his prayer for self-assurance. He had it now when the Jutish goddess whispered in his ear, "You are my first lover and I could not wish for better."

"I could have said the same words," he confessed, sending her into a renewed frenzy of lovemaking.

Two days passed sweetly before Valdor returned to his senses and remembered the task assigned to him. When he told her that he had to begin work, she said, "I will not be an ornament or a wallflower when you enter battle. I wish to fight alongside my man."

He gazed at her earnest expression and said slowly, "The Count of the Saxon Shore should be different from other men. He should have his own *skjaldmær*," he pronounced the word awkwardly, "I'll have you fitted with a legionary's armour and find you a decent horse. You can ride, can you not?"

"Can a jarl's daughter ride? What do you think?"

He would not tell her his true thoughts at that moment, which were that he had been forced to tame the two creatures he loved most in this world, Sparax and Svafa, where others had failed! He was not sure she would appreciate him comparing her with a stallion, however wild. He imagined how she would look in a legionary's uniform and liked the thought, so he took her to the armoury and had her fitted. First, he had to warn the armourer, "Do not say what you are thinking, soldier. This is my bodyguard and she can kill with her bare hands, so obey my orders in silence." *What a shame to hide such a splendid body beneath a cuirass* was his principal thought.

After which, his attention was immediately given to how best to compare this fortress to the one he had left in the north. He called over a legionary, one of his Branodunum party, and told him to find the *metator* who accompanied them.

Some minutes later, the wrinkled countenance was beaming at him before disappearing in a deep bow. "Show me around this fortress, my friend, I have been—*ahem*—somewhat busy and have had no time to explore. Perhaps you can point out the salient features of this fortress and we'll see how it differs from Branodunum.

"First, its history, Sire, this was a small fort built directly after the invasion of Britannia in the reign of Claudius, protected by earthworks. It was connected to *Durovernum*, the capital of the Cantiaci, by a road. It was strategically located at the mainland side of the entrance to the mile-wide Wantsum Channel, which separates the Isle of Thanet from the mainland. We'll see from the ramparts, and in yonder corner, once stood a lighthouse. Later garrisons did away with that because it was of more use to Rome's enemies." His dismissive laugh seemed to speak of earlier follies, but then he added, "Some four score years ago the decision was taken to build this stone fortress on the ancient Claudian site, so in some way acknowledging the sage choice of our forefathers."

"The first difference I noticed, Master Metator, is that this fortress is square-shaped, unlike Branodunum."

"You are right, lord, and this depends upon a choice you must make regarding the accommodation of a single legion, as here, or two legions as at Branodunum. Yesterday, I paced out the size of the fort. By my calculations, it covers an area of just over three hectares. I also measured the walls: the single rampart is ten feet thick at the base, tapering to eight feet at the top, with a height of twenty feet. It is a solid construction, which we should imitate, lord, following this example by the additional strengthening by an interior earthen rampart. The entire wall is surrounded by two external ditches, which I think you'll agree is an arrangement difficult for a foe to penetrate."

"Excellent, let's walk around the interior and you can indicate anything you believe worthy of consideration."

The two men took the buildings for granted, so the only feature the engineer wished to point out was the aqueduct.

"This runs inland to a freshwater spring, Sire. I believe the laborious choice was dictated by the marshy nature of this terrain, which might have dissuaded the choice of not digging a well, owing to the insanitary nature of the groundwater."

"I see. This kind of observation makes me realise that choosing a site for a fortress is not quite so simple a matter as I'd thought."

"Fear not, Count, I have found two qualified engineers in this fortress and we shall unite our expertise to your choice."

"Before choosing another site, we'll make a further comparison by riding to another nearby stronghold at *Portus Lemanis*, which I believe is but some 40 miles to the south from here and guards a large bay on the Channel coast. By drawing on the best features of all three, we should be ready to construct some new forts. I think we'll start here in the south, towards the west, before considering the east coast." He paused and smiled at Svafa, who had struggled to understand the long conversation. Next to her stood the legionary who had brought the metator. Valdor addressed him, "Legionary, find all the members of the group who came here and tell them to be ready to leave at dawn. Engineer, you tell your two colleagues the same message. Svafa, you and I will find some food and drink. We'll need an early night if we are to leave at dawn." He said this with a degree of innuendo that was not lost on her, and she leered at him.

12

Valdor's Antonine Itinerary took them through *Durovernum Cantiacorum*, the capital of the Cantiaci tribe. The *Duro* in its name spoke of a stronghold, and as they approached, they could see why. The strong stone walls with the interspersed towers were enough to dissuade any random band of roving pirates, although an organised army might be a different proposition. The thriving and bustling town contained a mixture of timber and stone buildings, but its role as a Romano-British *civitas* was clearly defined by the forum and basilica at the centre, the temple enclosure, and theatre. Sparax's shod hoofs clattered along the main road through the town while Valdor gazed anxiously at Svafa, but she seemed in complete control of her chestnut mare, despite the tendency to slide on the paving stones.

Although neither of them referred to this difficulty, they were glad to exit through the southern gate and take the crushed gravel road to Portus Lemanis, according to the Itinerary, some 16,000 legionaries' paces to the south, which was, therefore, sixteen miles away and could be easily reached before darkness cloaked the land.

Valdor realised he was nearing their destination when the invigorating salty sea air filled his lungs. He wondered whether

97

Carausius, given the clement late-winter weather, was preparing to sail southwards. It occurred to him that if he did, he would be able to see the *Classis Britannica* sail along the Channel. He would much prefer to be commanding a war galley than organising the construction of a chain of forts.

The difference between Portus Lemanis and the previous two forts was immediately evident to him as Valdor approached the gate. He had been informed that the fort had been rebuilt as recently as twenty years ago, and the novelties introduced included the projecting towers. He could count ten of them from his vantage point beside the road, although later, he was able to ascertain fourteen. Another curiosity struck him when he entered the fortress—the shape—whereas the other two had been regular, either square or rectangular, this fort had the unusual form of an irregular pentagon. Also, there was only one gate to enter the stronghold, but he noticed several posterns.

One attractive feature was the presence of a heated bath, where men and women mingled in unconcerned nakedness, luxuriating in the steamy water. Not for the first time, Valdor admired the ingenuity of the Romans and the civilising effect they'd had on the world. Certainly, the aches caused by the hours in the saddle eased in a delightful torpor. This lethargy was interrupted unexpectedly when an underwater invader grasped his genitals. Valdor removed the hand and, taking the wrist roughly and irritably, hauled the offender to the surface, only to stare into the beaming face of his woman. "Svafa! You're lucky I didn't break your arm!" She looked different with her bountiful locks transformed into lank dripping rat-tails, but she was still beautiful to his eyes.

"We've been in this water long enough. Come, we must dry ourselves and dress, for it is time to meet the fortress officials."

They walked naked, arm in arm, over a mosaic floor, depicting the god Neptune, back to the *laconicum*, a dry hot room, where towels and their clothes hung from pegs.

"I'll rub you down," she offered.

"I'm not a horse!" he objected, but allowed her to dry his back and to sprinkle a scented liquid over him. Feeling clean and invigorated, he went to retrieve his imperial purple cloak and diadem from his travelling chest. There were two sides to this decision: first, he had not worn them on the journey to avoid arousing unwanted attention; second, he now wished for the authority they would bestow in the presence of the unknown fortress commanders. So, dressed as the emperor's son, he headed across the compound, receiving closed-fist salutes from the soldiers. A carved stone near the wall caught his eye.

Valdor stood in contemplation in front of the altar stone dedicated to the god Neptune. Of course, he knew all the Roman gods and the tales surrounding them. The long-haired, long-bearded god holding his trident was the god of the ocean, and everyone knew about his violent temperament and lustful urges. Ocean storms and earthquakes were due to Neptune's bad temper, which was why the Roman naval legion, based here, sought to propitiate him at every appropriate opportunity.

As he stared at the carved dolphin and the sea horses surrounding the god, Valdor recalled his turbulent love story with the water nymph, Amphitrite, whom he had spied dancing on the island of Naxos. Upon seeing her, Neptune fell madly in love with her and had to take her for his own. Valdor had a similar tale to tell, but Svafa wasn't dancing; she was engaged in deadly fighting; still, like Neptune, he had lost his heart and had to possess the ferocious Jutish beauty.

Apart from dolphins and other oceanic creatures, Neptune was associated with horses and bulls. Valdor decided that he would ride Sparax up to this altar stone before departing this fortress to ask for the god's protection. He could not be too careful since he had to worry about Svafa's safety in these dangerous times as well as his own. His hand sought hers and gave it a squeeze, before he offered his arm and they walked together to the *praetorium* and, despite his high rank, Valdor felt nervous. Perhaps he was conscious not only of his youth but also of his barbarian origins so evident in the Jute on his arm. He knew that barbarians had risen to become generals in the Roman army, some had become senators and some, like Carausius, even emperors.

Much depended on the origins of the officials because there was still a minority of patricians who felt the purity of their Roman blood entitled them to feel superior. Luckily, the fort was garrisoned by troops raised in Tournai, the three hundred men based there known as *numerus Turnacensium*, with their officers of the same origin. The base commander, the *praetor*, was a consul, who, as Valdor had planned by his appearance, was honoured to welcome them and, as soon as pleasantries were exchanged, issued orders for a sumptuous meal to be prepared.

Valdor explained that his commission as Count entailed the building of further forts and, warming to this argument, Consul Titus Attius Marsus, was forthcoming.

"I have been in command here for four years, in which we have been subjected to pirate raids. When the barbarians decide to sail into our harbour, it is an easy matter to vanquish them. However, when they land in a bay farther west of here, it is a difficult task to move my men quickly enough to protect the settlements. I am sad to say that many peaceful farmers lost their livestock and property to these raids, not to mention the cost in lives in desperate attempts to repel them. The construction of more fortresses to the west, if located well, with perhaps a signal tower between us, would enable us to catch raiders in a pincer."

Aware of the precious nature of this testimony, Valdor listened carefully before adding, "I'm sure this can be done as a priority, Consul, but I must ask, do you have metatores in your ranks?"

"I'll call for him, at once. Perhaps you did not know, Count, that rebuilding began here in 270 and was only finalised some ten summers ago, before my arrival. The old fort was demolished and the stone reutilised in the new walls."

They continued conversing, especially about the Count's adoptive father because the consul knew very little about the new emperor. A man entered bowing to interrupt the dialogue, his neatly-trimmed grey hair, short and brushed forward to his brow, and his deeply lined face made Valdor smile. *Perhaps all engineers look alike!* he thought. As they spoke, Svafa lifted a domesticated weasel onto her knee and stroked its brown fur. Valdor wasn't sure whether he would have risked exposing his hands to those razor-sharp teeth, but the consul smiled and said, "This little fellow keeps us free of pests; he deserves petting." The Count smiled and said, "Honestly, I prefer cats, although I imagine the weasel is faster and fiercer."

"Ay, and can squeeze through narrow openings more easily. But let's return to more serious matters; Master Metator, the Count wishes to question you about the building of our fort."

"Sire, the fort was rebuilt on the site of a smaller and weaker one. As you will appreciate, the location is ideal as we stand on a hill overlooking the sea, so that we have excellent visibility over the Channel. You will have passed through the *vicus* that bestrides the road to Durovernum. The people can flee within these walls at the first sight of danger. The walls are twenty-six feet high and the ramparts almost thirteen feet wide." Valdor caught the pride in his voice. "We used recycled stone bonded with brick and some roof tiles to enclose 3.4 hectares."

"It's an impressive construction, Metator, but tell me, what would you improve if you had to start afresh?"

The engineer looked uncomfortable, "I'm somewhat a traditionalist, so I'd prefer a more regular shape, and although, fortunately, we have not been tested by a superior force, I can't help but think that against such a foe, we would need another larger exit than the several small posterns provide. I feel sure that our layout is limiting for a strategic response, but, Sire, we were conditioned by the terrain, hence the irregular shape."

"I see, but did you not gain by the location on top of the hill?"

"Precisely, Lord. Also, at the time of building, there was considerable danger in the offing, and by remaining on the same site, our defensive capabilities were not compromised."

"Consul, are you prepared to let your metator lend his expertise by coming along with my party to choose a site to the west?"

"How could I refuse such a worthy request?"

Before Valdor could continue the conversation, the weasel leapt off Sfava's lap and sped across the hall in a brown blur. The animal must have sensed the presence of a small rodent. The consul laughed, "Just doing his duty, as we all do, Sire."

"Even on weasels was a great Empire built," Valdor laughed. "We shall leave at dawn, but tell me, how far away is the bay you believe needs safeguarding?"

"To the west, 44,000 paces, lies a bay with a long sandy beach, which makes it easy for pirates to run their shallow vessels ashore. To make matters worse, it is at the confluence of three rivers, one of which is navigable, allowing inland penetration," said the consul.

"It's true, Sire, I know the bay," added the metator, "there is a peninsula projecting into a tidal lagoon and marshes. A small river runs along the north side of the peninsula." He smiled smugly, "You could say that the place is as ideal for a fortress as it is for an enemy incursion."

"We'll leave as the cock crows on the morrow to make a definitive decision. With a little luck, in the form of the gods sending us kind weather, we can begin levelling the terrain and digging the ditches. Consul, I'll need a large part of your men to work as labourers. Should raiding vessels approach your harbour, your men will be only a day's march away."

"The pirates will not know that we have reduced the garrison and will not dare attack the fort. I can spare two hundred and eighty men, for a score of men on the ramparts will be sufficient to give the impression of a full complement."

"Then, it is agreed. Master Metator, you will lead us to this bay. What is the state of the roads?"

"There is a ridgeway that will take us almost to our destination, while the last stretch onto the peninsula is sound. We have to avoid the surrounding marshland to the east, which will make an extra defensive feature. If we leave at first light, we can be there well before nightfall."

13

THE NEW CONSTRUCTION AT ANDERITUM, AD 287

WHILE VALDOR BUSIED HIMSELF BARKING ORDERS AT his hard-working men, he endeared himself further by grasping a shovel and setting an example—an emperor's son who cared little that his feet were covered in the mud at the base of the fifteen-foot-deep trench he was helping to dig. The men might not have been so happy had they shared in the conversation between Valdor and the metator: "By my estimation," said the engineer, "it will take 160,000 man-days to build the fort, which is another way of saying that it will take our 285 men two years to complete it."

"Then, I'll waste no more time in conversation," the commander said, grasping the shovel and leaping with a squelch into the trench. True, his manual contribution was useful, but the building work required all his organisational skills. He arranged for carts and oxen to be available to teams of woodcutters in the woodlands to the north of the peninsula. They loaded felled oaks for transport to the trenches, where these great trunks were driven as piles into the soft earth, destined to support the weight of the stone walls. Rubble and timber were thrown between them to aid in solidifying the foundations. Several weeks passed before the metator expressed himself satisfied with the preparations and declared the trenches ready to receive the stone needed for the walls.

"Regarding the stone, Sire, I calculate that we'll need eighteen vessels for a continuous supply over a working season of 280 days."

"Where will we get the ships, and what about the stone?"

"It's a question of 600 boatloads of stone, which I dread to think about how many wagon-loads that equates to: I'd hazard 49,000! So, we'll need oxen to haul them, too. All this must be done without delay, for every day is valuable."

"Ay, but where will we quarry the stone?"

"There is an isle that lies to the west, which provided the stone for Regulbium. It is the finest quality material, and the isle is known as Vindelis, which lies just over 100 sea miles from here. I have taken the liberty of sending a message for transport boats from Regulbium. Instead, Sire, you have the authority to requisition oxen and wagons from the surrounding area."

"I shall set groups of men to this task; it will come as a pleasant change from toiling in the trench."

After several days, the lowing of the oxen became a common sound, but the voracious cropping of the grass within the interior of the trench created another problem—that of obtaining sufficient fodder. At the last count, they now had 1,500 oxen and 250 wagons.

They were still waiting for the transport boats to arrive when a cry from a lookout warned Valdor that ships were in the offing. It did not require his sharp eyes to determine soon that these were not transport barges but war galleys. Approaching the harbour under full sail was the Classis Britannica. *Does Carausius think it necessary to inspect my work?* The thought made him angry, but he could not greet his adoptive father with a sour face. Before the emperor could disembark, he had time to wash and change into his imperial *sagum*. Besides, the heavy purple cloak would warm him, even if he had become used to the fresh wind off the sea. Sfava insisted that he wear the diadem, too. She seemed more excited than he to see the emperor.

"Father! How wonderful to see you, but what brings you here?"

Carausius bellowed one of his famous laughs and thumped Valdor playfully on his shoulder, "To see you, of course, my son!" The two men embraced.

"Not to check on my progress?"

Again, the trumpeting laugh, "Not at all! I know that you will deliver; indeed, at a first glance, I see you have made great progress, and the Spring is not yet here. Nay, I sailed into Regulbium to fill our casks with fresh water and found the place nigh on deserted. They told me that you were here with your wife. Now, I did not know that you were wed and so, I decided to come and see the spouse for myself."

"Father, I am not wed, but I have a woman. Sfava! Where are you? Come here!"

"Ah! A fine barbarian beauty! Just like you, Valdor! That makes sense, but why are you not wedded? You are a Jute, are you not, my dear?" Carausius' pug-like face came close to her, and he inspected her as a plebeian farmer might inspect a mule.

"Sfava is the daughter of a jarl, father, and she is a shield-maiden."

Carausius roared his laugh, drew his gladius, and lunged at the woman. Adroitly, she skipped aside and snatched Valdor's gladius from his belt in one motion. In a moment, feet apart and shoulders forward, she was ready to fight.

"Hold!" ordered Valdor, "You cannot fight your emperor!"

All work in the camp had ceased as the men gathered around to see their emperor, and now with these events, the atmosphere was heavy and tense. Carausius' bodyguard had drawn their swords and placed themselves between their ruler and the impertinent barbarian.

Once more came the guffaw, and the emperor ordered, "Put away your weapons, I like the girl's spirit! Valdor, she will give you a formidable heir! You must wed her at once before I sail away. Did you know that Maximian is preparing for an invasion of Britannia?"

"You will vanquish him, father. But about this wedding..."

"You're right. Things should not be done in haste. Besides, it takes time for a priest to convert pagans."

"By the gods! Father, do you expect me to become a Christian? Why?"

"Because one day, you'll rule the Britons. Diocletian is persecuting Christians, covering them in oil and using them as torches to illuminate the streets of Rome. The Britons rightly will not tolerate such inhumanity. I am popular because I am the restorer of the true spirit of Rome, Valdor. When I have defeated Maximian, you will wed your Jutish wildcat with a Christian rite."

His arm around Sfava's shoulder, they watched the Classis Britannica sail away to war in Gallia.

"I like your father; he is one of us," Sfava confided, "but I'll not abandon my gods for him."

"We don't know if and when he will return," Valdor said. He had foreseen her objections but said in a low voice, "I will wed you by hand-clasping when the walls are completed, and we'll have a great feast. Let's leave this Christian business to blow away in the wind."

Two days after the fleet's departure, the lookout called to Valdor— "The barges, Sire!"

Urging oxen onto barges is no simple feat, but all eighteen barges sailed for Vindelis with three oxen and the same number of wagons to each vessel. The beasts would be needed to transport stone from the quarry back to the barges. They would remain on the isle until 600 boatloads of stone had arrived at the peninsula. The name of the completed fort would be *Anderitum*, named after the great Ander Forest to the north that stretched across most of the south of Britannia.

Three days passed before the lookout repeated the same cry. Valdor broke off sparring with Sfava with practice swords. She hurried over to him to inspect his right forearm, where she had delivered a hefty thwack.

"It's nothing!" he insisted, eyes watering and jaw clenched, but when she touched it gently, he pulled his arm away, "Ouch!"

"You'll have a nasty bruise tomorrow. I'll go to collect the arnica plant in the woodland. I saw a cold well-drained place where it grows. I can make an ointment. You're lucky we weren't fighting with steel blades."

"Do not think you'd have got near me with a real sword, woman!"

She could see that his pride was hurt, but she would earn his respect on the battlefield when they fought side by side. She hoped that day would come soon. There was little work the men in the fortress would allow her to do; at least, searching for the herb would be more interesting.

On her way back to the woods, she noticed again that the fortress occupied all of the peninsula so that there was no room for a *vicus*, meaning that if Britons decided to live near the stronghold, they would have to build their settlement in the woods.

She left behind hectic activity as men toiled to unload blocks of stone from the barges in the harbour onto the wagons on the foreshore. This operation was made wearisome by the soft ground, which meant putting shoulders to the carts until they reached the harder ground of the winding track up to the heights of the peninsula. The quarrymen had faced the stone blocks and also provided sacks of broken tiles and bricks to be mixed with cement for the binding courses.

As soon as the first barge was empty, it sailed away again as if the respective captains were in a prestigious race. Inside the perimeter of the trench, the metator spoke with Count Valdor, "Sire, I think it would be best if we pace out four lengths of wall and mark them with pegs. Each length will be apportioned to a gang of labourers and be twenty-six paces long. What do you think?"

"You are the expert, Metator. Will the wall be the same height as at Regulbium?"

"This site is more easily defended, but it would be wise to keep the height."

The months went by and the three adjacent lengths were completed, with three more lengths started when a small boat carrying a messenger arrived with the news that Carausius had won a victory in Gallia, retaking possession of Gesoriacum, meaning that he had complete control of the Channel. Maximian did not have the ships necessary to challenge him at sea. Given the Emperor of the North's military skills on land, the Western Emperor was forced to sue for peace.

Valdor celebrated this news by giving his men two days off work and declaring a celebratory feast. Work resumed three days later when an unexpected visitor arrived. The well-dressed individual rode a fine grey stallion. He declared in a ringing voice: "I have come to seek Caesar Valdor Aurelius!"

"I am he!" Valdor strode towards the bearded individual, who dismounted and bowed. On closer inspection, the newcomer had grown a full beard to hide to some extent a severe wound that ran diagonally from under the left cheekbone across the mouth. A blade had slashed both lips, leaving the man with a permanent disfigurement that appeared to be a constant sneer.

"I am Allectus, Sire, treasurer to Caesar Marcus Aurelius."

I suppose you've come to see why I am spending so much money. Valdor thought, but said, "You are welcome to Anderitum, Allectus, although, as you can see, it is little more than a building site at the moment. Still, you may come to my tent and share a bottle of red wine and some bread with me."

"I thank you, Sire. I can see why you have been drawing considerable sums from the treasury. May I compliment you on your choice of location for what is going to be a fine fortress?"

So, I was right about your visit. He said tightly, "It is commendable that a finance minister has come to ascertain that the imperial coffers are not being wastefully drained."

"It is my duty, Count, as the emperor spoke of a series of similar strongholds along the coast. Judging by the state of progress of this fort, I can suppose it will be finished next year?"

"Our aim is to finish Anderitum by the autumn of 289."

Valdor found that he could not help but look at the scarred lips, which created the unsettling sneer, but now, the smirk increased as Allectus smiled, revealing the damage to his teeth caused by the enemy blade.

"In that case, there will be some respite for our treasury this coming winter before you start again, Count."

"Unfortunately, Jutish and Saxon pirates are directly responsible for draining our coffers. Defence comes at a cost, Minister."

"As we are well aware, Sire. I can see that you and your men are doing a magnificent job. This will be an impregnable fortress against the raiders and, undoubtedly, will stand the test of time." He raised his beaker of wine, "Here's to confounding the raiders and the future of Anderitum!"

"The future of Anderitum!" Valdor echoed. "I don't wish to be indelicate, Minister, but where did you receive your wound?"

"Fighting with Carausius, my general, in Maximian's campaign against the Bagaudae rebels. Those peasants were better armed than we imagined and although I slew my enemy, he wielded a fine Frankish sword to some effect," he pointed ruefully at his mouth. "I expect he'd taken it from a nobleman's corpse. I know, I took it from his, and sold it for a tidy sum." His laugh was harsh and bitter. "We won a crushing victory, you know. Isn't it absurd that Maximian, the ungrateful dog, has turned on his greatest general?"

"The latest news is that my father has defeated him and that he sued for peace, which was granted. My father now holds Gesoriacum."

"Mars be praised! Holding that port means that Britannia cannot be invaded."

Why the strange expression, then, Allectus? I'm not sure that I entirely trust you! Still, father clearly does.

Smiling in a friendly manner, Valdor offered his visitor another beaker of wine and the talk moved on to future foreseen expenses, which at this point, were little more than legionaries and quarrymen's wages.

The discussion did not prove to be problematic and the Count and the Minister parted on amicable terms. Deep down, Valdor was pleased to see him go, although he could not explain his antipathy. After all, the unsightly wound had been gained honourably, fighting for the Empire.

He was pouring his third beaker of wine when the tent flap opened and Sfava came in, carrying a bunch of yellow-petalled flowers and a linen cloth containing animal fat. She spread her treasures on the floor and sat, her legs curled behind her, as she shredded the petals into the fat and mixed them with the point of her knife. Valdor poured her some wine; she took the beaker in her left hand and drained it in one draught like a true warrior. He grinned, but she grabbed his arm, making him grimace.

"Sorry," she lied with a fierce grin, gently pulling the offended arm towards her. She smeared her blade in the greasy ointment and spread it along the outside of his forearm. Then, with a circular motion, rubbed it into his skin.

"There, you'll feel better tomorrow. Soon we'll be able to practise swordsmanship again and I'll do the other arm!"

"Unless I swipe you so hard across your arse that you won't be able to sit down for a week, balm or no balm," he growled, glaring at his shieldmaiden. But she laughed and, by surprise, kissed him ferociously.

Her wild, untamed nature had captured his heart. *See, she loves me or else she wouldn't have made the arnica ointment — the little vixen!*

14

ANDERITUM FORT, SEPTEMBER AD 289

THE COUNT OF THE SAXON SHORE SURVEYED HIS MEN'S achievement. The Anderitum fortress was now completed except for minor details. Some men were tamping gravel to make the walkway around the parapets sound underfoot. The walkways ran for each of the fifty yards between turret and tower. The towers were 28 feet tall and so that the users could move around undisturbed while carrying long weapons, the height between floors was 9 feet. Having only one floor over the 9-foot-high wall, the second floor of the towers was at a height of 20 feet. The killing range of a javelin hurled from one of these turrets was reckoned at 35 feet, so the area from the walls to the first of two ditches in front of the fortress was kept entirely clear. Some men were putting the finishing touches to the two ditches, the inner one was a *fossa fastigata* 20 feet wide and 6 feet deep and contained a drainage ditch or ankle breaker, 1 foot by 1 foot, to facilitate maintenance. The outer ditch was a *fossa punica*, 20 feet wide and 5 feet deep. Its outer slope made an angle of 30 degrees with the vertical and the inner one, 19 degrees with the horizontal. Woe betide any foe advancing on the stronghold out of the woods. He closed his eyes and imagined the excitement of defending the fortress against an advancing enemy. He realised that it was more likely that the garrison would leave the fortress through the 20-foot-wide gate of the *porta praetoria* to catch the raiders in a pincer trap. *Ay, all told, we've done an excellent job. It'll seem like child's play now to construct a signal tower between here and Regulbium. Then, I'll choose another site and begin all over again, farther down the coast.*

After the walls were completed, the legionaries had rapidly constructed timber buildings, which he now surveyed with pride: beside the road running through the *porta praetoria* were two important buildings—on the right a hospital and on the left the latrines. Between those and the stables in the corner was a stockyard. Across the road and beside the hospital were the baths next to a storehouse in the corner of the fort. All of these buildings were separated by the via principalis—which joined the two gates, the left and the right— from the headquarters that contained his room and those of the high-ranking officers. This building was flanked on either side by the barracks. Two more buildings behind the headquarters and between it and the last of the gates, the *porta decumana*, contained a granary and a workshop. Valdor fully intended to build another six of these forts copying this exact layout in the years to come.

(PORT OF GESORIACUM, SEPTEMBER AD 289)

Carausius stood abaft his flagship on the tower with Centurion Heidar beside him. The Emperor of the North had been so successful as a general also because he listened to his trusted men and sought advice. "The question, Centurion, is should I accept Maximian's offer of peace or press on to destroy him?"

"Sire, better the enemy you know. The Western Emperor is in disarray, and having defeated him so emphatically once, you can do it again. The Romans produce great generals all the time," he said prophetically, "one can never be sure from where or when the next one might emerge and prevail."

"Sound advice, Heidar. I shall accept Maximian's plea."

"Also, because, my Emperor, whilst you hold this port as tonight, there is no question of Maximian invading Britannia."

Carausius guffawed and slapped his thigh, "That's true enough, but we cannot stay here indefinitely, the men will get restless, not least me! I need to see my son wedded and wish to admire the fortress he has built."

For his part, Maximian realised that he could not defeat Carausius in Gaul and that he would have to indefinitely shelve his invasion plans, but he had no intention of losing the last battlefront—that of the ancient Roman art of intrigue—even as Carausius and Heidar discussed whether to accept his offer of peace, one of Maximian's envoys discussed treason with a bearded man of the disfigured mouth.

In the next four years, much would happen under Carausius' rule. Elsewhere, Diocletian continued to persecute Christians and, at his insistence, Maximian applied his co-emperor's first edict in his part of the Empire, which ordered the burning of the Scriptures and the closing of churches. The Western Emperor was reluctant to engage in the horrific excesses of Diocletian against the person of the Christians in his territory.

(PORTUS ADURNI, AUTUMN AD 289)

In Britannia, informed of the persecutions, Carausius engaged in encouraging the Church to convert pagans. For this reason, he visited his son, now engaged in building a square fort at Portus Adurni on a commanding position at the head of a large, safe harbour opposite the large isle known as Vectis. The emperor followed his adopted son into the praetorium, a timber construction made comfortable for Valdor as the walls, built of coursed flint bonded with limestone slabs, rose around them at a faster pace than had been possible at Anderitum.

"It is the beginning of October, son, I have no complaints whatsoever about the progress you are making with the forts—"

Valdor interrupted his emperor to describe eagerly his plans for further forts and their possible locations. Carausius listened indulgently and offered a few shrewd comments about locations and watchtowers, but Valdor could see that something was on his father's mind and that he refrained from broaching it while the Count so keenly outlined his future plans.

"Father, I can see that something is troubling you, will you not share your thoughts with me?"

"Ay, that is why I have travelled thus far, Valdor."

"What is it, then?"

"Are you informed about events in the wider Empire?"

Valdor shook his head, "Occasionally, something seeps through. I know, for instance, that you brilliantly defeated Maximian in Gaul. How I wish I had been there to play my part."

Carausius, typically, roared with laughter and thumped Valdor's shoulder, "There was no need for your strength, my boy. Your fortress at Anderitum is a much greater contribution; by the way, I've issued orders for it to be garrisoned by the *numerus Turnacensium* from Portus Lemanis, whereas that stronghold will receive surplus troops from overcrowded barracks elsewhere."

"Splendid! But that is not what is weighing on your mind."

"Nay, I confess that my heart is heavy for the sins of my co-Augustus."

"Maximian?"

"He is but a puppet manipulated by the demon, Diocletian. That is something I refuse to become! Do you have any idea of what he is about? I do not doubt that he is an able general; indeed, he was proclaimed emperor by his troops. Just this year, he defeated the Alamanii and usurpers in Egypt. But it is his persecution of Christians that concerns me. He claims to do the gods' will on Earth and calls himself *Jovius*. He organises games and feeds Christians—men, women and children— to wild beasts in the arenas. He crucifies many and, I hear, crosses line the main roads into Rome. Others are burnt alive to light the streets of Rome. I will have none of this in Britannia. We should never lose sight of what happened years ago when the Britons, led by the

Iceni, defeated Rome under Queen Boudicca. Many Britons, my people, have adopted Christianity through baptism and I wish them to practise their religion freely in my empire." He paused and asked for wine, draining his beaker in one gulp. Valdor scrutinised him, convinced that he had not yet heard what he had come to say. In this, he was correct, for Carausius went on to say as if he had not paused: "Which is why I have been baptised and pray for Diocletian to mend his ways—"

"What! You are a Christian, father?

Another bellow of laughter rent the air, "Exactly! You should see your face!"

Valdor placed a hand upon the table for support as his head began to spin. He could not easily absorb what he had heard. "But what about the old gods? Have you renounced them? Do you not fear their wrath?"

A long discussion followed in which Carausius echoed the words of the priest who had converted him. He was persuasive, but Valdor thought about his birth parents and their forefathers' beliefs. He satisfied himself that his adoptive father had no intention of persecuting pagans and was ready to let the matter drop when Carausius delivered a blow worthy of a *ballista* ball. "I want you and your woman to convert and be wedded in the Church by Christmas. Nay, I'll hear no objections! Either you do this, Valdor, or I will disinherit you and strip you of your rank and titles." Sfava, who had followed the debate with interest, buried her head in her hands but remained silent.

"I need to speak alone with Sfava, father."

"By all means, but I want an answer before long. I'll await it in my cabin aboard ship." He glared from one to the other and neither doubted that he would fulfil his threat.

When he had marched out, Sfava grabbed his empty beaker and hurled it at Valdor's head. He just managed to dodge out of the way. "I'll not abandon my gods," she screamed and rushed out of the praetorium and through the fort to the main gate, where she slipped out and ran towards the woods.

Valdor realised that it was pointless chasing after her, but he felt a hollow sickness in his stomach and his heart was beating too fast. He had experienced a similar feeling before his first battle. He wondered about whether he would ever see her again, for the one thing he knew about her was that she was as fierce in her beliefs as in her behaviour. Would she abandon Freya for the love of him? He doubted it, and his uncertainty increased as the day gave way to night. She was still somewhere out there in the forest, wild beasts and all. Maybe he would mourn over her mangled corpse sometime soon.

His immediate choice was whether to sit in self-pity or to get drunk, so he opted for the latter. The strong red wine, reinforced by fermented elderberry, which grew locally and saved the imported wine from Ostia from becoming little more than weak vinegar, miraculously did not cloud his powers of reflection. His sense of loss for Sfava gave way to rage at her selfishness—did his position as the emperor's son mean nothing to her? Well, he thought, *I can convert to Christianity to please father and find a pretty woman to wed.* Even as he thought this, he knew that no other woman could ever replace Sfava in his heart. He roared and hurled his empty beaker at the wall. Should he go in search of her? But it was dark and moonless that night and the forest was endless. She could be anywhere, assuming she managed to avoid the beasts. He thought of the irony: Diocletian threw Christians to wild animals and Carausius had driven a pagan to their fangs and claws. He shuddered as a wolf's howl rent the night air.

Slowly, he stood and bent to retrieve his beaker, hiccuped, and poured another measure of red wine and watched the bubbles winking at the brim before draining it in one gulp as he had watched his father do. After several more beakers treated simi-larly, he slumped across the table, his head resting in the crook of his elbow and he snored, oblivious to the world and his woes.

Dawn came and went and still he slept until a hand shook him roughly out of his comatose state. Slowly, he sat up, bleary-eyed and with a painful cramp in his right arm. He shook it to restore the circulation the pressure of his head had impeded. The brusque movement made him groan, fighting back the urge to vomit. But who had awakened him? He turned to gaze into the grinning face of his woman. "Sfava!" His tongue felt furry and twice its normal size and the word came out thickly but his heart leapt. She had come back to him! In her left hand, held by the ears was a dead hare—thank the gods, the only victim of last night had been her prey, not the other way around. But what would she say to him?

"Valdor, I cannot live without you. The night brought me counsel. I will do anything to stay by your side."

He rose unsteadily and accepted another beaker of red wine. "It is the best cure," she said as he looked doubtfully at the red liquid that had made him feel so bad, but he downed it and immediately felt better. As usual, she was right. "Wash and clean your teeth," she said. He obeyed and the cold water invigorated him and the sage-leaf paste made his mouth sweeter.

When he came back to her, he said, "We must go down to father's flagship and break our news. He loves hare, Sfava, make him a gift of it before we give him our consent."

"I can always trap another one," she said blithely.

"Weren't you afraid of the wolves, Sfava?"

"Ha, I can climb trees, wolves cannot!"

His laugh might have competed with Carausius' bellows, for he was truly relieved and happy; as was Carausius when he learnt of their decision. He accepted the hare with almost as much enthusiasm, summoning a cook at once. The next person to respond to his summons was a priest. "This is Father Wymond, he will instruct you in our faith. Centurion!" he bellowed and Heidar hastened into the cramped quarters.

"Centurion, tell the Count," Carausius grinned.

Heidar frowned in concentration and then, hesitantly in Latin, orated:

Credo in Deum Patrem omnipotentem,

Creatorem caeli et terrae.
Et in Iesum Christum,
Filium eius unicum, Dominum nostrum,
qui conceptus est de Spiritu Sancto,
natus ex Maria Virgine..."

He paused as if struggling to remember when Father Wymond came to his rescue, finishing the Apostles' Creed: *"passus sub Pontio Pilato,"* the priest droned on uninterrupted until the final *"Amen!"* Thus, giving Valdor time to think and ask: "Have you, too, then, Heidar, forsaken the old gods?"

The centurion removed his helmet and beamed happily at his old friend, "Ay, brother, and I hope you will join us. Father Wymond baptised me together with your father, our emperor. Eternal Life awaits those who believe in Christ."

Valdor turned to the priest, "How long will it take to prepare us for baptism, Father? We wish to wed in the faith," he put an arm around Sfava's shoulder. Before the priest could reply, Carausius intervened, "This is what we will do: Valdor, you take Father Wymond to your headquarters and he will prepare you every day until he considers you ready. When he does, he will baptise you in the creek that runs into the sea, yonder," he pointed vaguely at the cabin wall. Then, we shall prepare a great feast at Yuletide to be eaten after your wedding, which will be celebrated in the small Church of St Mary in *Clausentum*," again he jerked a vague thumb at the wall, "just up the river is the settlement. You are popular there, Count Valdor, because Saxon pirates sacked the place twice in the past and the inhabitants can see that your fortress will protect them henceforth."

15

PORTUS ADURNI, OCTOBER-DECEMBER, AD 289

Left to his own devices, Valdor might have embraced the cult of Mithras like many of his men. But he owed all his privileges to his adoptive father, not a man he would cross lightly. So, he followed Father Wymond's tutoring with great attention and ardour, paying special attention to the Annunciation and the Virgin Birth.

Yet, Valdor was endowed with curiosity and could not accept the priest's certainties when he retained the smallest doubt.

"Father, if the Archangel Gabriel was sent to Mary by God and she, a virgin, conceived Jesus, we must assume He was a divinity on Earth from His birth. Why, then, was it necessary for Him to be baptised in the Jordan River?"

The priest was a simple man and ill-prepared for such theological complexities, so he begged the Count for time. He hurried to search for the proselytiser who had baptised him. If anyone could explain these intricacies to the sceptical Count, it was Amphibalus. Father Wymond found the priest in Verulamium talking with a young follower called Alban. Amphibalus, a Roman Christian, had fled Diocletian's persecutions and recently baptised the ardent Alban. He recognised his convert, Father Wymond, and was intrigued to hear about Count Valdor. Here was a golden opportunity, he believed, to settle the mind of the emperor's son and complete poor Wymond's mission.

Several days later, the priests arrived and Valdor repeated his perplexity to the theologian. Amphibalus was perhaps the only person in Britannia capable of providing an answer. He listened carefully to Valdor's argument and complimented him on the intelligence of the question.

"Count, some of the leading minds in the Christian community over the last century have debated this very point, *in primis*, Irenaeus of Lyons and Justin the Martyr, who explained the events at the Jordan as necessary only for the sake of humanity; Jesus was not personally in need of the descent of the Spirit. For Justin, the Gospel narratives show evidence of the fruits of the Spirit in Christ, gifts that were later passed on to humanity in virtue of the baptism of Christ. Likewise, the baptism in the Jordan was and is a manifestation for the Christian community of the graces of the Spirit that are bestowed on Christians through immersion."

Valdor pursed his lips and frowned, gnawed at his thumbnail for a moment, then his expression cleared into an engaging smile. "Well, that makes sense, and I presume, priest, that if I submit to lustration in the freezing waters of the Itchen, I will receive the grace of the Holy Spirit, too?"

Now it was Amphibalus' turn to frown, and he said cautiously, "It behoves me to preach that the only begotten Son of God comes here, in order that whoever believes in Him should be saved, and whoever does not believe in Him should be condemned." He stared hard at Valdor, making sure that he had understood, but to be quite certain, added, "What I am saying is, ay, the Holy Spirit will come to you, Count, but any relapse into pagan practices or failure to renounce Satan's wiles, and the vessel of your body will be deemed unworthy to house it—"

Valdor cut the monologue short, "Your faith is demanding, priest, and I am but a poor, ignorant man. I wonder whether—"

Amphibalus took Valdor's hand and stared into his grey-blue

eyes, "Nay, Count, for one thing you *are not* is ignorant, maybe you are insecure. Remember from Father Wymond's teachings that God the Father spoke thus: 'This is my beloved Son, in whom I am well pleased,' as if to reassure His Son. If our Lord needed reassurance, wouldn't you know *you'd* need it?"

Valdor laughed, "Priest, it takes more courage to enter your religion than to go into battle!"

Amphibalus squeezed the hand and, finally, let it go, "You *are* going into battle, but against the invisible Forces of Darkness. Faith and prayer will sustain you, and you will not lose the war."

Valdor had much to reflect upon and, that night, for the first time in his life, prayed to the Christian God. It troubled him that he might not be ready to embrace this religion, but he woke in the morning with the conviction that he and Sfava should literally take the plunge into the gelid waters of the nearby River Itchen. Sfava's decisive nature and lesser propensity for intellectual struggle meant she had waited patiently for Valdor to decide for them both.

The Count accepted Father Wymond's plea to allow Amphibalus to conduct the ceremony, although he, too, would be in attendance to watch proceedings. The exiled priest surprised everyone by not leading them to the river, but to a small church between the fort and the stream. He explained that before baptism, the catechumen should renounce Satan and receive a first anointing with the oil of exorcism.

"Is that because you believe us to be possessed by evil, priest?" the quick-witted Count snarled.

"I wish you to do great deeds, son," Amphibalus reassured him, adding "and your jarl's daughter is by nature ferocious," he murmured this so low that not even Wymond standing beside him understood. He raised his voice, "Now it's down to the water for a triple immersion and the confession of faith."

Valdor and Sfava stripped naked on the banks of the Itchen and while he entered the freezing stream little-by-little, she flung herself with a great splash into the icy river, causing him to wince as the spray struck him. He managed not to curse, recalling that this was a spiritual moment. Amphibalus waded in and cupping his hands poured the water over the waist-deep Valdor's head while uttering prayers. He repeated the action twice more, then gave his attention to Sfava. When the Roman priest had finished, the goose-pimpled newly baptised, shivering and teeth chattering, grabbed the cloths offered by Wymond and rubbed themselves dry vigorously. They dressed hastily and Valdor turned to Amphibalus and glared. "Apart from cold, I feel no different, priest!"

"Nor should you, my son, the test will come and you will *know*. Now, let us go back to the church."

Inside the dimly-lit, simple wooden building, Valdor's eyes adjusted and he stared at the altar with its simple wooden cross. Amphibalus made his two converts kneel before it and, uttering a prayer, smeared them with the oil of thanksgiving, saying, "I anoint you with sacred oil in the name of Jesus Christ." He then laid his hands on their heads in turn and, again, applying oil, said, "I anoint you with holy oil in the Almighty Father, in Christ Jesus, and in the Holy Spirit."

It was at that precise moment that Valdor *knew* something had changed within him. Later, Sfava put it into words, "I felt a golden glow pass from the top of my head through my body to my toes. At last, I felt in touch with the divine."

"Ay, with the Godhead," said Amphibalus triumphantly and explained to her, "Daughter, you felt the Holy Spirit entering your corporeal body. Pray that He will remain forever within you. Do good deeds and love your man and your neighbours."

She began by acting as a nurse to injured labourers, bandaging blisters and making tinctures for sprained ankles. Valdor, instead, eased the pressure on the masters, whose exhortations had produced astonishing progress. On the sabbath, without explanation, he gave everyone a day's rest, which the men appreciated and redoubled their efforts the following day. In this way, the fort neared completion as advent approached. Only Valdor and Sfava knew what this meant, but they were surprised when, as the last gateway tower neared completion, a horn sounded to announce the approach of a ship. Valdor bounded up the twin tower at the other side of the east gate and peered seawards. Indeed, there was a ship, he smiled, recognising the vessel as his father's flagship. Disembarked, Carausius led a small party up to the east gate, where three blasts of a horn opened the great oak doors to admit the emperor and his contingent into the square, 9-acre enclosure.

As he embraced his father, Valdor peered over his shoulder to espy with pleasure the features of the priest, Amphibalus, whom he had not seen for months following the baptism.

"My dear son," Carausius began, "I am well pleased. This fortress is almost completed and, although you have not yet been called upon to fight, we have destroyed countless pirate vessels in the east coast estuaries. Don't worry, I predict that you'll be honing your blades in the spring to repel the marauders, who are coming in waves." The emperor turned and gestured to Amphibalus, who hurried to stand next to him. He addressed Valdor with "Greetings in the name of Christ our Saviour, Count. I hope you have said your prayers and read the Bible that I left you."

"I have, and expect some lively discussion with you, priest. But all in good time. Come, you must be weary, let's enter the praetorium, where you shall have warmth, food and drink."

Gathered around the hearth, supping Valdor's fine red wine, served by Sfava, the conversation soon turned to their conversion.

"Amphibalus survived my co-emperor's persecution of Christians in Rome. Some friends hid him and smuggled him aboard a trading vessel directed to Britannia. He tells me that you have a fine mind and posed him some acute questions before he baptised you."

"I'm thankful that it was he who performed the rite, father, because I know it was efficacious."

"Good, you may ask why I brought Amphibalus with me."

"Why, father?"

Carausius roared his typical laugh, "To add to your sacraments, of course."

Valdor looked puzzled, "I don't understand."

Again, the bull-like bellow of laughter, "Holy matrimony! There's no reason that you and Sfava should not marry in the Church. Yuletide is in the offing and Christmas is a good time for your nuptials. Who better than Amphibalus to conduct the service?"

"There is no church in the fort," Valdor said gloomily.

"Nay, but he tells me there is one down by the river. It's enough that it's consecrated. Afterwards, we'll have a great feast. I've brought a host of cooks with me. We should go a-hunting in the forest together tomorrow. I have a fancy for venison," another roar of laughter made Valdor smile. "It's a splendid idea, father. They say that bear steak is exquisite, but I've never tasted it. Sfava found a bear den while collecting herbs to treat men's aches and pains. She can lead us to it." He turned to his woman, "Can you find it again, do you think?"

Her quizzical expression made his smile widen, for he knew she was challenging him. "I reckon that means ay, you can!"

"If you're after bear, we'll need spears, not just bows and arrows," the emperor mused. As if remembering something important, he turned to his cornicen, "Outside by the gate," he jerked a thumb, "three blasts if you please!"

The soldier picked up his horn, draped it around a shoulder and hurried out.

Three resonant blasts followed, and Valdor wondered what their purpose could be.

Soon enough, the cornicen returned, leading a small group into the building. To his immense pleasure, Valdor recognised his Batavian friends: Faldrek, Heidar, and his cousin, Johar, accompanied by Father Wymond.

Carausius howled another of his laughs, "You should see your face! Close that mouth and welcome your brothers in Christ!"

"What! My friends have become Christians?"

125

"Ay, fully-fledged, thanks to Father Wymond. I thought it best that my most trusted bodyguard shared my faith. When they heard that you had converted, they decided to do the same."

Valdor leapt to his feet and embraced them each in turn. He called Sfava. "This is my woman, Johar, it's time you found one like her," he paused and considered, "well, perhaps a little less savage!" Sfava backhanded a slap, but Valdor was ready and caught her wrist, "See what I mean!" and Carausius bellowed again.

Amid the hilarity, Faldrek looked serious and said, "When we came through the gate, I couldn't help but notice—it's ingenious."

"What?" asked Johar, "I didn't notice anything."

"You have a good eye, my friend," Valdor smiled at Faldrek, "but I take no credit. It was my metator."

"What are you talking about," Johar asked grumpily.

The emperor, too, looked intrigued and stared at Valdor expectantly.

Valdor smiled and said, "Faldrek's right, the gates of Portus Adurni are of particular interest: they are indented inwards, so as to trap the enemy in an area exposed to walls on three sides. That is, if we ever get the chance to fight the pirates," he added gloomily.

"Cheer up, my boy, I'm sure you will, for these Germanic tribes are coming in increasing numbers to these shores. Thank the Lord they cannot venture forth in these winter months, so we can enjoy our firesides," he stretched out his hands over the hearth.

Christ's Mass approached and Carausius busied himself with organising the ceremony unbeknown to Valdor. The first he knew of any such arrangements was on the day itself, the eve of the celebrations for the birth of Christ. Carausius ordered them to march down to the small church by the Itchen. Valdor gazed with curiosity at a plump matron dressed in white and at his bride, who wore a veil over her face. He wondered at these oddities. The Romans were as reluctant to surrender their gods as the pagans were, so in these early days of Christianity, Carausius made sure to appease the old divinities at his son's nuptials. The ceremony was simple and conducted by Father Wymond. However, the matron chosen by the emperor took Valdor's right hand and placed it in Svafa's, the *dextrarum iunctio*. The matron was the personification of Juno or of Concordia. She only backed away when the priest wrapped his stole around the joined hands and declared the couple man and wife. Then he addressed God in prayer, citing Tobias, "You made Adam, and for him you made his wife Eve a helper and support. From these two the human race has sprung. You said, 'It is not good that the man should be alone; let us make a helper for him like himself.'" Then, the priest blessed the couple and they exchanged the gold rings Carausius had provided. It was that simple and, amid the well-wishers, Valdor and Svafa returned to the fortress. There, they found more surprises.

The emperor had been busy with craftsmen for some time. He presented the couple with a large gold glass medallion. Their likenesses were beaten into the gold foil before it was encased in green glass, the couple stood, half-turned with right hands joined and between their heads was the *chi-rho* symbol. The magnificent piece was intended for display on a high table and it certainly caught the light and affirmed the Christian marital status of the spouses.

The surprises did not end there because the emperor presented Svafa with an exquisite silver cosmetics case, its lid inscribed with the slogan *Dulcis Anima Vivas*—Sweet Soul May You Live!—a nod to the concept of Eternal Life.

Carausius brought to an end the wedding occasion by announcing that they should be in the forest before noon to hunt for the bear or a deer. The Batavian centurions, Valdor and two of his preferred officers each withdrew a heavy spear from the store-room as did the emperor.

The ever-practical Johar also coiled a rope around his shoulder and down to his hip. Svafa, instead, not wishing to carry a heavy pole, withdrew three javelins. Some of them also carried a bow and wore a quiver of arrows. These were more suitable for deer hunting should the bear not be found. Svafa led the way into the forest and pointed out various herbs to her husband, explaining their doctoral use until she came to a clearing, where a track led away through dense undergrowth. It was narrow, so they were forced to move in single file behind her. After following this trail for several minutes, she stopped and spoke to Valdor behind her. "This fork to the left leads to a small clearing where there is an outcrop of rock. There are signs that a bear has dug a den under the overhanging rock. We should move swiftly and silently if we want to slay the bear." Valdor passed the instructions back and Svafa took the fork, halting when she reached the glade. "It might be a little early for hibernation," Valdor said doubtfully. "But if we wake the beast, it will be enraged. I see the opening under the rock." He pointed out the crevice to Heidar. "I'll go and poke my spear into its den," said the centurion. "Usually they are not very deep, just big enough for the creature to turn around on its litter of leaves."

"Be careful, Heidar, we'll have our spears ready in case the animal attacks."

They moved forward silently, Svafa hanging back slightly as the men approached the den.

Heidar lowered his spear, holding it parallel to the ground, his left hand grasping the pole ahead of his right. He assumed a half-walking, half-squatting position and drew near the entrance. Only a foot away from the hole, he thrust his spear forward. The other men formed an arc behind him, their spears all pointing at the den.

A squeal followed by a growl came from the den and suddenly, Heidar fell backwards as the spear was knocked sideways out of his hand. Before anyone could react, the brown bear emerged, preparing to pounce on the supine figure of Heidar. Even as the moaning bear sprang, a javelin thudded into its chest, rapidly followed by another. This second strike was enough to send the creature toppling backwards, which was when Carausius lunged forward and buried his spear deep into the beast's chest. To make quite sure, Valdor plunged his spear into the bear's throat and there could be no doubt that it now lay dead.

Johar dropped his spear, leapt forward and bound the bear's front paws together. He hacked through the rope and proceeded to bind the hind paws. That done, Valdor inserted his spear so that two men at each end could raise the prey onto their shoulders to transport it back to the fortress, where it would be skinned and butchered.

Heidar, somewhat pale, got to his feet, his first thought being to thank Svafa for her prompt reaction that had likely saved his life. But the emperor reached her first to congratulate her on the accuracy and power of her throwing. "After all, I see that my son's claims were not exaggerated. You are truly a shield maiden and I thank you for saving my centurion."

The fierce light in her eyes thrilled him and he knew why Valdor had chosen her to be his woman. But her words pleased him even more. "Lord, I wish only to fight beside my husband in your cause."

"You are as impatient as he is, but trust me, the pirates will come in the spring and worse for them if you are to greet them, my daughter!" he guffawed.

They trudged back to the fortress eagerly anticipating the two evenings of feasting that awaited them. Tonight, they would sample bear steak for the nuptial feast and on the morrow, roast geese for the Lord's birthday.

16

DUBRIS, KENT AND THE SOLENT, AD 289-90

CARAUSIUS, A MENAPIAN COMING FROM THE LOWER Rhine, was a seasoned sailor and already knew the ways of Frankish raiders. He enjoyed his peaceful Christmas and shared his fireside reflections with his son.

"I have experienced considerable success against the pirates, Valdor, but it cannot last unless I change things."

"You'll have to explain, father, I've been fully occupied with fort building and know little about your maritime adventures."

"It's a question of ships, my boy. The Frankish vessels have much in common with the 'Celtic' shipbuilding methods of my area of the Rhine. I have captured several and studied them. They have a strong keel and are carvel-built. The Romans use the immensely strong but time-consuming Mediterranean method of shell building," he explained the two techniques to the ill-informed Valdor. "So, you see, if we adopt the Rhine building technique, we can produce more craft quickly to match the increase in pirate numbers that I expect."

"But doesn't that building method mean that the ships are less watertight?"

Carausius roared with laughter, "The priest is right! You ask astute questions, my boy! It does! That's the importance of caulking. We'll stuff the joints with fibres and smear tar over them. That solves the problem. There are other gains, too. Let me explain. The mast step takes the form of a heavy transverse frame with a notch to hold the mast. The mast can take a light, lateen sail and there are twenty-six oars and a steersman. The vessels I captured are sleek with a shallow draught, drawing only about eighteen inches of water. They are about sixty feet long by ten feet broad: fast and manoeuvrable."

"Certainly, more so than our lumbering war galleys," Valdor mused.

"Exactly! But if we match them, we can intercept and defeat them. At present, they can easily escape us even by rowing up shallow rivers. I have ordered the building of scores of a ship type called a *scafa exploratoria*—a fast, 20-oared, camouflaged warship to be used for scouting and interception. I'm afraid that the triremes and Liburnians are no longer of much use to us. We must and will adapt! Since I became emperor, the land has prospered, to become largely free of piracy."

"I can see the benefits of the new ships," Valdor scratched the back of his head, "they will be cheaper and easier to build with a good performance—"

"Ay, and they'll require only a third of the crew of a Liburnian, meaning I can deploy my manpower more efficiently."

"Is the rumour true? Has Maximian taken Gesoriacum?"

"True, but much worse, he has defeated our Frankish allies to gain control of navigation on the Rhine. My scouts tell me that he exploited the tribal rivalries and is forming a fleet up at Trier. When spring comes, he'll proceed to the mouth of the Rhine and launch an invasion of Britannia." Carausius smirked, "But we'll be ready for him, son. During the next few weeks, I'll rearrange my legions, they will man your shore forts. You will be ready to counter any attack that sets foot on our shores. I will have every available vessel gather in the east coast estuaries but will send you a patrol for the Solent Channel. Together we'll defeat Maximian and confound his intention to re-take Britannia." The emperor of the North did not bellow his famous laugh, but frowned and stated prophetically: "Sooner or later, the Western Empire will find itself a better general than Maximian. My boy, do you know how many emperors have been murdered due to their lack of success? Failure in battle means loss of confidence and shortage of pay. My men have a lack of neither. Learn from me how to cultivate popularity." Now he trumpeted his famous laugh.

"How many?"

Carausius looked puzzled, "How many, what?"

"How many emperors have been murdered?"

"I don't know the exact number, but it goes as I said: defeat, lack of pay, debasement of the coinage to find the silver with a consequent inflation in prices, then revolt. Look, as recently as Gallienus, about the time you were born, he alone had to suppress 18 usurpers in his nine-year reign, only at the end to be murdered by his own officers. The empire was on the brink of collapse, then along came Diocletian and his reforms, of which I am proud to have played my part." He peered at Valdor and placed a hand on his arm, looked apologetic, and said, "This is your heritage, my son. Only success is acceptable."

"Then, it is success we'll achieve, father."

The emperor kissed his son's hand and agreed, "We'll have success!"

Winter gave way to spring and Valdor finished the work on Portus Adurni. He was considering what to do next when the warning blast of a horn sent him scurrying to an observation post. His heart thudding in his chest, he peered out to sea, relaxing at the sight of two familiar triremes leading half a dozen lighter ships into his harbour. His father had kept his word about reinforcements. He remained patiently at his vantage point and watched the pleasant sight of an entire legion disembarking from the two triremes. He identified the Capricorn shields of II Augusta and the figure of Legate Vitulasius leading his men to the trail up to the fortress. Valdor hurried down to wrap his imperial purple cloak around him and place the diadem over his fair locks.

To the usual three blasts, the great gate swung open and Valdor hurried to greet his welcome visitor. "Legate, you are just the person I would have wanted to take command of this fort. I'll soon leave you in charge." He explained the novelty of the defensive gates and how best to lure the enemy to destruction then, went on to negotiate for the ships. "I suggest that my cousin, Centurion Johar takes command of the triremes and patrolling the Solent. I will command the six smaller vessels and take them to the site of my next fortress."

After much reflection, he had decided on a strategic location facing Gallia—at a place named Dubris—the site of the estuary of the Dour. The planned fortress would, therefore, be in close contact with Portus Lemanis to the south and Regulbium to the north.

He was delighted when the shallow draught of his flotilla allowed him to moor in the River Dour. At this site, two lighthouses called the Pharos stood on the eastern and western heights. They were constructed soon after the Roman conquest of Britannia. Valdor chose the western heights for his fortification and climbed up to inspect the 80-foot-high lighthouse to see whether it could be incorporated into the planned defensive walls. His metator urged him, instead, to consider constructing, as the earlier Classis Britannia fort, below the western heights on the west bank of the Dour, but building anew, ignoring the old fortress. When the metator marked out the line of the foundations, the corners of the two forts did overlap. The older fortress would be a profitable source of stone for the new one. The new fort enclosed a number of civilian buildings to the north of the earlier fort and the west wall went straight through the west end of a Painted House. Valdor also inspected this *mansio*, which the metator considered in an ideal position for his fortress. The army came first, so he would sequester the building, demolish it, and incorporate its foundations into those of the 10 feet thick walls. The foots of the *mansio* walls could be embodied into the ramparts. He inspected the many multi-coloured panels framed by fluted columns, each with a motif dedicated to Bacchus, the Roman god of wine. As a Christian who appreciated wine, Valdor was saddened to tell the owner of the *mansio* of his decision.

"Friend, it is better to lose your home to the Roman army, than to lose it to Frankish raiders along with your life. Defence of the Channel is paramount. I will see you are compensated."

Demolition and the beginnings of the foundations began the next day. The surplus stone from the *mansio* was immediately built into the wall foundations. Valdor was pleasantly surprised to find baths quite close to the *mansio* and made good use of them, soaking himself while his metator took control of the layout of the fortress. The worthy engineer decided to reinforce the walls at intervals along its length with great stone bastions and ditch nearly 40 feet wide and 10 feet deep. Within the walls, he planned a dozen timber-built structures, metalled roads, and a postern gate with a footbridge. The ancient military bath house would be reused within the walls, which would delight his commander, the Count.

(THE SOLENT, AD 290)

Initially, Johar was irritated at being fobbed off with the two lumbering triremes while his cousin and commander took a sleek *scafa exploratoria* and the other five to Dubris. He sent the other trireme to the eastern approach of the channel and stationed his own at the western entrance. He understood that the two vessels guaranteed safety to a long stretch of the south coast and this made him feel better about his appointed task. During the first six weeks of patrolling, he was first startled by the strong and variable currents, which he studied intensely until he knew them intimately. At this point, he began to hatch a plan to defeat the pirates. He was certain that when they approached from the east, they would see his sister ship and deviate course to pass the northern coast of Vectis to then veer into the western entrance.

His scheme involved subterfuge. He would let the raiders believe that he was frightened of them and make as if to flee.

Everything went to plan when a dozen lateen-rigged Frankish ships appeared and Johar apparently fled. But he led them in hot pursuit into the treacherous currents where his three banks of oarsmen were able to pull out of danger. Alas for the raiders, each with only a third of Johar's available rowers, they were unable to save themselves from being dashed and wrecked on the rocky shore. The Franks who survived the devastation to reach the land were slaughtered by the II Augusta legionaries, who had been warned by their watchtower of an imminent incursion.

A more successful patrolling of the Solent was unimaginable, and Johar rejoiced in his feat, giving his crews three days' respite in the harbour.

(DUBRIS, KENT AD 290)

The fortress was half built when Valdor received news of a likely raid on his stretch of coast. It was extremely difficult to foresee where the pirates would choose to penetrate the land. However, he took his six ships deeper into the Dour estuary where a reed bed grew and backed his camouflaged ships among the tall canes. From the water, they were practically invisible. He had left instructions with a horn blower placed on the seventh floor of the western lighthouse to alert him with three blasts if he spotted pirates entering the Dour estuary.

The wait was long and boring, hardly relieved by the teeming fowl that occupied the reed bed. The men were becoming restless, the tedium made worse by Valdor's strict orders not to speak. He did not want voices alerting the enemy. At last, three horn blasts came from the Pharos, but Valdor held up a warning hand, ordering his crews to wait. He wanted to see the foe for himself to evaluate the odds.

He saw eight vessels rowing towards them, which made the stakes about even. He had the advantage of surprise, so he dropped his arm, and simultaneously his six vessels shot forward abeam of the foe. His archers in the prow had easy pickings, decimating the enemy crews before they realised they were under attack. The current swung Valdor's ships parallel to the Saxons so that his oarsmen hauled in their oars and became javelin throwers. These wreaked more havoc than the archers. Valdor's was the first boat to grapple an enemy and heave it to his hull. The commander himself, closely followed by Sfava, jumped aboard the enemy craft, swords drawn and shields raised. There was no need for shouted orders. His men knew their roles, and they followed their two leaders to overcome the marauders. The beauty of his success, repeated along the river by the others, was that not only did they slaughter the enemy, but they also seized the Saxon ships undamaged, thus more than doubling the size of their flotilla.

Valdor ordered a celebratory feast for all his men, including those in the garrison who had not been involved in the triumph. Sfava boasted that she had slain one more Saxon than Valdor's three, and he knew this to be true, although, as he pointed out to her, she had run a risk with the fourth that he would not have taken. She laughed; "I only did it because I'm more agile than you, and the swine was about to strike you from behind with his axe. I saved you, my darling commander." He knew that this was true, too, and was grateful and indebted to her, but knew that she had exposed herself to the very peril he had faced. She was indeed more agile, but on a blood-smeared deck, footholds were uncertain. He would have to think long and hard about taking his shield maiden into another battle.

(BLACKWATER ESTUARY, ESSEX, AD 290)

Built shortly before Carausius came to power, the fortress of *Othona* at the edge of the Dengie Peninsula was ideal for control of the estuaries of the rivers Blackwater and Colne, the latter leading to the important city of Camulodunum. It was here that Carausius had taken his newly-built fleet of fast interceptors and here that he added to his crews, reinforcing them with the *numerus fortensium* of the garrison. Before leaving Branodunum Fort, he had made arrangements to reinforce all the east coast garrisons because his scouts were certain of Maximian's invasion. The scouting patrol ship he had sent out sailed at great speed into the Blackwater Estuary and rowed over to the flagship. "Sire, the invasion fleet is on its way. I believe it is heading for the Yare Estuary. If we move quickly, we can trap them there."

"Excellent!" Carausius grinned. "I have added to the garrison at *Gariannum*, so we are well prepared. We sail at once!"

Whether Maximian expected to be opposed by cumbersome triremes or was ignorant of Carausius' new fleet, he was caught cold by the manoeuvrable interceptors and, much as had happened almost contemporaneously in the Dour Estuary, his fleet was overwhelmed by the disciplined troops who grappled and triumphed over Maximian's vessels. The engagement was short and bloody and ended with Carausius deliberately allowing his co-emperor to escape with six other vessels.

"Why, Sire, did you let your sworn enemy escape?" asked Centurion Heidar, who shared the emperor's confidences.

Carausius bellowed his famous laugh, "Because, my friend," he said triumphantly, "he will never again dare to launch a seaborne invasion after today's debacle." In this, Carausius was correct and far-seeing. For the moment, at least, Britannia was firmly in his grasp.

17

NORTHERN GAUL, AD 290

Carausius slapped Heidar on the back. "You're going home, Centurion!"

The former smith's apprentice stared at his emperor slack-jawed. What had he done wrong to deserve exile? He had thought that his commander was in an excellent mood after his crushing defeat of Maximian. Strangely, the deafening laugh seemed to confirm as much.

"You should see your face, my boy! Anyone would think that you don't want to return home. We're all going, you know."

Heidar's mouth shut with relief. "To Batavia, Sire?"

Another slap on the back. "That's where you are from, isn't it?"

"Ay, but—"

"*But* Batavia is in Maximian's hands, you were about to say. And that's the point. He was able to invade Britannia because he could sail unimpeded out of the mouth of the Rhine. We have to put a stop to that. We don't want him making a habit of it!" He bellowed another laugh at his joke. "The sea conditions are fair. Gather your men and bring them on board my flagship. I want you by my side, Centurion."

As predicted, the crossing was calm for the season, and

Heidar, standing in the stern with his emperor, enjoyed the breeze ruffling his hair and breathing in the salty tang, and, to crown his enjoyment, he was going home. But that, in itself, promised to be problematic. He turned to the stocky, curly-haired figure beside him and shared his doubts.

"Sire, I have spoken to some recent recruits from Batavia, and they tell me that the sea level has risen and that the land has subsided. Together it means a higher water level of twelve feet. Good farming land has been flooded. A decurion told me that agriculture has been ruined by inundation together with a lack of manpower. People are leaving to seek a better life elsewhere. He said that the area between the Scheldt and the Rhine is so wet and swampy that it cannot truthfully be described as 'land' anymore. I dread to think what has become of my village, Sire."

The emperor frowned and ran a hand over his curly blond beard. "Heidar, you have provided me with one of the reasons for all this piracy. These fellows want plunder right enough, but I'll wager that given half the chance, they'll seize good farm land in Britannia without thinking twice."

Heidar nodded thoughtfully. "You can't really blame them, can you, lord?"

"Our duty is to protect our people. If the new settlers clear woodland and pay their taxes, while living peacefully beside our people, I can see no harm in their permanence. You know I've been recruiting men from your area. They prefer to fight for me than to struggle to make a living. After all, I guarantee them pay and food!" The sea breeze carried away his guffaw.

On entering the Rhine, Heidar gazed with trepidation at the flooded fields. Where crops once grew, waders splashed in search of worms or small fry. Carausius' new vessels handled beautifully in the river, so steering into the turbulent confluence of the Waal was no problem. Heidar looked longingly ashore as they rowed past the small group of houses that once comprised his village. What he saw was desolation. Not one emitted smoke, but that was hardly surprising as they had moved their families to

Britannia and to a better life. Water, at least a foot deep, lapped against doors and walls.

"Look, sire, that building yonder, it was once the smithy where I toiled, but now the roof has caved in!"

"Times change, Centurion! Surely, you have no regrets?"

"None, Sire. But life plays certain tricks. If Faldrek had not fled from his Roman pursuers, who knows? I might still be beating red-hot iron bars in that hovel, or sweeping out muddy water. Soon, I'll use these arms to beat your enemies, God willing."

"Ay, my friend, it's not far now to Noviomagus Batavorum if my memory serves me well. We'll enter the harbour and then besiege the fortress, for it controls the whole reach of the Waal and Rhine lands."

Heidar blew out his cheeks and released his breath slowly.

"What?" said the emperor. "Do you think it an impossible task?"

"Well, Sire, we have brought no siege engines."

Carausius' lips curled. "Then we shall pray for ingenuity. Look! Up there is the fortress!"

The dominating site of the citadel did nothing to ease Heidar's fears. This wasn't the homecoming he'd anticipated when they set sail from Othona.

On arrival in the port, they found three of Maximian's warships. Onboard, the scuttling around suggested anxiety at seeing such a large naval force entering the harbour.

"These are three of the vessels that we allowed to leave with Maximian. So, news has arrived of his defeat," Carausius nudged Heidar. "Centurion, go to the ships and find out whether they wish to join our fleet or die a noble death. Put it to them in those terms."

"Ay, Sire, we'll see how faithful they are to their emperor."

As a Batavian warrior, Heidar considered loyalty a prime and immutable quality, so he prepared himself to receive insults and, as a neo-Christian, was prepared to turn the other cheek with dignity. At his approach, he was surprised, therefore, when a decurion scrambled up the ladder to the quay to meet him. Heidar delivered his message, and the decurion laughed bitterly. "Centurion, you should know that my crew are on the verge of mutiny; they have received no pay from the emperor even after they traversed the North Sea twice at his command. The other two ships will tell you the same tale. Indeed, they detached from Maximian to berth here as we did. I believe that the other three ships have rowed upstream to Trier."

"Are you saying, Decurion, that you accept to join on the Emperor of the North's terms?"

"I presume from his reputation that Caesar Marcus Aurelius Mausaeus Carausius will pay my men for their service?"

Heidar smiled: "Nobody among us ever speaks against our emperor because he pays in good coin punctually. Rest assured; I shall intervene personally on behalf of the three crews."

The two officers clasped wrists and grinned at each other. Heidar could not blame his erstwhile enemies for not following a leader who exploited their loyalty without reward.

"One last thing, Decurion, has news of Maximian's defeat reached the garrison?"

"Ay, it has, and it must be said that the commander and his men are largely auxiliaries raised by the same emperor and transported here from Dacia. I think you'll find no love among them for Maximian."

Heidar hurried back to his emperor to assure him that the three ships would unite with his fleet. He explained the price for their loyalty. Carausius roared mirthfully, "The world is made up of men who want the same thing—money to buy strong drink and women!" He ended his homespun philosophy with a guffaw. "Centurion, fetch your comrade Faldrek to me. He can help carry the bags of silver to the ships. You have given my word, and it will not be broken: a promise is a debt, my friend."

Soon, Heidar withdrew three bags of silver coins and took them with Faldrek to the moored vessels, where cheers from the crew greeted them along with cries of 'Hail Emperor of the North!'

Carausius listened to this with pleasure, even if his smile was cynical. These were not the first, nor would they be the last men he had brought into his ranks with undebased silver coins bearing his portrait.

When the two centurions clambered aboard, he called them over.

"Hark, my most trusted and able Batavians, I have another task for you. Go up to the fortress and deliver this message. 'The Emperor of the North has no quarrel with them, but if they do not surrender the fortress, no ships will be allowed to unload wheat. They will be permitted only barley for their bread.'"

Bread was made from barley, but in Italy, almost all bread was made from wheat, and barley was usually reserved for animals. Forcing men to eat barley—the lesser grain, the grain of beasts—was nothing more and nothing less than a way of underlining a unit's shame and exclusion from the rest of the army.

The two centurions exchanged a grim smile, bowed, and set off up the winding track. The message was insulting, and Heidar worried about their reception. Had not the decurion stated that these men were mainly Dacian auxiliaries? Dacians were renowned for their fierce pride. He discussed this with Faldrek as they approached the gate.

"Let's hold back on the barley and use it *in extremis*."

"Very wise," his comrade agreed.

The fortress commander, a Dacian consul, received them amicably, with a jocular smile, "So, the conquering heroes have arrived!"

"We bear a message from our emperor, Caesar Marcus Aurelius Mausaeus Carausius, Consul. He wishes to make it clear that he has no quarrel with the garrison here, but, as you are aware, needs control of this stronghold to avoid further attempts at invading Britannia."

"Until now, this fortress has been under the sovereignty of

Emperor Maximian, Centurion. Yet, we have been ineffective because the emperor had no interest in preventing pirates from leaving for Britannia. Indeed, I'd say he positively encouraged certain Germanic tribes to depart for your shores; hence his stubborn refusal to equip us with interceptor craft. However, his defeat to your illustrious emperor—a great general, by the way—changes everything. Most of my men are Daci and feel no particular loyalty to the Western Emperor. Of course, the same could be said for the Emperor of the North. The difference is that your Caesar pays his men, whereas Maximian provides coinage the traders snub. It is practically worthless. I have a message for Carausius," the centurions noted that he pronounced the name with due respect. "Tell him that Noviomagus Batavorum is his, on one condition, which is that my men receive a fair indemnity for the surrender of a fortress that they have loyally garrisoned for his foe."

"We shall bring you his answer within the hour, Consul."

Carausius agreed to these terms but with a condition of his own. The Dacians would be replaced by a cohort of Batavians led by Centurion Faldrek. The Dacians would receive their pay but would serve in Britannia after swearing loyalty to the Emperor of the North. The Dacian troops greeted the announcement of these conditions with a raucous cheer and the chanting of the emperor's name. Heidar surveyed the strong walls and thanked the Lord that taking Noviomagus had not come to a battle. He blessed his intuition not to insult the Dacians by comparing them to animals.

The consul made his way to the flagship and spent a considerable time speaking with his new emperor. Heidar was not privy to their conversation but noted Carausius' keen interest in the other's words. It would not be long before Heidar knew more than he would have liked about the consul's discourse. The emperor called him over to explain.

"The consul is going to fetch his men, who will return to Othona with me. Your cohort of Batavians will remain here under your command, Heidar, but such a fortress cannot be governed by a centurion. I am raising you to the rank of consul."

Heidar knew he was too young for this rank, but if that was his emperor's wish, who was he to argue? Also, he was confident of his relationship as centurion with his men. They would give him unswerving loyalty. His musings were interrupted by the emperor's next words: "I'm leaving you half of the ships, Consul, for it is time to go on the attack. I learnt from the garrison commander that the largest number of pirate ships leaving the Rhine are from one tribe in particular—the Chauci. I want you to row upstream, raid inland and slaughter the lot of them, seizing every available seaworthy vessel. Once that is done, you will regularly patrol the estuary, making sure that no bands of pirates sail for Britannia. Any questions?"

"None, Sire. My men will not disappoint you."

"I am sure of it, Consul Heidar. Now, gather your troops and lead them up to the fortress."

Heidar's 480 men filed past the descending garrison, making the new consul realise how seriously understaffed his garrison would be. He knew that some Roman consuls commanded an army of 20,000 men, but at a quick assessment, he could see that the Noviomagus garrison was no greater than 800. A rapid exchange of information with the retiring commander proved informative. Heidar particularly appreciated the suggestion of enrolling auxiliaries from the Chauci, once he had defeated their chieftains. One important fact also emerged: it appeared to the Dacian consul that the Chauci had been largely absorbed into a Saxon confederacy, so Heidar might have to press as far inland as the upper Weser. The friendly officer summoned four men from his ranks. "These men are expert scouts and know the Germanic territory well. They will be of no use to me in Britannia, so consider them my parting gift to you."

No sooner had Heidar established himself in the luxurious praetorium and ensured that the emperor's bags of silver were locked into a steel-banded chest with no less than four locks—the departing consul had consigned him a key ring and a cynical witticism about poor-quality coinage—than he summoned the four scouts and seated them at a large table. Across this, he spread a map of the river systems in the area. The men seemed perplexed.

"What is your worry, good fellow? Share it with me."

"Consul, we'll need to reach here," his finger jabbed the chart midway down the upper Weser. "Marching there would be folly, as the land is dense with impenetrable woodland and the tribes are expert at ambushing enemy incursions. We need river craft, but—"

"You were going to say *but* we have no ships. That's where you are wrong! The emperor is leaving half his fleet in the harbour for our use."

The relief on the scouts' faces was palpable. One was already tracing a route with a finger along the river Elbe.

At dawn, Heidar stood on the ramparts and watched the fleet sail out of the harbour. As he stared, he felt a pang, realising that the departing Carausius was more than his emperor, for he had become his friend. He and Valdor, and his other two close friends, owed everything to this remarkable man: their rank, place in the world, wealth, and safety of their families. He would serve his emperor-friend to the best of his abilities. As the departing fleet became dots in the distance, his eyes moved to the vessels Carausius had left him. He counted them and considered that, again, the emperor had shown his military acumen. He knew how many men Heidar had at his command and had calculated the necessary number of ships. Tomorrow he would lead the expedition to re-establish his lord's military presence in Northern Gaul. His only regret was that Valdor and Johar were not here to share in the glory, but he did have Centurion Faldrek. He collected the invaluable chart of Germania and summoned him to his room, where he outlined his plan to take the Saxon chieftains by surprise.

18

LOWER SAXONY, AD290

History has a way of repeating itself, which is why a good general should be a student of its military aspect. Heidar was not a scholar, but history also allows for the idiosyncrasy of individuals to emerge. The Batavian was inexperienced but had the instincts and intuition of a great general. Knowledge of what had happened in the Teutoburg Forest in the autumn of 9 AD might have made him even more cautious when he disembarked on the Elbe and pressed into the forests of Lower Saxony. It may have been that Publius Quinctilius Varus had been inept or unlucky, but the Germanic leader Arminius had ambushed and slaughtered three Roman legions in the woods. Heidar, aware of his inexperience, arranged his men so that battle formation could be achieved in moments while still making progress along the trail. He sent scouts, now forging ahead, who explained that they had found the heartland of the Saxon confederation between the Elbe and the Weser.

Heidar was correct in thinking that a surprise attack could not be launched from the water. The forest cloaked their approach and kept them safe in an overnight encampment. The new day brought them to a large settlement made of primitive turf houses dug into the earth, their roofs only a few feet above the ground.

At a quick glance, Heidar estimated 200 houses. In the centre of the community stood a larger wooden building that must have been a hall, perhaps, hoped Heidar, the chieftain's residence. He decided to attack that building, giving instructions to slay anyone who resisted.

The Saxon warriors who emerged from their bunker-like homes were tall, strong blond or red-haired men. They wielded axes or long swords, but charging Heidar's steadily advancing defensive formation, they were no match for the disciplined Batavian regiment whose swift gladius stabs took a deadly toll from behind their curved shields as the Saxons raised their weapons to strike.

The cries and screams had alerted the occupants of the hall, who barred the stout oak door. Since access without a battering ram was impossible, Heidar ordered straw and wood to be piled against the walls and fires lit. But before striking the tinder, the men used their blades to hack away the dried clay daubed between the wooden uprights so that they could smoke out the occupants, or they could alternatively choose to choke to death.

Meanwhile, he was content to allow men to run away into the forest. His vague plan was to take an important hostage and, in any case, to provoke other tribes into emerging to seek vengeance. It was easier to provoke the enemy into coming to him than to find their lairs in these dense forest lands.

The dry wood caught and crackled, and soon Heidar's men were backing away from the flames and smoke. After a while, the sound of an iron bar hitting the floor rang out, and the doors swung back. The gigantic form of a blond warrior emerged, trying not to cough, but snarling as he crouched over a battle-axe held at the ready in both hands.

"I want him alive!" Heidar shouted, which made his men's task much harder. Their discipline and training paid off as half a dozen curved shields cramped his swinging room and pushed him back against the wall. Persistent short stabs to his bare, muscular arm made him drop the axe, and the sag of his shoulders meant the encounter was over. Heidar ordered him to be bound, ignoring the stream of oaths in an unknown tongue. Five other men staggered out of the building, coughing and spluttering, careful to lay their weapons at their feet. They had emerged in time because the roof had caught fire, and the whole structure was now in flames. Again, Heidar shouted orders to secure the captives and gave further instructions to ignore the women and children peering fearfully from their tiny doorways. He had achieved what he wanted and, as a Christian, was not prepared to slaughter the innocent.

He led his men back into the forest, sending out scouts as a precaution and ringing a clearing with guards. His next move involved interrogating the prisoners. He tried speaking to them in his native tongue and noticed that there was comprehension in the eyes of the captive, but he obtained no cooperation. He wanted to know where the enemy kept their ships and where they were based. His questions met with a stony silence and even a spit, which stirred him into slapping the offender across the mouth with the back of his hand.

Not achieving anything, he ordered a small fire built near the prisoners. As the branches caught and created glowing embers, he seized the bound spitter by the hair and dragged him towards the flames. Holding the man's face for a mere second over the heat, he said, "You will tell me what I need to know; otherwise, I'll hold your face in the flames." He was prepared to do this, but fear loosened the fellow's tongue. The language was not so different from Heidar's own, close enough to understand. The captive revealed that there was a river basin some miles to the west, where the Saxons kept their vessels moored. He added death threats, revealing that the tribes had united their forces in the area and their numbers were far greater than Heidar's puny force.

Restraining a desire to cut the man's tongue in retaliation, instead, he asked who the giant prisoner was. "That is Arnulf, son of Fulbert, the chieftain of our tribe and one who will make Rome pay for what it has done today."

"Always assuming that Arnulf, son of Fulbert, survives this day," Heidar said sourly—Batavians showed no fear to their enemies. He called over the only scout remaining in the camp and referred to the news of the river pool to the west. "I want you to find it and return to me with its precise location and distance from here." The scout departed, well aware of the danger of his mission without the consul's dire warnings.

The danger of lingering in the forest became clear towards the end of the day when a score of Saxons intent on rescuing their leader were surprised in their furtive approach by the Roman watchmen. A skirmish ensued, which showed how closely matched, in terms of valour, were the tribesmen and Heidar's force, which sustained its first casualties. Only when alerted to combat and the disproportionate numbers overwhelmed the would-be rescuers did the fighting end in the slaughter of the Saxons. Heidar ruefully ordered the burial of his six dead comrades and the burning of the Saxon corpses.

If he had not learned about the Saxon vessels, he would have beaten a hasty retreat from the perilous area he had penetrated. It was now crystal clear why Maximian and others before him had established a line of fortresses along the Rhine-Danube axis and rarely ventured beyond it into the densely forested area. As he lay on his heavy woollen sagum, trying to snatch some sleep, he pulled the cloak closely around his shivering body; his restless thoughts also kept him sleepless. It would be futile to retreat without completing his mission, which was now so near and yet so perilous.

Towards morning, when he at last had sunk into sleep, a gentle hand shook his shoulder.

"Sorry to wake you, old friend, but first light is nigh, and our scout has returned with news." Heidar shook his head to chase away the sleep and peered blearily into Faldrek's concerned visage.

"Fetch him to me, Centurion, I need to splash some cold water on my face to clear my thoughts." In truth, he wanted to pray for guidance. He had seen what the Saxons were capable of and did not want to blunder into danger.

His scout was reassuring, up to a point. "Lord, the Saxons have placed a guard upon their ships, but I counted only a dozen. There are sure to be more. If we move early, we can reach them by noon."

"Good work, my friend, you will lead us, but a small advance party will accompany you to look out for danger in all directions."

"Ay, that would be as well, lord." The scout approved of the commander's wise precautions.

As the sun rose to almost overhead, with Heidar wondering how much farther to the river, a runner from the advance party bent double in front of him to catch his breath. When he straightened up, he pointed in the direction from which he had come, gasping, "A trap, Consul, but we can circumvent it. There's a track off to the left, which will take us to the enemy's rear. There are at least a hundred Saxon warriors waiting for our arrival, but I killed their scout myself." Heidar stared at the blood-spattered forearm of his scout and congratulated him, "Well done, friend, you've earned extra pay. Now, lead us to the fork in the track and we'll attack from the rear with javelins."

The Saxons were hiding in a hollow not far from the main track, which made the javelin throwers' task easier. At the silent lowering of Heidar's arm, more than 400 javelins hailed down on the unsuspecting backs of the lurking force. The survivors turned and ran, shouting up the slope to be met with the second wave of javelins. Many were parried this time, but some achieved their purpose. Heidar wasted no time in forming his troops into seven eight-square phalanxes.

Even with matching numbers, the Saxons would have struggled against this defensive formation, but with Heidar's skilful manoeuvring, their task became impossible. His Batavians surrounded and annihilated the enemy force in less than half an hour. Heidar's scouts assured him that the way to the river was now clear.

A small fleet of some thirty vessels lay moored in the calm water of an ox-bow lagoon formed by the meandering river. The consul's cohort raised their shields and lined up along the bank. They were met by desultory and ineffectual archery. Heidar had Arnulf pushed forward in front of the shields and called out, "Surrender your ships or we'll cut his throat here and now!"

The stunned silence that followed made the consul fear that his threat would be ignored until a voice shouted, "We'll exchange the ships for your captives."

"We agree to this proposal!"

One by one, the boats rowed to the bank and were occupied by legionaries. When the last one was taken, Heidar and his body-guards handed the captives to a tall, red-haired Saxon with a livid scar down his right cheek.

"Tell your fellow chieftains to stay away from the North Sea, for we shall destroy any vessel intent on leaving the Rhine Estuary for Britannia. We'll be ready and waiting in strength." Heidar said, thrusting his face into Arnulf's before bounding aboard one of the boats.

One of his four Dacian scouts explained to Heidar how they had to follow a long detour, taking a circuitous route necessary because the Wadden Sea, with its shoals in the area between the Weser and Elbe estuaries, was unnavigable. They rowed well into the evening until the dim light made navigation impossible. A temporary camp was established and, aware of the danger of a night-time attack, Heidar tripled his guards and arranged for regular rotation.

Apart from distant wolves' howls, the night passed peacefully. An early morning start brought them to the turbid waters of the Weser estuary, where they raised sail and travelled westwards into the mouth of the Elbe. They rowed for hours upstream until they came to the place where they had left their ships days before. Heidar was relieved to find his small crews untroubled and the ships unharmed. The guards reported having seen only three men the day before. From their sooty aspect, they believed them to be charcoal burners, out collecting wood with a small handcart. Anyway, the entire fleet was now ready to make the return journey to the river Waal.

The consul was confident that his force could handle any adversary except a united tribal army, but he expected to arrive at Noviomagus unscathed with a fleet sufficient to patrol and dominate the estuaries on the North Sea, exactly as Carausius wanted. In addition, the Saxon fleet had been depleted and the enemy would have to rebuild its naval strength. Heidar smiled wryly at the thought that the Saxons might now gather together and launch a revenge attack upon Maximian's border fortresses to the south. He doubted they were bright enough to understand that Noviomagus should be their objective.

19

BRITANNIA, AD 291-293

THE COUNT OF THE SAXON SHORE WENT ABOUT HIS
duties largely untroubled for a long period in which raids had
become infrequent. He toured the fortifications, old and new,
adding reinforcements of men to garrisons where necessary.
Among his other activities was the construction of intermediate
watchtowers, either in stone or timber depending on the avail-
ability of material. On three occasions, his enforced absence from
combat persuaded him to join in the pursuit of sporadic pirate
incursions. Twice, he led by example and wetted his sword, but on
the other occasion when the Saxons veered and headed back
towards the Continent, he called off the pursuit, considering it
wiser to remain in British coastal waters.

In April 292, Sfava bore him a son—*his little warrior*, the
proud father called him—and his world offered him everything he
had ever wanted: a beautiful family, power, status, and wealth,
friends, and respect. This blissful state of affairs could not last, he
told himself many times, for he lived in a harsh world liable to
sudden shifts and dangers.

The first erosion of his solid foundations of happiness arrived
when the news that his cousin Johar had been smitten by a Saxon
axe while intercepting a raid. The message came to him while on a

visit to Rutupiae, where he had gone ostensibly to supervise the last of the work completing the new fort. His real reason was to sample the famous oysters—renowned as the best in Britannia—and to attend a gladiatorial contest in the amphitheatre with its capacity of 5,000 spectators.

Rutupiae, with Dubris close by, made a perfect supply station for the whole south-eastern area and the twin presence of the fortresses ensured prosperity to the Canti, now free of marauders.

As is often the case, the more carefree and entertained an individual becomes, the more Life seems challenged to swipe an unexpected low blow. A messenger rode into the fortress, sought out Valdor, and informed him, "Sire, your cousin is grievously wounded and struggling between life and death; he is asking for you."

"What happened? Where is he?"

"At the new fort at Portus Adurni. A Saxon axe laid him low and now, the doctors are fighting to save his arm if not his life."

Valdor took three ships and sailed to the harbour, making sure his crew comprised two capsarii.

Entering the sick room, Valdor gazed at the fevered brow of his cousin and at the pallor of his cheeks. His two capsarii were already in conversation with the doctors of the base. After what seemed an eternity, one of them came over to Valdor and spoke gravely. "Lord, I wish you to give me one last chance to preserve the arm. The doctors here have given up on saving it and decided on amputation. They fear the onset of gangrene, but my examination reveals that there is still time to intervene. In our capsae, we have the necessary potions. If I can sedate the patient, staunch the bleeding more effectively, and remove some rotten flesh, who knows, the gods may smile upon us."

"Let it be so!" Valdor waved everyone out of the room except his two capsarii. He sat on the edge of the bed and took his cousin's hand, feeling its unnatural coldness. He closed his eyes and preferred to pray to his Christian God that the two doctors might succeed. The one he had spoken to explained as he mixed scopolamine with red wine before operating, that the plant extract caused drowsiness and amnesia. Leaving nothing to chance, given the gravity of the patient's condition, he took out a phial of clear liquid and carried it to the patient's lips, pouring a few drops into his mouth. Valdor watched his cousin swallow while the doctor explained, "It is an extract of the seed of the poppy. Under its sedating influence, he will feel nothing. Now we must operate on the arm, Sire, will you see that we have a brazier and a searing iron as well as boiled water? It will be of greater use than holding the centurion's hand, for see, he is quite insensate now." Valdor sprang up and hurried to organise the necessities.

On his return, he watched as the doctor took a scalpel and began to remove dead flesh around the gash. Next, he soaked a cloth in vinegar and applied it to the wound to disinfect it and prevent infection. He called out, "Honey, wine, and olive oil!" A legionary brought them on a tray and, as the doctor mixed them, he explained, "This will stop inflammation and prevent the wound from going bad." After applying this mixture, he cauterised the slash, then took a curved needle and fine catgut and stitched up the wound. "He'll be lucky to boast about this scar to his sons!" the doctor grinned. "Sire, we have done all that is possible; the rest is in the lap of the gods. Do you want us to organise a sacrificial rite?"

Valdor gazed severely at the doctor. "Nay, you have done what you can. I shall say my own prayers as I vigil over my cousin. Go! I'll send for you if his situation changes."

The doctors bowed out of the room and murmured, unheard by Valdor, that the Count had abandoned the gods of Rome. Would he be punished with his cousin's death for this? For his own part, Valdor took his hand again and peered at the sutured arm. Undoubtedly, his capsarii had done a precise job on it. *If only we had come sooner!*

Valdor reflected on the importance of having specialist doctors in every fortress. The local doctors had done their best but faced with a severe wound had blundered around. His capsarii, instead, had operated swiftly, *but is it enough?* He looked lovingly and doubtfully at the young fisherman's son with whom he had shared his childhood. The Count sat for hours in this attitude, but his restless mind was working on establishing a school for capsarii. His project was to have a competent surgeon in each Saxon Shore fortress. Lost in these thoughts, he suddenly realised that Johar had been unnaturally still for too long. He placed a finger under his nose, hoping to feel breath upon it. Nothing! Having no doctoral knowledge to speak of, he leapt up and called for his doctors, who came running.

He pointed at the supine figure, "I fear he is dead!"

A doctor sat on the bed, still indented from where Valdor had been moments before. Gently, he did what the Count had failed to think of doing. He pressed two fingers to the patient's wrist and felt a weak but steady pulse.

"Sire, he is alive! The unnatural stillness is due to the opiate. It will help with the recovery. Your centurion is strong, but even he will require time for healing and convalescence."

"The Lord be praised, he lives! Thank you, thank you!"

The hours passed until Johar groaned and his eyelids opened. He tried to speak but only made a croaking noise, yet he managed to squeeze Valdor's hand. The Count called for the doctors, who had expected some sign of revival and were ready with a beaker of mead. Gently, one placed it to Johar's lips, easing him more upright with an arm behind his shoulders. Valdor stared on in approval and wondered if he imagined the slow return of colour to the cheeks.

"Let him sleep, lord, you can talk tomorrow."

"Ay," Valdor acquiesced, thinking that maybe his cousin had overcome the worst.

Once out of the room, a doctor halted him. "When he is back on his feet, he'll need to rest that arm for some time. It will be a slow healing process."

"I understand. Hark, doctor, what do you think about teaching your profession to eager young men? We can begin here in this fort if you consent. I want rigorous standards, mind you. You must work only with those who show promise."

"I consent, lord. It is a splendid idea."

"I fear that I will bring you more patients for them to practise on, since my aim is to clear these waters of raiders."

For the rest of the sailing season, Valdor assumed command of naval operations around Vectis. He was driven by the twin desire to rid those waters of the pirates and to avenge his cousin who was convalescing and recovering well. The Frankish pirates, in particular, proved able seamen and difficult to capture. However, in the first month of his command, he overcame two pirate vessels and, although he would have been happy to enrol the crews or enslave them, he was compelled by their ferocity to slaughter them.

The first boat they encountered in the next month brought Valdor a memorable unpleasant incident. Warriors do not wish to be reminded of their mortality, but that is what happened. Upon grappling and boarding the Saxon vessel, Valdor came face-to-face with a gigantic chieftain. He wielded an axe and, despite himself, Valdor thought about Johar's wound and took an involuntary step backwards. This was the first time he ever hesitated in battle. Hesitation is usually fatal and would have been on this occasion, except for the quick wits of Valdor's centurion, who hurled a javelin with all his might that impaled the Saxon under the raised arm about to deliver the fatal blow. The great Saxon toppled and fell to the deck, and such was his strength that he tried to pull the dart from his body. In a mist of rage, no doubt associated with his cousin's injury, Valdor leapt on the Saxon and finished him with his short sword, effectively breaking the Saxon resistance.

Four of this crew agreed to enrol in the Roman army as auxiliaries, two flung themselves into the sea and drowned. The others surrendered and awaited their fate; Valdor set them labouring tasks, such as building a defensive wall around the high-status villas on the nearby Isle of Vectis at a place called Brerdynge by the locals, or working on raising the height of the old lighthouse on the prominent headland.

Vectis had no towns, but was a fertile isle with a mixture of wealthy farmers and a smattering of poorer peasants who worked the less productive land. The new slaves eyed the recent construction of an aisled farmhouse with a mixture of wonder and envy. In their wildest dreams, they could not compare this stone-built marvel with their wattle and daub homes in Saxony. They were not allowed inside, or their eyes would have boggled at the mosaic floors with their images of dolphins and sea nymphs. What they saw was enforced because they had to work the furnace used to parch the crops of Celtic beans that they had previously harvested and carried back.

Valdor's brush with death did not dishearten him, but he had to find time to inspect the new lighthouse and purchase some red wine directly from the press because the islanders took advantage of the south-facing aspect and light, chalky soil to dedicate themselves to viticulture and bottling and storage of wine. Argue as he might, Valdor did not pay for the several flagons he had chosen because the farmer was so honoured to provide for the emperor's son that he insisted on making a gift of the wine and pressed on him a variety of fresh produce, which had to be carried to his ship. This perishable cargo gave the Count a good reason to return to nearby Portus Adurni to check on his cousin's progress, where his wife and son provided companionship to Johar as he convalesced.

As he strode through the gates of the fortress, he found Johar fighting a legionary, both using practice swords.

"Johar! Are you crazy? It's too soon for this!"

"I'm going easy on him, Sire," grinned the legionary.

"Oh, aye?" snarled Johar and redoubled his efforts. In moments, the legionary's wooden sword sailed through the air, and the blunt tip of Johar's pressed against his adversary's throat.

Valdor clapped, "Very impressive, cousin, but aren't you liable to spring your stitches with all this vim and vigour?"

"You've lost track of time, cousin. How long have you been at sea? The doctors removed my stitches weeks ago, and I began by lifting weights. I wanted to see if I could fight again, but this apology for a warrior has scarcely made me break a sweat. What I need is a tall Saxon chieftain!"

The Count shuddered, "That's exactly what neither of us needs! Come indoors, and I'll tell you about my meeting with one such over a beaker of Vectis wine."

Little Caurus, named after his grandfather, flung himself into his father's arms.

"I swear you have grown since I sailed out a few months ago. Where's your mother?"

The tiny finger pointed towards the kitchen. *Of course, she's sorting the vegetables.*

Slowly savouring the wine, Valdor stared hard at his cousin, "Are you completely healed with no pain?"

"It's as good as new!" Johar flexed his arm and waved it around extravagantly.

"Just as well I didn't arrive a day later, cousin, those butchers had decided to amputate. That's why I set up the doctoral school."

Johar's mouth dropped open. "Really? They were going to amputate?"

"Ay, in their ignorance, they wished to prevent gangrene. But if it makes you feel better," he gazed around to make sure Sfava wasn't in the offing, "I found myself in the exact same situation as you—facing a giant Saxon chieftain. If it hadn't been for my centurion's quick reactions, I wouldn't be here now. I hesitated, something I never do, and he would have finished me but for Livius' javelin."

"It seems we were both fortunate."

"Ay, but good fortune cannot last forever," Valdor said ominously through clenched teeth, but as it would turn out, with prescience.

20

PORTUS ADURNI AND BRANODUNUM FORT, AD 293

For a number of years, Carausius had maintained that sooner or later a competent general would emerge to sustain the western Empire. Following Maximian's failure to invade in 289, an uneasy truce with Carausius began. Valdor wondered whether when that day came, it would be with or without the presence of Emperor Maximian? Maximian tolerated Carausius' rule in Britain and on the continent but refused to grant the secessionist state formal legitimacy. Neither Carausius nor Valdor understood that Maximian was not the main threat to their newly established equilibrium, but Emperor Diocletian. For his part, Carausius was content with his territories beyond the Continental coast of Gaul. However, Diocletian would not tolerate this affront to his rule.

Valdor had established hearth and home in the fortress of Portus Adurni, where the milder climate and bracing sea breezes, with the strategic outlet into the Solent, granted him the possibility of controlling the south coast of Britannia and the approaches to the Channel.

He watched his son grow sturdy and headstrong—a miniature Valdor but with Sfava's fierceness—would he ever get to know his father's homeland? On occasions, Valdor would sit and reflect on his early life in Batavia. In truth, he had left his village when he was no more than a boy. The world he had grown into was dominated by Rome. And Rome, in the shape of Carausius, had evaluated him, seen his worth, and promoted him to wealth and rank beyond his imaginings.

To maintain his position and enjoy it in peace with Sfava, Caurus, and the newcomer, the bouncing Lavinia, was his heart's desire. He had his cousin based here, although Johar spent much time at sea, patrolling the coasts of Vectis—too much, because he hadn't found time to choose a wife. As his commander, Valdor felt responsible, for it was he who sent Johar forth to sweep the sea clear of pirates. Often, he would join the fleet, leaving the command to his relative. He had seen him frolic with a slave girl on his last sojourn in port. Yet, as a centurion and commander of the fleet, Johar had the wealth and stability to set up home with the daughter of some high-ranking citizen. The problem was that Johar used Valdor, or rather, Sfava as his model, and where did one find such a spirited goddess? Valdor made a silent promise to search for a bride for his cousin.

He also missed Heidar but was happy for his best friend, who had become his adoptive father's closest counsellor. Carausius had decided that given Valdor's preference for the south coast, he would establish himself at Branodunum Fort on the east. He recalled Heidar from Noviomagus, replaced him with Faldrek, whom he also raised to the rank of consul. The distance to Branodunum meant that visits were increasingly rare and, indeed, Carausius had not yet seen his new granddaughter.

As for Faldrek, he was clearly doing his job, which could be seen from the reduced number of Frisian, Frankish, and Germanic raiders leaving the Rhine estuary. Valdor missed his old friend and wondered when they would meet again. Did Faldrek enjoy breathing the air of home? One thing was sure, their home-land was not what it had been in their youth. There was little or no possibility of recreating the fertile fields of yore. Where crops had once grown was now marshland or worse. Building a villa on

Vectis and farming there in their old age was more appealing. But would events allow such a peaceful outcome? A man could dream, but Valdor had seen and done enough to differentiate between fantasy and reality.

The most unlikely component of a reunion was Faldrek; ironically, he was the nearest to their origins, but the farthest from his friends. Rome, in the shape of Diocletian, remained vigilant and, faced with Carausius' secession and further challenges on the Egyptian, Syrian, and Danubian borders, he realised that two emperors were insufficient to manage the Empire. Carausius' prediction that a new formidable general would emerge came to fulfilment.

On 1 March 293, at Milan, Maximian appointed Constantius to the office of Caesar. On the same day, Diocletian did the same for Galerius, thus establishing the *Tetrarchy*, or 'rule of four'. The reforming emperor made Constantius understand that he must succeed where Maximian had failed and defeat Carausius.

As a general, Constantius was everything that Maximian was not, and he met expectations quickly and efficiently, and by the summer of 293 had expelled Carausian forces from northern Gaul.

Constantius stood under the gateway to Noviomagus and spoke directly to the commander, Faldrek, inviting him to open the gates, "Consul, as Emperor, I wish to laud you for the commendable work you have done in clearing the Rhine delta of pirates. This has not gone unnoticed in Rome. However, you will realise that you cannot continue in the service of the usurper, Carausius. I order you, in the name of the Empire, to open the gates."

Faldrek looked with concern at the four legions disembarked on Batavian soil and considered his position. He owed everything to Carausius. It would be the meanest betrayal to surrender the fortress to his rival. He wondered whether he could negotiate passage to Britannia for himself and his most trusted men? This thought prompted his reply: "Caesar, I require a few minutes to parley with my senior officers. My reply will soon be forthcoming." He turned away from the rampart to do so and had no time to defend himself as three Dalmatian officers drove their swords into his chest and stomach.

Together, they hoisted his body to the rampart of the gate tower and flung it down under the hoofs of Constantius' rearing horse by way of reply. The Batavians, faithful to their consul, could do nothing except watch as the great gates swung slowly open and Constantius rode triumphantly into the fortress followed by the eagle standard bearers. Rome had retaken possession of Noviomagus Batavorum at the expense of one of Batavia's most eminent sons.

Meanwhile, not only was Constantius preparing to overthrow Carausius, but Maximian also plotted to do the same. As autumn headed into winter, Heidar and Valdor separately learnt of their friend's demise and the fall of Noviomagus.

Carausius cursed and warned Heidar, "We have to reckon with a *real* general." He wrongly added, "We have nothing to fear from Maximian, but we must ensure that all our shore fortresses are completely garrisoned and ready to resist this so-called Constantius I. We'll see who is the more capable general—he or I. I want you to travel swiftly to Count Valdor and explain my requirements." Neither man would realise what a portentous decision this would prove to be and how mistaken Carausius was, for once, in his assessment of the political situation.

Heidar decided that sailing down the coast and rounding Kent was a better solution than riding across country. Although autumn had shaken the leaves off the trees, the sea was grey but relatively calm. His voyage was undisturbed by raiding vessels, his only sightings being Roman trading vessels legitimately plying their trade.

When, at last, he reached Portus Adurni, after the usual pleasantries, he exchanged versions of Faldrek's demise. The two accounts differed: Valdor had the correct version, but Haidar insisted that their friend had led his forces out to engage Constantius and had died gloriously in battle.

"Who told you this?"

"A Batavian trader."

"Well, there you are, then. One of our own, wishing to glorify Batavian prowess. Look, knowing Faldrek, if he'd had any chance of making a stand or escaping, he would have taken it. Nay, he was disloyally betrayed, as I learnt—it's the only explanation."

"Ay, you're right. First there were four. Now we are three! Where's Johar?"

"My cousin is patrolling the Solent. I dare say he knows of your arrival and will join us when he can. But come, see my treasures." He led Heidar to his private chamber where Sfava was playing with the children. She leapt up and embraced Heidar before lifting Lavinia and handing her to the warrior to hold.

"Heidar, you are another, like Johar, who needs to find a good woman to give you children as Sfava has to me."

Heidar ran his fingers through the silken blonde hair and let the little fingers twine around his large forefinger. "I have thought about it; indeed, your father is insistent, but Valdor, how can I make such a move when our emperor is under threat? First, we must secure Britannia for him, then I'll set about hunting for a wife. I have a fancy for a red-haired Briton!"

Sfava laughed, "I'll say one thing for you Batavians, you do not care for an easy life. If Valdor thinks he's tamed his wildcat, just because I've borne two children, he's got another think coming! Graahr!" She bared her teeth and made a feline scratching gesture with her hands.

The following day, to Heidar's delight, Johar's fleet docked in the harbour below. The commander brought a surprise with him. It was not unusual for the Classis Britannia to capture prisoners and enrol them as auxiliaries. Most of these men were either Saxons or Franks, but on this occasion, Johar brought Jutes and handed them over to a centurion to be whipped into shape. He brought his real surprise with a rope tethered around the neck like a mule: another captive shield maiden. His first thought was to make a present of her to Sfava, who would be sure to welcome a compatriot, and one as fierce as herself. Things did not quite work out as planned because he was not expecting the presence of Heidar.

While the old friends embraced, Sfava directed her attention to the crouching creature staring with malevolent grey eyes, who now addressed her, "What are you doing here with the enemy, Sfava Hibaldsdottir?"

"You know me!" Sfava cried incredulously.

"Your father and mine fought often enough over land, back home. Ha! Now they are both dead and we are here."

"You are Jarl Egred's daughter, but which one? Estrith or Inga?"

"Inga, but what is it to you, who cohabit with the foe?"

"These men are Batavians, Inga. So, not so different from us. They have served Rome to make Britannia safe and risen as reward for their valour. My husband is the emperor's adopted son."

Inga spat on the floor. "Give me a sword and I'll kill him!"

"The only sword I'll give you is one between your ribs!" Sfava leapt forward and drew Johar's blade before he could move. Now she held everyone's attention as she circled the red-golden-haired woman like a prowling cat ready to pounce. But Johar jerked the rope attached to Inga's neck fiercely, pulling her off-balance and causing her to stagger straight into Heidar's welcoming muscular arms. He pinned her to his broad chest and refused to release the writhing, spitting Jute.

Valdor drew his gladius and placed himself between his wife and the newcomer.

"Hand me that blade, Sfava, it's an order!"

A stream of oaths greeted his words, but she could hardly fight the father of her children, whom she dearly loved. "Punish her then," she sulked, handing the gladius back to Johar.

A momentary silence fell over the hall, although Inga tried

stamping on Heidar's foot. This only made him squeeze her tighter and, breath forced out of her lungs, she ceased her writhing to sag forward in his arms. It was he who spoke, "Sfava, Johar gifted her to you. Let me buy her—this is the red-haired woman for me!"

Sfava snorted, "Buy her? Nay, I'll *give* her to you. I don't want her!"

Heidar unclasped his arms and gently eased the chafing rope from the captive's neck. No sooner had he raised the noose above her head than Inga dodged sideways and flung herself on Sfava, bringing her crashing to the floor. Her fist raised to smash into Sfava's face, when a giant hand clasped her wrist. The former smith, always strong to those who knew him as a youth, had become an athletic and mighty warrior. Now, he picked up Inga and raised her in the air above his head, oblivious to her venomous kicks that had no effect on his cuirass.

He looked her in the face and said, "Isn't it enough for you, foolish woman, that a consul wishes to take you for his wife?"

"Wife?" the Jute echoed, all the fight going out of her body as he lowered her and bent his face to hers. He half-expected her to spit in his eye, but instead, her lips sought his and she kissed him passionately as Sfava called for ale. The first beaker she offered was to a beaming Inga, who quaffed it in one wild gulp, her eyes sparkling.

"We shall be friends, Inga; you have chosen the best man in the fortress, bar one," she said hurriedly, glancing at Valdor, who smiled. Soon, influenced by drink, they danced and caroused until Valdor brought an end to proceedings.

"Heidar, Johar, I need to speak with you about serious matters," he panted happily, "we can leave Sfava and Inga to catch up on their various news, always hoping they don't harm each other," he added, warily eyeing the two wildcats. Sfava was more interested in showing off her children, so he need not have worried, since Inga had helped her mother raise Estrith and Hild, her younger sisters. Capable of slaying a warrior in battle, Inga was gentle and playful with children.

Valdor made sure to take a flagon of Vectis wine to a table and, seated around it with his lifelong friends, poured three beakers full to the brim. He raised a beaker in a toast before his thirsty friends could move, "To Faldrek!" he said simply.

They echoed the toast, and Heidar said gloomily, "If Carausius hadn't recalled me to Britannia, it could have been me in his place."

"We'll talk about Faldrek in the days to come, first we have our duty to consider," said the Count. "It's clear that now Constantius will not halt at Batavia. From there, he'll strike at Britannia." In this, he was incorrect, for something more terrible would happen first.

Unable to see into the future, Valdor divided the shore fortresses into three groups, keeping those nearer home to himself and sending Heidar to those more north-easterly, culminating in Branodunum Fort. Johar, principally, would deal with the Kentish strongholds. "We must each ensure that every fortress is well-armed and its garrison up to strength ready for when the invasion comes. Be prepared to move men quickly from inland stations to reinforce the coastal contingents. Also, ensure that watchtowers are properly manned and supplied with coal to act as visible beacons. That's it for now. When you have finished, report back to me."

"Not to the emperor, Valdor?" Heidar asked.

"Nay, to me. I might have to organise a land army in conjunction with sea manoeuvres. I need you both here."

"Very well. I'll tell Inga I'll wed her," his voice slowed and he sounded doubtful, "...when I return. But that's a problem, isn't it?"

"Nay, Heidar. You'll wed her with her customs. Later, calmly, you can persuade her to convert to Christianity, just as Sfava did."

"Do you think she'll consent?"

"I don't know, but you'll be wed anyway!"

"Now, let's set about what we must do so that we are ready for any eventuality." They would have been, except for the unexpected upsetting Valdor's plans.

Fortunately for the timing of subsequent events, Heidar decided to start at Branodunum and work his way down the coast, not on the contrary. His motivation was to reunite with Carausius to describe his new granddaughter and to share his news about Inga. He considered the emperor as close a friend as Valdor and could not wait to share a glass of wine and these confidences.

While Heidar sailed north, Carausius and his treasurer, Allectus, were discussing the apportioning of pay to various garrisons. The treasurer's disfigured smile unsettled most who encountered it, but Carausius paid it no attention, considering it a badge of honour. Unfortunately, there was nothing honourable about Allectus' intentions. He had been in constant contact with Emperor Maximian and had his head turned by false promises. Allectus, as his scarring testified, was a valiant warrior proven in combat, but he was also a coward. He knew that he could not overcome Carausius in a fair fight, which was why, with insinuated doubts, he led his emperor to the steel-banded coffer containing the imperial treasure. The locking system required four separate keys and the final one held by Carausius himself. After the treasurer had opened the four-lock sequence, the emperor bent to insert his key in the central lock. Swift as a striking serpent, Allectus plunged his sword with all his might into his emperor's back, hissing, "Die, usurper!"

He now had to enact the next part of his plan. Over the past few weeks, Allectus had gathered a group of Frankish mercenaries, sufficient to seize the fortress. The coffer was open and he could pay his accomplices, so the leaders came in, as arranged, and, leaning over the body of Carausius, he grasped three bags of silver and handed them to the Franks. He cleaned his bloody blade on a drape and said, "We need to find a scapegoat for the assassination."

The Frankish chieftain hurried out of the room and returned moments later hauling a pale-faced slave, a callow, gangly youth, who had never shaved. He flung the poor creature over the body of the emperor, pushing him into the blood pooling around the body, and grinned at Allectus and nodded. The treasurer did not hesitate but plunged his sword into the slave's defenceless body three times. The Frank took his own sword, dabbed the blade in the blood, and forced the slave's fingers around the hilt.

"I'll swear the slave stole my sword while tidying my room. You will say that you caught him in the act of murdering the emperor and dealt with him on the spot. Now let us go to conserve these bags of silver. Give us some time before calling for help."

The Franks left the strongroom and Allectus smiled grimly. He helped himself to the emperor's key and closed and locked the treasure chest with all five.

His wild cries for help brought guards running; as speechlessly, Allectus pointed at the bodies. When a centurion arrived, Allectus grasped his arm. "When I came into the room, I found this wretch—what is he? A Briton? If only I had come a few moments sooner, I could have saved our beloved emperor. Where did he obtain that sword? What now, Centurion? We must appoint a new emperor."

"Caesar Marcus Aurelius was a fine general. We need someone as worthy as he," the centurion said thoughtfully, keeping his counsel for the moment. "We should deliberate carefully, but let's fling this wretch to the crows and wash and prepare the emperor for entombment."

From the doorway came a loud cry, "Long live Emperor Allectus!" It was the leader of the Frankish mercenaries. Figures half-shrouded in the gloom of the corridor behind him took up the cry, and they, too, had a Frankish accent. The Centurion wisely continued to keep his thoughts to himself, for he favoured the emperor's son, Caesar Valdor Aurelius, but he sensed that nominating him would lead to his demise and bloodshed within the fortress. There had been too many Frankish auxiliaries taken on lately for his liking.

At the first opportunity, the centurion sidled out of the room and went to seek several trusted officers to share the news of the murder. They took a fortuitous decision by slipping down to the harbour with other trusted men. It was a lucky move because as they prepared to sail southwards to find Valdor and proclaim him emperor, Heidar's ship nosed into the harbour. The centurion recognised him and waved him over.

"Caesar Marcus Aurelius is dead—murdered—they are blaming a British slave, a mere youth, but I say it was the treasurer, Allectus! They are declaring him Emperor. Beware, friend, the fortress is in the hands of Frankish mercenaries."

Heidar stood in stunned silence for a moment. It was hard to take in that he had lost a dear friend as well as his emperor.

"Never! This cannot be!" Heidar cried. "Quick, we must return south and install Count Valdor as Caesar. It is his right: Carausius declared him Caesar Valdor Aurelius." The two ships sailed away, their occupants unaware of the coup taking place in Branodunum where the Franks, rewarded with bags of silver, ensured that Allectus was pronounced Emperor of the North. The few foolhardy dissenters were immediately slaughtered.

21

VALDOR STARED WHITE-FACED, HIS HANDS BALLED INTO fists as Heidar explained the events in Branodunum. He passed through such a range of emotions in mere moments that he determined to avoid making an impulsive decision. For the moment, he would push vengeance to the back of his mind. With Carausius dead, his position most definitely had changed, but he needed to think calmly about his next move.

"Heidar, my old friend, ahead of us stretches a road with at least three forks: the question is which route to take? Remember our oath back on Torik Isle? Each of us would always support the others until death intervened. Faldrek is dead, so whatever we decide, we'll commit to as a threesome."

"Where's Johar?"

"Back out patrolling the Solent."

"When he returns, we'll sit down and consider the different options together."

"Ay, I'm in no state to choose right now. I just want to slay my father's murderer. Oh, the irony! A usurper accusing Carausius of usurpation."

"The only urgent decision I wish to take," Heidar said, "is to wed Inga as soon as possible."

"Not today, my friend. In the midst of tragedy, we'll have a celebratory feast for your wedding. Hold off a couple of days so that I can make arrangements."

As if a dark thundercloud had rolled away and the sun blazed forth, Heidar's countenance cleared, sporting a broad grin. "I'll go and tell Inga the news!"

Valdor sent a ship to bring Johar back to the harbour, little realising that the few days' grace he had insisted on would prove so momentous. Rapidly apprised of events in Branodunum, Johar spat, "We should march north at once, gather legions, and destroy the murderer."

Valdor put an arm around his cousin's shoulder and said calmly, "Ay, that's one option, but remember the oath we took on Torik. Whatever we do will be the result of a joint decision and, you wouldn't want to miss Heidar's wedding, would you?"

Two days passed, in which Valdor and Sfava made arrangements for the great feast. On the eve of the wedding, the praetorium fell silent relatively early as everyone took to their beds. Valdor was in a dark mood owing to the emperor's murder and, a rarity this, repulsed Sfava's amorous advances. She, instead, lay drifting in and out of sleep, which was fortunate because she perceived movement in the bed-chamber. She always kept her sword on the floor next to the bed and, although she was uncertain about whether she heard breathing, her hand grasped the hilt and she threw back the covers, swinging out her legs and standing upright. This movement provoked an onslaught by the intruder, and the dim light cast by the moon piercing the small window high in the wall saved her, for she was able to parry the thrust of a gladius. The clash of steel and her scream to Valdor for help roused him from his slumber.

Without a moment to spare, he was on his feet, drawing his gladius from its sheath and springing at the second interloper. Valdor was at a disadvantage because he was barely awake and naked down to the waist; the price he paid was a slash across his upper arm, luckily not his weapon arm, but a shock that enraged him, waking him completely. Even so, he was pressed backwards by his armoured assailant and would likely have been killed had not Sfava smitten her opponent's throat, sending him crashing lifeless to the floor. She immediately saw Valdor's predicament and leapt onto the bed, bringing her Frankish sword down with all her might onto the nape of the infiltrator's neck.

"I am cut!" Valdor spat. "Father was right, by adopting me, he placed me in danger."

"I'll light a taper, we need to—oh, God! The children!" Sfava dashed out of the room to the children's chamber. She almost tripped over a dead body, and her heart seemed to leap into her mouth. She burst into the room, sword raised, and discerned a figure. Gently stroking Caurus' head with one hand and sword in the other, stood Inga, her white shift spattered with blood.

"Inga! What? —"

A throaty laugh preceded the Jute's words, but it held a bitter tone. "I heard the clash of steel and your cry. My first thought was for the babes. She pointed at the corpse, "He had come to slay little Caurus, but it is *he* slain!" Valdor arrived with a blazing torch to light the scene. "The children?" he could barely utter the words for anxiety.

"Safe, thanks to Inga! She's no longer my friend, but my sister! She saved our son."

Valdor laughed, "More than a sister, just look at you two! Twins more like!" He had a point; there they stood, in matching white blood-spattered shifts, swords in hand and hair tousled. Sfava's concern had shifted, "The children are asleep, come on, let's move the body! Oh, let me see that wound! Straight to the hospital with you! You were so insistent on opening an infirmary, but pull a cloak around you!"

Sfava and Inga, smiling at each other like true sisters, dragged the bodies of the legionaries out of the praetorium to find the guard on the door slumped with his throat cut, which explained much.

The following morning, that of Heidar and Inga's wedding

day, the time had come to take a decision. The three Batavians sat together and considered the events of the previous evening. "It's Allectus' handiwork," Valdor said, "without a shadow of doubt. He knows that if I make the slightest move, I'll have the legions in Britannia behind me, whereas he can only count on his Frankish allies. He sent men to kill me and my son because, as the legitimate heirs to Carausius, who was so popular with the legions while alive, we'd be a constant threat to his position."

"Well, it's clear then," Heidar said, "we should move north and gather men like a rolling snowball gains in size until we have an irresistible force. Then we can oust the usurper."

"Then what?" Valdor replied, "You seem to forget some important facts, my friend. Diocletian was unwilling to tolerate Carausius, and now he has a competent general, raised to Caesar, readying an invasion of Britannia: I refer to Constantius. It will be his task to overthrow Allectus."

"So, do we wait, defend ourselves, and then defeat this Constantius?" Johar, who was the slowest of the three, asked.

"Nay, cousin. We cannot hope to combat the Empire. Besides, I have no wish to become emperor. I have already risen beyond my wildest dreams."

"Speak plainly, Valdor, what is it you intend to do?"

Valdor pursed his lips, "It is easier for me to state what I *don't* mean to do. I will not remain in Britannia while Allectus is in power. That can only lead to our murders—where he has failed once, he will try again, or as an alternative, I'll be forced into a civil war to take his place and, as I said, I don't want that."

"So, where will you go, cousin?"

"Don't lose patience, Johar. Have we not seen how leaders will gladly accept reinforcements? I propose to take a legion and sufficient ships to Gesoriacum and offer my sword to Constantius. My long-term aim is to return in some role to Britannia. Are you both with me, or do you have alternative suggestions?"

His friends sat in silence until Heidar grudgingly said, "If

Constantius respects our ranks, joining him will gain us all revenge on the traitor Allectus. That sits well with me."

"Me, too!" Johar said quickly, who found agreeing far easier than ruminating.

In the afternoon, the hand-clasping ceremony, held in the courtyard in front of the ranked legionaries, by its very nature was a rapid affair, culminated in the throaty cheers of the rank and file. The heartiness of the roar, sufficient to drown the ubiquitous mewling of the ever-present swooping gulls, reflected the popularity among the men of the newly-wed centurion. There was scarcely a man present who would not willingly have changed places with Heidar as it was universally acknowledged that Inga was a Nordic beauty. Word had not yet circulated about the death of the emperor, so the prospect of a celebratory feast and indulgence in wine on such a splendid day, clear enough to see Vectis Isle from the fort, created a joyous atmosphere.

Valdor doubled the watch for the celebratory feast much to the disgruntlement of those chosen, but he did not want Allectus sailing into the harbour with an army and attacking during the revelling. He ensured they received food but did not allow them wine until the end of the watch that coincided with the onset of night. It was a long night. Valdor deliberately allowed the stock of wine to be entirely depleted, for he did not intend for anyone to remain in the fortress in two days.

As the Count of the Saxon Shore, he had every right to send to other fortresses, requisitioning ships. He would need a numerous fleet to transport the entire garrison to Gesoriacum.

The day after the feast, not only Heidar was the worse for wear but also most of the garrison. Valdor had expected this and contented himself watching the harbour fill with the *scafae* that was the basic warship of the Classis Britannica. The fleet was completed by several horse transport vessels and the *liburnae* to transport food and drink for the legion.

By the afternoon, the hangovers were cleared by the fresh sea air so that the ships could be loaded and Valdor chose a suitable moment to address the men, assembled in front of the praetorium. He chose to speak from Sparax's back, which enabled the men to see and hear him better. He began thus: "Soldiers of Rome, it is my solemn duty to inform you of an act of treason. On the eve of our recent nuptial celebrations, an attempt was made to murder me and my family in our beds." The reaction, although not deafening, was loud, for it is a notable noise when thousands murmur chorally. Valdor allowed this to sink in before raising his bandaged arm for silence. He indicated the binding, "I was lucky enough to receive only a scratch, but you will wish to know who was the principal behind the attempt. Let me inform you..." he paused and called for water, his throat refreshed, he shouted again, "...it was none other than my father's murderer— ay, Imperator Caesar Marcus Aurelius is most foully slain—his treasurer, the traitor Allectus. This coward has declared himself the Emperor of the North. Be it known, that I, your legitimate commander have, like you, sworn loyalty to Rome, not to a usurper. I have brought ships to sail to the headquarters of the Western Emperor Constantius I with the aim of uniting my forces to his to reconquer Britannia. You must choose, brothers, whether to remain in this fortress or to sail at dawn with me."

Now the incomprehensible shouting was deafening, and it took Valdor much effort and coaxing to control Sparax. Valdor lifted his wounded arm again and winced. He cried: "Fellow soldiers, you will each go to your centurion and communicate whether you will stay or will sail with me." He touched his chest with his right hand and then his forehead in a sign of respect. By jumping from Sparax, he made it clear that his speech was concluded.

Valdor was much loved and respected by men he had commanded, even those in other garrisons, so it was no surprise when a series of centurions entered the praetorium, hobnails ringing on the paving stones. Their message was always the same —the men were faithful to him and to Rome; they would sail at dawn. The Count was gratified, knowing that the backing of an entire legion made his bargaining position incontestable, not to mention the fleet of *scafae exploratoriae* and sundry quinquiremes he had available.

The sea was rougher than of late, but Valdor did not want to delay departure. Many men suffered sea sickness, but generally, the mood was good with much speculation about Emperor Constantius. The discipline of Valdor's sailors meant that despite the heavy sea, the fleet was not dispersed. By mid-afternoon, the water had become less choppy until by evening and their arrival in the estuary, the harbour water was calm. Valdor retrieved Sparax, mounted him, and disembarked, prepared to open a new chapter in his life.

22

GESORIACUM, AD 293-294

THE UNANNOUNCED ARRIVAL OF A FLEET AND AN entire legion caused alarm in Gesoriacum. Valdor rode with a small group of officers, including his trusted friends. The approach of a dozen horsemen made the serried ranks in front of the shore fortress appear absurd. Valdor had chosen not to dress in his imperial purple cloak and diadem but wore the crimson cloak and helm of a centurion.

At the sight of what was clearly a peaceful encounter, Constantius urged his horse forward to meet the newcomers. Valdor halted his a few paces ahead of the emperor and sprang to the ground, holding Sparax's reins. Reciprocally, Constantius dismounted, which gave Valdor the opportunity to kneel before him.

"Hail Caesar, we come from Britannia, and I, Valdor, *Comes littoris Saxonici per Britanniam*, bring you an entire legion and fleet in the service of Rome. I also bring news. My father, the Emperor of the North, was treacherously murdered by his treasurer—"

"I am informed, Count, and I gladly accept your men and ships, but cannot say whether I accept *you* until you have answered some questions."

"Sire?"

"Your father fought against his emperor, Maximian, and defeated him. Did you take up arms with him against the legitimate ruler?"

"Impossible, Caesar, for I was charged with constructing defensive fortresses, and that is what occupied me during the battle."

"Can you honestly say that you have not fought against the imperial army?"

"I can. Although I fought on occasion with Carausius, it was always against Rome's enemies, including pirates, with some success."

"Finally, Count Valdor, if I accept your sword, what are your expectations?"

"Sire, I renounce any claims to my adoptive father's inheritance but would appreciate my officers and myself maintaining our ranks."

"I see you wear the helm of a centurion. I confirm your ranks. If you conduct yourself well, Centurion, I may well confirm you as Count when we re-conquer Britannia."

"Thank you, Sire, I would ask for no more."

"Bring your men into the fortress. We shall talk further in the Principia when they are settled in."

Valdor looked around him, whatever doubts he had about the fortress accommodating his Legio XX vanished. To his expert eye, Gesoriacum was about twelve times bigger than Dubris. The two men walked side by side into the Principia.

Soon seated facing each other across a table, the emperor and Valdor talked about the political situation.

"You have Batavian origins, is that not so?"

"It is true, Caesar."

The emperor smiled, "That could be useful since my first task is to reclaim Batavia from the Franks."

Valdor frowned, *Surely you took Noviomagus when Faldrek died.*

As if he could read his thoughts, or alerted by his perplexed expression, Constantius said, "It is true that I took Noviomagus, but since then, I have been diverted from the task of retaking the rest of the country. Maximian's most urgent priority was for me to recapture Gesoriacum, which I did. There remains unfinished business beside the Rhine. Have you not heard that the Franks have retaken Noviomagus?"

"Nay, that's news to me."

"We shall have to march north to re-conquer Batavia. That will be your first campaign with me. Only once the Rhine delta is in our hands can we contemplate an invasion of Britannia."

"But surely, Caesar, if you hold Gesoriacum—"

"Are you not aware that the usurper, Allectus, has made an alliance with the Franks? He's an astute devil, not to be underestimated. Nay, we have to march on Batavia first to nullify the Frankish threat to our rear."

"The year is drawing to a close, and the weather certainly not improving, Sire. At this time of year, we can expect heavy rain and when I was last in my homeland, not so long ago, I was appalled at the flooding, mostly due to a rise in sea level. Rain will make matters worse. I suggest postponing the campaign until spring."

Constantius snapped, as if resenting the advice he had sought, "I had already decided that we'd await spring. How I detest sitting hand in hand!"

The rest of the year passed uneventfully, although Constantius began to appreciate Valdor's intelligence and became more confidential in his conversation. Early in the New Year, Valdor was wandering around the port with Sfava and Heidar's wife, Inga. The women were interested in buying cloth for dressmaking. Allectus had spies in Gesoriacum, who had received instructions to eliminate Valdor when a suitable occasion arose. It was difficult, if not impossible, to act while the centurion was safely within the Roman fortress. Wandering the chaotic streets of the port among traders' stalls was another matter, especially since he was accompanied by two women. The three spies considered it an easy task to dispense with the women and then slaughter the centurion. To make sure, they enrolled a couple of Frankish mercenaries. Five men against a man and two women seemed to promise only one outcome.

Sfava studied a sample of silk imported from Asia and, despite her apparent distraction, out of the corner of her eye, noticed suspicious characters approaching Inga from behind. She had no time to draw her weapon, but swung the bale of silk forcefully into the midriff of the nearest assassin. It was enough to save Inga and alert her companions, whose swords flashed forth in seconds. The would-be killers were unaware of the prowess of Jutish shield maidens—to their cost. So, surprised, one Frank and a Roman spy fell dying to the ground. Now, evenly matched, Valdor overcame another of Allectus' spies, and most likely the two women would have prevailed, except that a patrol from the fortress came running to restore order and, recognising the centurion, captured the assailants and marched them back at spear point to the stronghold. Warily, Sfava continued her scrutiny of the gaudy silks.

Having purchased material to her liking, the trio returned to the fortress, where Valdor was immediately summoned to the emperor, who said, "This is Allectus' handiwork. But well done, Centurion, you slew three of the assailants and protected your womenfolk as a true Roman officer should."

Those two don't need my protection!

Constantius stared hard at Valdor as if assessing his value. Measuring his words, he said, "The question now is, what to do with the two prisoners. I could have them crucified outside the gates, but I have an idea. Little escapes my notice: it is clear that the men of your legion hold you in great esteem, but you have to win the respect of the other legions here. This is my proposal; nay, my command. Centurion, you will fight both adversaries in the arena outside the port at dawn tomorrow. In that way, the men will see what a valorous centurion they have and will be willing to follow you in battle when need occurs. Besides, it will alleviate their boredom. To incentivize your opponents, I will promise them their freedom if they overcome you, which they will not!"

"They tried to murder my woman, Caesar, I need no other motivation to slay them." Valdor bowed and hurried away to hone his *gladius* and break the news to Heidar.

"But that's unfair, two against one," his friend objected. "I'll plead with Caesar to let me fight by your side."

"If you value our friendship, you'll do no such thing. I ask only that you look after my family if I fail." Valdor explained why the emperor wanted him to fight superior odds.

"It makes sense only if you have to lead a ragbag legion of auxiliaries, Valdor. Our men would follow you into the jaws of Hell."

"Ay, the emperor knows that."

Heidar frowned and said, "The Frank had a long sword when he was captured. If they give it back to him, you'll need a good shield."

"I've already thought about that; I have my Capricornus shield gifted to me by Legate Vitulasius of the Legio II Augusta. As yet, I have never used it in battle. It's sure to bring me luck and, at least with the Roman, intimidate him, for the fame of *that* legion precedes it."

"Good, and whatever you do, seize the initiative, Valdor. Do not hesitate!"

"You mean well, old friend, but you begin to annoy me! I am away, I must make sure the tip of my *gladius* is well honed."

Invigorated by the sea air and watching the sky from behind a barred gate on a fair, somewhat variable day, with clouds scudding across the sky, sending sudden beams of light through the breaks in the murky grey patches, Valdor waited patiently as the stadium filled with rowdy legionaries. There was excitement in the air as men took or placed wagers. Staring out across the arena's ground of beaten sand, Valdor saw his opponents stride from another gate into the centre of the circus. The Frank was a head taller than the Roman, and both were fully armoured and wearing helms.

Valdor's body was well armoured, too, and he smiled grimly as he adjusted the cheek-guards of his *galea*. The thought of his transverse centurion plume heartened him because he knew that his aspect would be fearsome for his adversaries. Suddenly, a cranking sound and the squealing of hinges accompanied the slow opening of the barred gate. He did not rush out but allowed the tension to build as a sector of the crowd—his men—began to intone his name.

That enthusiastic noise was nothing compared to the great roar that coincided with his emergence into the arena. It was clear that the spectators wanted him to win. The odds seemed stacked against him, so a good price was quoted for his victory, which, in turn, meant greater vocal encouragement.

He did not need Heidar's advice, for he had already decided not to hesitate. He thanked the Lord that his left arm, supporting his shield, had fully recovered from the first assassination attempt. Merely thinking about the cowardly assault on his family and, now, the repetition the day before, sent adrenaline surging through his veins. His adversaries clearly had a plan because they stood back-to-back, motionless. This allowed Valdor time to devise a countermeasure; suddenly, he ran in a circle past the Roman, ignoring him, turned, lowering his shield to a collective gasp from the crowd, who sat forward as the Frank raised his long sword. Without breaking stride, Valdor swung the shield upwards fast, using the metal-rimmed edge to strike his opponent violently under the point of his chin. He continued running, ignoring the deafening cheers, to stop several yards farther on, sending sandy dust flying from under his caligae. He turned with a raised shield and surveyed the scene. The Roman was vigorously shaking the prone figure of the unconscious Frank. He obviously had no stomach for a fair fight. Valdor realised that it was to his advantage that the Frank remained senseless, so he broke into a run directly towards the legionary, who leapt desperately to his feet, raising his shield.

At the sight of the Batavian centurion charging him, his nerve broke, for he was not a veteran soldier, but a spy hired to enact a cowardly murder. The craven-hearted assassin turned and ran towards the edge of the circus. Valdor, instead, reached the Frank who was stirring. The tall, bearded warrior struggled to stand, but Valdor was too quick for him, kicking his chin and dropping him back to the ground amid shouts and chants of 'kill, kill, kill!'

His opponent was helpless, but so had been little Caurus in Britannia, prey to assassins; thanks to Inga, his son was alive. This thought was enough to make Valdor strike the Frank's throat with the sharp point of his gladius. He sprang to his feet and raised his bloodied blade to the heavens as the sated crowd shouted his name, not just his own men, but the whole stadium rocked to the repetition of *Valdor! Valdor!*

He took a deep breath, knowing that the contest was not over and not yet won. It would be folly to believe it so because the other had run to cower against the perimeter wall. Valdor admitted that it was not a bad ploy because the wretch's back was covered. But he might turn it to his advantage. He would play on the villain's mind. Slowly, shield raised full on, displaying the Capricornus; slowly, swinging his gladius in a nonchalant circular motion, he advanced with slow determination, playing on the legionary's nerves. With every step forward, the crowd chanted his name louder, in time with his step. The slow advance ceased at ten paces from the cowering figure, who nevertheless held his gladius at the ready, only to be replaced by a sudden surprise dash. Valdor sprinted at his opponent, arriving shield-to-shield with a mighty clash and pinning the man's shield with all his might against him, trapping him helpless between the oncoming shield and the wall. His situation impeded him from wielding his gladius so that the centurion, with no such problem, was able to pick off the other's sword arm with a series of short, sharp thrusts that shredded the legionary's forearm, causing him to drop his weapon to the delight of the crowd, which took up again the familiar chant 'kill, kill, kill!'

The beaten man dropped to his knees, letting his shield fall to the ground. He stretched out his arms, one bloodied, in supplication as the disgusted soldiers encircling them bayed for his death. Valdor dropped his shield to free his hand to grab the man by the hair and pull him painfully into the centre of the arena. His eyes sought the emperor and for the first time, he realised that Heidar, Inga, and Sfava were privileged to be seated in his box.

Marching the man to the area in front of the box, Valdor gazed at Emperor Constantius and their eyes met. Almost imperceptibly, the emperor's head nodded, so Valdor tugged at the hair, pulling his head back and swiftly used his razor-sharp gladius to slash the man's throat. A rousing cheer greeted this bloody act and men demanded their winnings. In an act of disdain, Valdor placed a boot on the dead man's chest. He raised his sword, first to Caesar, then to the four quarters of the arena. In an afterthought, he ran to retrieve his shield, which he was certain had played a psychological part in his victory.

He was sure that he would carry it to further triumphs in Batavia in the months ahead.

23

GESORIACUM AND BATAVIA AD 294

THE HARBOUR AT GESORIACUM WAS LOCATED IN THE 'Anse de Brequerecque', a small bay off the Liane estuary located below the fortifications. On the waterfront, Valdor watched a wooden crane swing a large, sturdy net laden with perfectly round stone missiles over the hold of a cargo ship, and a legionary wound a handle and lowered them down. This was the third such netful since he had been in attendance. He strolled over to the labourer to ensure that *ballistae* had been previously deposited in another cargo vessel. He also discovered that they had loaded a battering ram, so, satisfied, he strolled back to the fortress. A sharp cry to the gatekeepers, and the heavy wooden door swung back to admit him.

An acute observer, Constantius could not resist a smug smile as he glanced at Valdor making his way across the courtyard. The idea of a gladiatorial contest had proved compelling. Whoever the centurion passed smiled at him and fisted his chest in respect, and Valdor's proud bearing indicated his appreciation. There and then, the emperor decided to entrust an army to the Batavian's leadership.

In his right hand, he held a suitable provocation to spur Valdor on to greater determination—if he should need it—which he doubted. Nonetheless, he called the centurion over to him and opened his hand, saying, "Centurion Valdor, you might find this interesting." He handed a coin showing the bearded and cuirassed profile of Allectus with the legend IMP. ALLECTUS around the edge. His expression grim, eyes blazing, Valdor turned the coin and saw a galley under a set of compasses on the reverse. His hand clenched over the coin until his knuckles became white, and he only slowly handed the offensive piece back to his emperor, who said, "This was given in change today at the fish market to one of my cooks. He wanted to know if it was legal tender. I exchanged it for a coin bearing my portrait, Centurion. Keep the coin. It will remind you, if needed, who your enemy is."

"I swear to God that I'll slay him, given half a chance!"

"Tomorrow, you will lead an army to Batavia. Take Noviomagus and drive the Franks out of your homeland. That done, leave a strong garrison and ships in the harbour, then sail back here and we'll invade Britannia. I have the utmost faith in you, Centurion Valdor. There's no need for me to raise your rank, for you are a Count. I'll announce as much to the army."

"Thank you, Caesar, I'll not fail you." *So, he's going to keep me as Count of the Saxon Shore! Thank the stars!*

The following morning, the emperor convened Valdor's *Legio XX* Valeria Victrix and another legion, the glorious *Legio VI Gallicana*, largely made up of Illyrians from the Balkans. These were renowned fighters but they also had a reputation for intolerance towards inefficient officers. Murders had been known. This made the emperor's speech all the more important.

"Legionaries, you sail within the hour for Batavia, where you will retake the region for Rome under the command of my friend and general, *Comes Saxoniae Litoris*, Valdor. Once you have achieved this objective, some of you will return and together, we shall invade Britannia. Comrades, onwards for the glory of Rome!"

Ha! He kept his word and used my highest title.

This short speech was met with thunderous cheers and all eyes turned to Valdor when he drew and raised his gladius, "*Ave Caesar*, Hail Caesar! For the glory of Rome and Emperor Constantius I!"

Ten thousand voices took up the cry and the emperor beamed with satisfaction at his chosen commander, who went to the stables for Sparax and proudly led two legions on the short march or, in 600 cases, short ride, to the harbour.

All aboard, they sailed with a seasonable following wind past the Grey Cape into the Strait of Dubris. To the east, the coast of Gaul, with its cliffs and sandy beaches, flashed in a blur while to the west, the white cliffs made his hand clench over Allectus' coin. The invasion of Britannia and his revenge could not come soon enough. At this fair rate of knots, they cleaved into the North Sea, never losing sight of the eastern coast, thus avoiding the dangerous, well-known sandbank of the *Infera Insula*. Legend had it that this sandbank was once a fertile isle.

Bearing north-easterly, they came to the sodden mouth of the Rhine and sailed into the estuary. Orders were shouted on each ship, sails furled and oars deployed as they rowed into the confluence of the Waal. Fifty-two nautical miles of fatigue to the beat of drums resounded over the water from one ship to another, drowning the cries of waterfowl in the reed beds, stretched before them along the Waal as far as the harbour at Noviomagus, which was their destination.

Arrived at the quay, his men requisitioned oxen and carts before taking command of the loading bays and unloading the weapons and missiles from the cargo ships. His officers had readied the men on dry land so that the two legions were ready to march up the trail to reach the levelled ground under the fortress walls. The eight double-yoked ox carts lumbered uphill after them. At the head of the army, Valdor halted Sparax and ordered the cornicen to blow three blasts of his horn. The gates remained stubbornly shut, but a Frankish officer appeared on the gate tower and refused to admit the Roman army.

"Your decision is the worse for you; this means war!" Valdor cried.

He withdrew his men out of range of archers and javelin throwers, then waited for the ox carts to creak their way to him. Meanwhile, he organised a *testudo* formation around the unloaded battering ram—an oak trunk with a steel sculpted ram's head at its extremity—swinging on leather bindings in its wheeled cradle. The ram thundered against the stout, barred oak doors to no avail as missiles and boiling oil, launched from the ramparts, had no effect on the Roman shields held overhead, effectively creating a protective roof.

Exasperated, Valdor withdrew the testudo and organised the ballistae so that all three were aiming at the same spot on the oak doors, where he believed, from memory, the bar was placed. This took some time, but the veterans were not restless. They knew that alternatives to storming through the gates would be costly in the number of lives lost. Instead, the Frankish onlookers from the ramparts prayed that the barred doors resisted the bombardment. The ballistae were wound to maximum tension and the engineers alerted their commander to their readiness.

He raised and dropped his hand, so, with amazing accuracy, three massive stone balls almost contemporaneously smashed into the oak doors. The noise was reverberant and the only astonishing thing was that the doors were still intact. "Three more!" yelled Valdor. He had a good supply of missiles and was prepared to use them all, but he wanted to concentrate his fire on the same spot. It proved to be a wise decision as the second volley, while failing to demolish the doors, had weakened the steel brackets holding the bar in place and created a small visible gap between the doors, forcing one back slightly.

Encouraged, the Count ordered another volley, whose thunderous impact was matched by the hoarse roar of thousands of legionaries as the doors caved in under the enormous impact. Valdor ordered his cavalry forward at a gallop and the heavy infantry centurions urged their men to run forward, shields raised against missiles from above. But the resistance was weak, both in number and in morale, since the garrison was so obviously outnumbered. More Franks surrendered than fought. The gallant fighters met a bloody end, so their courage and opposition were futile. Soon, the fortress belonged to Valdor. His only task now remained to send scouts along the river in both directions to ensure there were no other Frankish enclaves.

The scouts returned the following day, assuring him their reports were negative. This was mostly due to the sodden terrain and the desertion of farmsteads.

Considering his mission accomplished, Valdor convened the Illyrian commander and explained that he intended to leave the *Legio VI Gallicana* as the garrison with a commensurate number of ships, should they be needed for embarkation. To his relief, the centurion accepted the orders without a qualm, grateful to Valdor for the sound strategy used to capture the fortress-citadel that had left him with minimal casualties.

All aboard the vessels, Valdor's fleet rowed with the Waal's favourable current very swiftly as far as the mouth of the Rhine. There, the choppier water of the river mingled with the tide of the North Sea and an idea came to Valdor.

He could transform the return voyage into a reconnaissance. His knowledge of the Britannia shore forts was second to none, and he might well contribute to his commander's thinking. Thus, he sailed straight across the sea to near the British coast where he surveyed the two forts, which were considered as one site, guarding the entire Yare estuary. Without entering the estuary, which was not his intention that day, he made out the form of Gariannonum Fort, its curious name derived from the Celtic language, meaning 'babbling river.' He remembered that this fortress was commanded by a cavalry garrison, the Equites Stablesiani.

Valdor cursed himself for the thoroughness that had characterised his construction work. The other fort, surrounded by imposing walls, was also protected by treacherous marshland, although on the far side from his viewpoint, there was an extensive civilian vicus. It was one thing to construct a fortress with defence uppermost in mind, another to plan an assault, altogether a more difficult prospect. Perhaps the other fortress, built before he took over responsibility for the Saxon shore, the one guarding the river Waverley confluence with the Yare, might be more vulnerable. He would report this to Constantius. Satisfied with his inspection, Valdor's ship led the fleet down the east coast, where he reached the territory of the Cantiaci. He knew all about these forts, their strong and weak points, and began to abandon his earlier idea of Gariannonum. At the end of the day, much would also depend on the mustering of Allectus' army. Still, any information he could give to Constantius would be useful, especially if the usurper barricaded himself in one of these fortresses. After his experience at Noviomagus, nothing seemed too formidable to overcome with the right approach.

The Count studied the Rutupine shore, whose oysters were considered on a par with those from the Italian Lucrine Lake, or so he had heard fellow officers declare. What he remembered most fondly of Rutupiae was the major quadrifons triumphal arch, one of the biggest in the Roman Empire, which was erected around AD 85 to straddle Watling Street, the main road from the fort to Londinium. He sighed at the memory and the significance of the monument and felt a surge of pride at his role as the Count of the Saxon Shore. He considered himself, justly, a part of the history of Britannia. He closed his eyes and remembered the arch as if seeing an image of it in front of him. Its position and size were due to its being built to celebrate the final conquest of Britain after Agricola's victory at the Battle of Mons Graupius.

He prayed to the Lord that he, too, would win a battle against Allectus, although he doubted that even if it should come about, it would not merit an arch almost 82 feet high with a façade of high-quality Italian granite, adorned with sculptures and inscriptions like that of General Agricola. That arch, which he saw so clearly in his mind's eye, standing as it did between the port and the province, signified formal entry into Britannia. What could he hope to achieve of greater importance? Nothing. He could only hope for victory and vengeance for the murder of his adoptive father.

As the white cliffs of Dubris slipped past, barely registering on his distracted mind, he knew that the time had come to return without further delay to Gesoriacum. He would arrive in triumph with the emperor's promise that on achieving his mission, they would set about the invasion of Britannia. Momentarily, he thought about his birth father, Caurus, and with a pang realised that Namuta had never seen his namesake, her tiny grandson. When he re-conquered Britannia, he would remedy that situation.

24

GESORIACUM, PORTUS ADURNI AND LONDINIUM, SEPTEMBER, AD 296

NATURE CONTRIVED TO DISPLAY EVERY SHADE OF GREY, in the sea, in the sky, and even in the drawn faces of the garrison. A few adventurous gulls, driven from precarious nests in desperation to seek food, were snatched mid-air by gale-force wind and flung, ruffled-feathered, in a different direction. The winter of 295-296 was the most severe in living memory.

If Valdor had not abandoned the pagan gods for Christianity, he would have thought they were conspiring to prevent the invasion of Britannia. How could it be right that a murderous usurper thrived while his justiciar waited impatiently on the other shore of the raging sea?

If only Constantius had kept his word more than a year ago and allowed Valdor's fleet to sail for Britannia! The irony was that the emperor's scouts had reported on the strength of the shore forts—those he had created. The decision to delay departure apparently provoked Neptune's wrath. The North Sea became unnavigable for Valdor's ships and had remained that way until the summer of 296. Even so, preparations were slow, and only by the end of August, were his daily prayers answered. Constantius' fleet sailed in several divisions, one under Valdor's command, another under the praetorian prefect, Asclepiodotus. The emperor's dithering meant that his division was the last to leave Gaul.

As if to taunt him, Nature decided on one last flourish. She wreathed the approach to Vectis in thick fog. Allectus' fleet was concentrated there, and Asclepiodotus used the conditions as an excuse to sail well wide of the isle to avoid the enemy. Instead, Valdor, knowing the Solent well, sailed recklessly at considerable speed too close to the island. His years of patrolling saved him, as despite the veil of grey, he discerned a dangerous headland. His alertness served a dual purpose: first, it gave him his position, and second, it saved his fleet from certain shipwreck. He changed course, and, sure of himself, directed his ships into the estuary under the fort of Portus Adurni, which he had built.

Since he had conveyed the entire garrison to Gesoriacum, the fortress was weakly defended, commanded by a centurion who had remained at the time on his sick-bed with the ague. Now fully recovered, he had worked miracles to transform an ill-disciplined collection of scoundrels into a respectable unit to hold the fortress. His joy on seeing Valdor was immense, and the gates were flung open to receive the new garrison.

The following morning broke with welcome limpidity. Valdor watched a fishing boat sail out of the estuary into the calm Solent, little suspecting that the wretch had other than fishing on his mind. He wanted to gain good coins for reporting what he had seen to Allectus on Vectis. His mission became more urgent when halfway across the strait, he saw Asclepiodotus' division sail into the natural harbour of *Noviomagus Reginorum*. This fleet almost came to grief, its crews unaware of the shallow spit that presented a navigation hazard at all states of the tide. Fortunately, only one ship foundered there. The others dealt with the fast tidal stream at the entrance to the harbour with considerable expertise. Nonetheless, once his men had disembarked, Asclepiodotus decided to burn the ships. He did not want them falling into the hands of his enemy, and, besides, he was an able general on land and did not care for the restrictions of naval warfare.

From his vantage point on a turret of the fortress, Valdor saw the smoke of the conflagration. He could not imagine that Asclepiodotus had burnt his vessels, but having seen his division enter the north side of the Solent, recognized that the fire appertained in some way to the praetorian prefect.

Meanwhile, on Vectis, the fisherman told Allectus everything he had seen and for his troubles received three silver coins. The usurper, devious and cowardly, stripped himself of outward signs of command, posing as an ordinary legionary, in case the forthcoming battle went against him. Even if he died, he did not want the enemy desecrating his body.

He directed his fleet towards the smoke and, disembarking his force, immediately realised his tactical inferiority to Asclepiodotus. Wily and craven, he ordered his men to retreat aboard the ships, for he knew that the prefect had burnt his and could not pursue him out of the harbour. Reasoning with his own yardstick, he did not expect the other division to leave the safety of its fortress at Portus Adurni. Therefore, Valdor had the advantage of surprise. Allectus knew that he had to remove Constantius' force from its stronghold if he wished to retain his position of emperor of the North, so he disembarked in the harbour under the fortress. Concentrating their gaze inland, his lookouts were slow to spot the oncoming naval division, which had turned about from the high water of the Solent, heading for Noviomagus Reginorum, and veered instead back into the same estuary of Portus Adurni. By the time Allectus' force was aware of the disembarkation of the enemy, its commander, concerned at being trapped between the fortress and the newly arrived force, formed his army into a defensive formation.

Consumed by hatred for his father's murderer, Valdor had only attack on his mind, which, anyway, was his preferred battle tactic. He arranged his veterans of the XX Legion into a wedge formation, placing himself at the front tip of the triangle, leading by example, closely followed by his Batavian officers and then the veterans, attacking the enemy centre. No army in the world could have withstood these able soldiers, and, with the tactic repeated in two other wedges along the enemy front, the three wedges thrust well into the foe. When these formations expanded, the enemy troops were pushed into restricted positions, making hand-to-hand fighting difficult for the less experienced legion of Allectus, largely composed of Frankish mercenaries. This was where the short legionary gladius was useful, held low, and used as a thrusting weapon, while the longer Frankish swords became impossible to wield.

It soon became clear to Valdor that victory would be his, especially because Heidar had wrested the eagle standard from the foe, a sure sign of imminent success. Indeed, the adversary received orders to retreat and, gathering together, headed northwards along a Roman road towards *Calleva Atrebatum*, where undoubtedly, Allectus expected to reinforce his numbers. Valdor was in no hurry to pursue the routed force but sent an envoy to fetch Asclepiodotus' division.

For the moment, the triumph had a bitter taste because there was no sign of Allectus' insignia. Arrogant as ever, and reinforced, Allectus now felt sufficiently superior to Valdor's army to not remain behind the solid walls of Calleva Atrebatum. Instead, he placed his army in the same defensive formation that had cost him dear the previous day. Also, the arrival of the other division took the usurper by surprise.

Valdor spoke rapidly with Asclepiodotus, an experienced general, who nodded wisely in agreement and allowed repetition of the tactics of the previous day. Allectus had fewer Franks in his formation, but the confidence of Valdor's force compensated for the increased presence of Roman legionaries in the enemy ranks. The tide of battle soon swung in favour of Valdor and the praetorian prefect. Even so, there was no sign of his hated foe. The Count wondered whether Allectus was cringing behind the city walls, watching the progress of the engagement, which inexorably swung in favour of his foe—the deceased emperor's adopted son.

The battle still raged and Valdor noticed an enemy enclave

seemingly intent on defending someone at its core. He fought his
way through and at last found what he sought. Although Allectus
wore the armour of a simple legionary, his men were determined
to protect him. Had Valdor not had the advantage of having met
the usurper, he would not have recognised the disfigured face.
There was only one like it, so with a bloodcurdling cry, emanating
from suppressed fury at his father's murder, Valdor pressed
forward, stabbing and thrusting, closely followed by his most
trusted friends and the expert veterans of XX Valeria Victrix.

The coward fought with the desperation of despair as he saw
his handpicked bodyguard falling before the fighting valour of his
adversary. With horror, he recognised the murdered emperor's
son, whose eyes blazed with hatred as he neared him. With his
own malevolent yell, Allectus leapt forward to finish the job of
slaying father and son. It was his undoing because his foothold
betrayed him, slithering on blood, he lost his balance and Valdor,
infused with demonic energy, was onto him in a flash. His gladius
pierced at least three inches through the leather cuirass, such was
the might of the thrust impelled by pent-up rage. The Batavian
followed it with a slash to the throat, possibly unnecessary, since
the first thrust was mortal, but undoubtedly satisfying as he
watched the light of life dull in his victim's eyes. "For Carausius!"
Valdor shrieked like a man possessed, and standing astride the
corpse, let the fighting proceed around him as he offered a prayer
to his deceased adoptive father: *Father, I have avenged you this
day. I pray that now your soul may rest in peace at the bosom of Our
Lord. Amen.*

Valdor felt a great weight removed from his shoulders and
again thrust himself into the fray. Soon, a rout followed towards
the town. Heidar lagged behind. He had seen his friend exult over
the body of what seemed to be a lowly legionary. He had not seen
Allectus; nonetheless, he had heard Valdor describe the disfigured
mouth, so he recognised the corpse for whom he was. Unknown
to his friend and commander, for love of Valdor, Heidar beheaded
the body and carried the head to town. Outside the main gate to

the amphitheatre, he sharpened a stake and planted it with Allectus' head impaled on it. "Behold the usurper!" he cried, and numerous legionaries gathered, curious to see.

"Long live Caesar Valdor!" someone called, and the cry was taken up by many voices until Valdor rode up and called for silence.

"Nay," he shouted, "I have sworn fealty to Emperor Constantius. This victory today is in his name. Long live Caesar Constantius I!"

Unknown to Valdor, Constantius' division had been separated by the fog from the others, and he had rowed up the Tamesis, where he saved Londinium from an attack by Frankish mercenaries who were now roaming the province without a paymaster, and massacred them. At the very moment that Valdor declared his loyalty, Constantius was riding into Londinium, where he was hailed by the Britons as a liberator. That very afternoon, he had a die cut for a gold medallion describing himself with the wording: *redditor lucis aeternae*, 'restorer of the eternal light', by which he meant Roman rule.

The triumph was essentially Valdor's and to some extent Asclepiodotus', for Constantius had arrived after the battle. On hearing that the emperor was in Londinium, the two generals marched their men there, where Constantius received them with great honour.

"Centurion Valdor," said the emperor, "I hereby confirm you as Count of the Saxon Shore. You will resume your duties forthwith. It seems I have business in the far north of the land, where trouble is stirring."

"Sire, your wish is my command; forgive me, but my greatest desire is to retire on Vectis with my family. I would like to settle there, build a villa and plant a vineyard to enjoy my old age."

The emperor looked at him benevolently, "I have heard reports of your loyalty, Count. This is what we will do. You will come north to aid me in my conquest of the Picts. That achieved, you will suggest a successor to build more fortresses and fend off the pirates. You will, however, retain the rank of Count for your retirement."

"Thank you, Sire. I could ask for no more. I'll look forward to seeing and pushing beyond Hadrian's Wall. I have never travelled so far north."

"The noble Hadrian found the Picts fearsome warriors. Every time he tried to move into their territory, they successfully drove him back. That was over a hundred years ago. Did you know that they fought completely naked, using only spears? Although, some say they painted their bodies in different colours. Reports have come to me that the Picts are attacking the forts along the Wall."

"We can deal with those savages, Sire. I look forward to it."

25

BRITANNIA, AD 299 - 306

THE EMPEROR EXPLAINED TO VALDOR THAT THE Pictish crisis had calmed, meaning there was no immediate danger from the north. His scouts were monitoring the situation but as far as Constantius was concerned, he smiled benignly, Valdor could go to Vectis and make a start on his retirement plans.

"Sire, might I suggest Centurion Heidar take over the shore defences? He has worked with me and knows what is entailed. I was going to build a fortress near the mouth of the River Exe to complete the southern line of strongholds and to protect *Isca Dumnoniorum*."

"Then that is what we will do. I'll make him the Count on the understanding that if I should need you—you remain a count— you will come with all haste to *Eboracum*."

"Eboracum, Sire?"

"Ay, I have chosen it for its strategic location, especially with unrest to the north of the Wall."

Valdor had a cart built, making it into a comfortable travelling wagon with a luxurious interior. He requisitioned oxen to haul it and a chestnut mare. With these, he travelled on Sparax to Branodunum, where he arbitrarily removed his parents from their employment, explaining, "Father, I'll need you to take over a vineyard and produce quality wine. Your previous years of farming in Batavia will stand you in good stead. Mother, you will continue to make bread. I'll have an oven constructed according to your requirements. We shall all live together on an island with a milder clime than this east coast, where the wind cuts to the bone: it's no place for the aged."

They travelled south, and Sfava and little Caurus joined Namuta in the wagon, much to his grandmother's delight. The crossing to Vectis was uneventful, except that they were joined by a small craft containing Johar, who had retired from the army. He explained that he wanted to resume work as a fisherman and to live close to his only remaining relatives. In an aside to Valdor, he confided that on Vectis he hoped to find a Briton who pleased him so that he could wed her and start a family. Valdor took everyone to a fertile inland area on a strategically defensible height, known as Robin Hill.

He took his father and Johar aside to describe his vision: "I want to build a bath-house and an aisled building linked by a corridor on this side of a courtyard that will stretch down there to the south. I will have a mosaic floor with a dolphin motif in the bath-house and underfloor hypocaust heating in the main building. Then there will be outhouses, barns..." he paused, "...come over here, father, see how the land rolls away down to the south? Imagine it cleared of trees and planted with rows of vines. I'll bring labourers to start work next week. For a while, we'll have to camp, military style," he chuckled. Johar clapped him on the back, "Who would have thought that you would have become a wealthy landowner in Britannia when we set out to sea with no destination in mind? What folly that was, eh, Valdor!"

"Ay, but we had to save Faldrek. Poor Faldrek! He was unlucky. How he would have loved it here, don't you agree?"

"If only Heidar could join us. I'm going to love it, too, I know. Now I must go to choose a site near the sea for a small house, not a grand villa like yours, Valdor."

"Not too small, Johar. I'll help you with funds, for I have

been very fortunate. Besides, I'll regularly send servants down to buy fresh fish from you, so it's in my interests that you establish yourself comfortably."

They laughed, and their enthusiasm for a new lifestyle was evident to anyone, who, like Caurus, could see the joy illuminating his son's face.

The months passed, and the buildings sprang up like mushrooms; inside, however, work was slower because the master craftsmen, the mosaicists, worked with precision and could not be rushed. In the villa, once the hypocaust was installed and the pavement laid, these master craftsmen created a magnificent mosaic of the legendary Medusa, with hissing snakes for hair.

Outdoors, a barn was adapted for a wine press, with large barrels ready for the first grape harvest. Caurus had overseen the planting of twenty-seven rows of 100 vines on a hectare of prepared land. Namuta requested a wood-burning oven, with a granite slab as a baking surface. Valdor organised the transport of the slab from Dumnonia; that done, he oversaw the stacking of wood obtained from the vineyard land clearance.

Johar made his own nets on a frame by the shore. His house, not a villa, but a fine *mansio*, overlooked a bay where he dragged his fishing boat onto a sandy beach when not in use. In that bay, without venturing far, he caught flounder and mullet and school bass, rays, mackerel, and bream in the summer, whereas in late autumn and winter he netted cod without risking turbulent waters.

Inland, Valdor built a small church near his villa and employed a priest from the mainland. Johar's wedding with the Briton, Valda, was the first such ceremony there, followed months later by the baptism of their baby boy, Enyon.

Everything would have been auspicious, had it not been for the news arriving from Rome. Emperor Diocletian had begun persecuting Christians and had issued edicts ordering the destruction of the cult throughout the Empire.

Therefore, when a messenger arrived on Vectis from Constantius, demanding Valdor's presence in Eboracum, he feared the worst. He travelled, determined to fight for his faith, expecting never to return to his family on the isle. He had expressly forbidden Johar from travelling with him, demanding that whatever happened, his cousin should protect his family. His main hope was that the island was too far from the rest of Britannia and his family and small church too insignificant to interest Constantius; yet, he had summoned Valdor to Eboracum.

The emperor's welcome reassured him somewhat and an explanation for his summons was soon forthcoming. The Picts had breached the wall and invaded the north. "You owe me a favour, Valdor. I presume you know about the persecution of Christians according to the imperial edict?"

"I have heard terrible reports from other parts of the Empire, Caesar."

"I have limited myself to demolishing a handful of churches for appearance's sake, but have not harmed a single Christian. My son Constantine and his mother, Helena, are both Christians, which is why I have brought Constantine here. You will meet him soon, for he is marching with us. Helena is hiding, safe in her home city of Drepana in Bithynia."

He assures my loyalty by playing on my Christianity, but he has it anyway.

Constantius studied Valdor's face as if trying to read his mind, but continued, "There are those, notably Galerius, who married Diocletian's daughter, who use my leniency towards the Christians against me with the Emperor, but he will not prevail. I have put plans to work so that when Diocletian and Maximian no longer wear the purple, Constantine will do so."

Now, I understand! He wants me to befriend Constantine and become his trusted general in Britannia.

As if reading his mind, Constantius said, "I am placing you and Constantine each at the head of a legion, and I will command a third. Fetch Constantine!" he bellowed at a servant. "We shall march north at dawn on the morrow; so, we need a strategy to defeat these savages."

Valdor rode Sparax next to Constantine, mounted on an equally fine stallion on the long march north. The Picts retreated ahead of them beyond the Wall, which marvel, Valdor surveyed for the first time, noting how it stretched up hill and down dale for miles.

The Roman forces advanced past the Firth of Forth, razing villages and sending refugees ever deeper into lands where the harvest was already beginning to wane. As the native population became more desperate, the Romans carried out the plan the three generals had devised in Eboracum; namely, they grew better stocked by ransacking the provisions that the fleeing Picts had left behind.

The scheme worked perfectly until one band of Picts decided that the best way to end the Roman advance would be by assassination: this unstoppable army would descend into chaos, they believed, and, leaderless, would hurry to retreat to winter quarters.

The Picts chose to make the attempt during the pagan festival of Samhain. While Roman eyes were dazzled by the bonfires lit to keep wicked spirits at bay, a small group of Pict soldiers adopted the ancient practice of guising: wearing masked costumes to approach a neighbour's house. Under the half-moon, they wandered about, wearing cow heads and hides amid a small herd of stray cattle, which was eagerly snatched up by Roman scouts. By this subterfuge, they entered the Roman camp and evaded the sentries long enough to sneak up to the luxurious tents of the Augustus and his generals. There they shrieked and attacked, slaying everyone they could reach before Valdor and Constantine, fighting shoulder-to-shoulder, cut them down.

The attack did not entirely fail. Among the dead officers was Constantius' son, Constantinus, by his first wife. The emperor, thanks to the harsh clime, had fallen ill, and announced the retreat to Eboracum to mourn. By January, the broken-hearted father also passed away, leaving behind his two younger sons by his second wife, Helena.

Constantius died on 25 July 306, endorsing Constantine as his successor. The legions hailed him as Rome soon broke into civil war.

"I will leave you temporarily in charge of Britannia, Valdor, until I have overthrown my rival Maxentius. I know you dearly wish to return to your isle and you have my benediction to do so as soon as I am undisputed ruler of the Empire."

Valdor arranged to meet Heidar in Eboracum and devised a plan to ensure that Britannia would remain loyal to Constantine. The Picts settled for a period of peace, which made his task that much easier.

"Heidar, I'll make Eboracum my base and strengthen the east coast shore fortresses. You will use Camulodunum as yours, and from there reinforce the southern shore fortresses. We must make certain that Britannia does not fall to other usurpers. Constantine will ensure that our religion is respected throughout the Empire."

A messenger arrived at Eboracum to inform Count Valdor that Constantine had defeated Maxentius at the Battle of Milvian Bridge. The new emperor immediately pushed the Edict of Mediolanum, legalising Christianity. When he heard this, Valdor immediately departed Eboracum for Camulodunum, where he encountered Heidar.

"My dear old friend, I leave Britannia in your hands, for now, unless I have to defend my home and family, my fighting days are over. Since leaving Torik Isle, we have achieved much. Now, the time has come to enjoy my father's first vintage by the fireside with Sfava and my mother, not to mention little Caurus, who will soon be taller than I! Remember our oath on Torik: I expect it still to bind you—when Emperor Constantine allows you to retire, come and join Johar and me on Vectis. Sfava would love to have

Inga close by, and we can all live in peace on an isle that does not flood."

THE END

ABOUT THE AUTHOR

Award-winning author, John Broughton, was born in Cleethorpes, Lincolnshire, UK in 1948, just one of the post-war baby boomers. After attending grammar school and studying to the sound of Bob Dylan, he went to Nottingham University and studied Medieval and Modern History (Archaeology subsidiary). The subsidiary course led to one of his greatest academic achievements: tipping the soil content of a wheelbarrow from the summit of a spoil heap on an old lady hobbling past the dig. Fortunately, they subsequently became firm friends.

He did many different jobs while living in Radcliffe-on-Trent, Leamington, Glossop, the Scilly Isles, Puglia, and Calabria. They include teaching English and History, managing a Day-Care Centre, being a Director of a Trade Institute, and teaching university students English. He even tried being a fisherman and a flower-picker when he was on St. Agnes Island, Scilly. He has lived in Calabria since 1992, where he settled into a long-term job, for once, at the University of Calabria, teaching English. No doubt, his "lovely Calabrian wife Maria stopped him from being restless.

His two kids are grown up now, but he wrote books for them when they were little. Hamish Hamilton and then Thomas

Nelson published six of these in England in the 1980s. They are now out of print. He's a granddad and happily the parents wisely named his grandson Dylan. He decided to take up writing again late in his career. When you are teaching and working as a translator, you don't have time for writing. As soon as he stopped the translations, he resumed writing in 2014. The fruit of that decision was his first historical novel, The Purple Thread. The novel is set in his favourite Anglo-Saxon period. Subsequently, he has published eighteen novels set between 450 and 1066 AD, including three trilogies, with Next Chapter Publishers. They also published Angenga a time-travel novel linking the ninth century to the twenty-first. This novel inspired John Broughton to write a series of novels about psychic investigator Jake Conley, whose retrocognition takes him back to Anglo-Saxon times.

In order to put his writing versatility to the test, he embarked on a series of detective mystery novels set in London with the Metropolitan Police, who have to deal with a criminally insane serial killer in The Quasimodo Killings; The London Tram Murders and The Thames Crossbow Murders. The latter was voted among the best twenty-five independent books of 2022. Heartened by this venture, he completed a fourth and fifth mystery The Thames-Tigris Connection and London's Psycho Cyclist. To widen his experience of genres he decided to write an apocalyptic novel entitled The Remnant, a science-fiction novel. However, he returned to his first love with a historical saga, Expulsion, about the expulsion of the Vikings from Dublin and the subsequent diaspora. The Reversed Hermit is his first novella. Newly committed to historical fiction, he embarked on Rhodri's Furies, which is Book 1 of an early medieval Welsh trilogy, The Bretland Trilogy, of which Avenging Rhodri is Book 2, Hywel the Good—is Book 3. The Wyvern's End is Book 3 of the Wyrd Trilogy.

To learn more about John Broughton and discover more Next Chapter authors, visit our website at www.nextchapter.pub.

Printed in Great Britain
by Amazon